21世纪高等学校规划教材

DAXUE YINGYU SHIYONG JIAOCHENG (2)

大学英语实用教程(2)

主　编　徐莉芳　陈永生

副主编　刘新华　李宝芬　张秀菊

参　编　段雪芹　周　军

主　审　Dewan Benjamin

中国电力出版社

http://jc.cepp.com.cn

内 容 提 要

本书为 21 世纪高等学校规划教材。

《大学英语实用教程》共分四册，每册都以对话、课文及语法三部分形式表现，内容新颖实用、条理清晰、通俗易懂、针对性强。本书为第二册，重点为句的讲练。在每单元里采用一个主题，分别用对话和课文的形式来培养学生的听、说、读、写、译全方位的实际表达技能。在语法部分中，以非英语专业学位考试大纲要求为主线，更加注重实用性和针对性。每单元之间既相互独立又互相呼应，且单元中的对话、课文、语法都配有相应的习题及参考答案。

本书可作为高等院校非英语专业教材，也可作为高职高专院校及远程教育、业大、函授等学生的基础英语课教材，并可作为成人非英语专业学位考试的参考用书。

图书在版编目（CIP）数据

大学英语实用教程（2）/ 徐莉芳，陈永生主编. —北京：中国电力出版社，2009

21 世纪高等学校规划教材

ISBN 978-7-5083-8307-1

Ⅰ. 大⋯ Ⅱ. ①徐⋯ ②陈⋯ Ⅲ. 英语－高等学校－教材 Ⅳ. H31

中国版本图书馆 CIP 数据核字（2008）第 212031 号

中国电力出版社出版、发行

（北京三里河路 6 号　100044　http://jc.cepp.com.cn）

航远印刷有限公司印刷

各地新华书店经售

*

2009 年 2 月第一版　2009 年 2 月北京第一次印刷

787 毫米×1092 毫米　16 开本　12 印张　287 千字

定价 **20.00** 元

前　言

　　本书是 21 世纪高等学校规划教材，内容新颖实用、条理清晰、通俗易懂、针对性强。

　　《大学英语实用教程》共分四册。每册主要由对话、课文及语法三部分组成。对话部分以提供的主题示例训练学生实际交流及表达的能力；课文部分侧重对语言点和语篇整体的理解，为非英语专业的学生在学位考试中的阅读部分打下坚实的基础；语法部分中，结合学生英语基础知识和基本能力的实际，针对非英语专业学位考试大纲要求，有的放矢。在内容上，全面覆盖考点，重点突出，系统性强；在形式上，题型新颖，有利于学生能力的训练和培养；在编排上，注意由易到难的阶梯性、针对性和适用性。

　　本套教材的每个单元紧密配合，又不重复；单元内的内容又相对独立，可根据学生的实际情况调整侧重点；并且，每个单元中的对话、课文、语法三部分都配有相应的练习。

　　本书为《大学英语实用教程（2）》，作者为北京科技大学等高校的一线英语教师，他们具有丰富的教学与实践经验，以确保本套教材教学的可操作性、针对性及实用性。

　　本书由徐莉芳、陈永生主编，刘新华、李宝芬、张秀菊副主编，段雪芹、周军等也参加了编写工作。

　　在编写过程中，参考了大量的书籍和资料，有些内容难免引自其中，在此对原作者表示诚挚的谢意！同时对许多给予帮助与支持的同事、朋友，一并表示衷心的感谢。

　　由于编者的能力和水平有限，书中难免有不足或错误之处，恳请广大读者批评指正。

编　者

2008 年 10 月于北京科技大学

目　录

Unit 1　Students' Life
Communicative Samples

Conversation 1

(Lucy and Mary are chatting after class.)

Lucy: Hi, Mary. What are you doing?

Mary: I'm trying to take an English literature course for this term.

Lucy: Take Professor Holt's class. I had hers last year.

Mary: Really? What's she like?

Lucy: Fantastic! I think she's really a good teacher.

Mary: Why? What makes her so good?

Lucy: For one thing, she's really funny.

Mary: Yeah, but I want to learn something.

Lucy: Don't get me wrong. She's funny, and if someone's funny, you pay more attention.

Mary: What do you think of Professor Vance?

Lucy: He's boring. Everyone falls asleep in his class. And it's hard to talk with him.

Mary: Ok. I'll try to get into Professor Holt's class.

Lucy: You won't be sorry.

Conversation 2

(Some students are going to graduate from middle school soon. They are talking about the future.)

Jim:　Only three months to go! So, what are you going to do after you graduate, Peter?

Peter:　I'm going to go to college in Ohio.

Jim:　Have you decided what you're going to major in?

Peter:　Uh-huh. I'm planning to study engineering.

Jim:　That's a good field. And what about you, Simon?

Simon: My father is going to give me a job in his company. I'll probably work there about a year so I can learn the basics.

Jim:　And what are you doing after that?

Simon: After that I'm going back to university to get my degree in business.

Jim:　　That sounds very practical. How about you, Fong? What do you plan to do next year?

Fong:　　I'm planning to take it easy for a while. I'm going to spend some time traveling in Europe, but I'm coming back after that for studying.

Jim:　　How long will you be there?

Fong:　　Well, I'm leaving in June and coming home for Christmas, so I'll be there for about six months.

Jim:　　Well, it seems that everybody has got plans for their futures.

New Words and Expressions

asleep	/ə'sli:p/	*adj.*	睡着的，睡熟的
basics	/'beisiks/	*n.*	基本，基础
boring	/'bɔ:riŋ/	*adj.*	令人厌烦的，枯燥的
degree	/di'gri:/	*n.*	程度，学位
field	/fi:ld/	*n.*	旷野，领域
future	/'fju:tʃə/	*n.*	将来，前途
literature	/'litəritʃə/	*n.*	文学（作品），文献
professor	/prə'fesə/	*n.*	教授

Exercise 1: Complete the following sentences.

A: Hi, Mary. What are you doing?

B: I'm trying to ＿＿＿＿＿＿＿＿＿＿＿ (选门英语文学课程) for this term.

A: Take Professor Holt's class. ＿＿＿＿＿＿＿＿＿＿＿ (我去年听过她的课).

B: Really? What's she like?

A: ＿＿＿＿＿＿＿＿＿＿＿ (棒极了)! I think she's really a good teacher.

B: Ok. I'll try to get into Professor Holt's class.

Exercise 2: Fill in the missing letters.

l_ter_ture　　profess_r　　f_ture　　　de_ree　　　_sleep

f_ntast_c　　b_ring　　　_asics　　　_ttent_on　　f_eld

Paragraph Reading A: On Applying for a College

The task of being accepted and enrolled in a university begins early for some students, long before they graduate from high school. These students take special courses to prepare for advanced study. They may also take one or more examinations that test how well prepared they are for university.

In the final year of high school they complete applications and send them, with their student records, to the universities which they hope to attend. Some high school students may be required to have an interview with representatives of the university. Neatly dressed, and usually very frightened, they are determined to show that they have a good attitude and the ability.

When the new students are finally accepted, there may be one more step they have to take before registering for classes and getting to work. Many colleges and universities offer an orientation program for new students. In these programs, the young people get to know the procedures for registration, university rules, how to use the library and they receive student advice. They also learn about other major services in the college or university.

Beginning a new life in a new place can be very confusing. The more knowledge students have about the school, the easier it will be for them to adapt to the new environment. However, it takes time to get used to college life.

New Words and Expressions

ability	/ə'biliti/	n.	能力，才干
accept	/ək'sept/	vt.	接受，认可
adapt	/ə'dæpt/	vt.	使适应
advanced	/əd'vɑːnst/	adj.	先进的，事先的
application	/ˌæpli'keiʃən/	n.	请求，申请
attend	/ə'tend/	vt.	出席，参加
attitude	/'ætitjuːd/	n.	态度，看法
confuse	/kən'fjuːz/	vt.	困惑，使糊涂
determine	/di'təːmin/	v.	决定，确定
enroll	/in'rəul/	vt.	登记，入学
frightened	/'frait(ə)nd/	adj.	受惊的，受恐吓的
graduate	/'grædjueit/	n.	毕业生，研究生
interview	/'intəvjuː/	vt.	接见，面试
major	/'meidʒə/	vi.	主修
offer	/'ɔfə/	vt.	提供
procedure	/prə'siːdʒə/	n.	程序，手续
register	/'redʒistə/	vt.	记录，登记，注册
representative	/ˌrepri'zentətiv/	n.	代表
require	/ri'kwaiə/	vt.	需要，要求
task	/tɑːsk/	n.	任务，作业

Exercise 3: Select the answer that best expresses the main idea of the paragraph reading A.

1) Why do some high school students take special courses in universities?

A. Because they take an advantage in the application of the university.

B. Because they prepare for advanced study and university life.

C. Because they show that they have a good attitude and the ability.

D. Because they can gain more school marks.

2) What does the word "applications" probably mean in the paragraph?

A. It is a formal, usually written request for something.

B. It is a method, idea, or law in a particular situation, activity or process.

C. It is an agreement for something at an agreed time and place for some special purpose.

D. You are glad when you realize something good.

3) From the passage we can infer that _____.

A. it is quite easy for students to adapt themselves to college life

B. many colleges and universities offer an orientation program for new students

C. the students have no difficulty in beginning a new life in college

D. it is not easy for students to adapt themselves to college life

4) What's the passage mainly about?

A. The passage is mainly about the reason why some high students take special courses in university.

B. It's mainly about what the students should do to go to college.

C. All the students should do apply for a college.

D. What the students should do is to keep a good impression in the interview.

5) Which of the following is **TRUE** according to the passage?

A. The students are nervous in the interview because it's very important for them.

B. Many colleges and universities offer services for new students to help them to adapt to college life.

C. In order to go to college, students have to hand in their applications and records.

D. All of the above.

Exercise 4: Fill in the blanks with words and expressions given below. Change the form where necessary.

enroll	application	attend	require	interview	representative
determine	attitude	register	procedure		

1) I wrote five _____ for jobs but didn't get a single reply.

2) What is the company's _____ towards this idea?

3) Please let us know if you are unable to _____.

4) Her encouragement _____ me to carry on with the work.

5) She decided to _____ in the history course at the local evening school.

6) When she was still at school, she had her first _____, for a job in a shoe shop.

7) What's the correct _____ for renewing your car tax?

8) By law we are required to keep a _____ of births and deaths.

9) Are your opinions _____ of those of the other students?

10) The urgency of the situation _____ that we should make an immediate decision.

Exercise 5: Definitions of these words appear on the right. Put the letter of the appropriate definition next to each word.

1) _____ confuse　　　　a. to become suitable for new conditions

2) _____ ability　　　　b. to cause to be mixed up in the mind

3) _____ task　　　　　c. full of fear

4) _____ orientation　　d. a person who has completed a university degree course

5) _____ adapt　　　　　e. the power or qualities that are needed in order to do something

6) _____ advanced　　　f. to take or receive something

7) _____ frightened　　g. position or direction

8) _____ offer　　　　　h. a hard work that must be done

9) _____ graduate　　　i. to hold out to a person for acceptance

10) _____ accept　　　　j. far on in development

Exercise 6: Translate the following sentences.

1）他们刚一到飞机场，老师就告诉他们这消息。

2）学生花了两个半小时才做出这道数学题。

3）我觉得现在为他的死而哭泣是没有用的。

4）作为一名中国人，我们应该把一生奉献给祖国。

5）我们上星期参观了这位科学家曾住过的房子。

Paragraph Reading B: Examination

Examinations are a common headache to students all over the world. They all detest them, but they are all being domineered by them.

Nowadays, examinations have become a popular form of testing. They can almost dominate one's future. If we want to obtain a diploma, we must first pass the exams. If we do not have a diploma, we may not find a good job easily. That is the reason why all students are nervous and pale when they are sitting for an important examination which may concern their future.

Do not only think of the harm that they bring, but think of the good they may do for us. If we do not have exams, we may indulge ourselves in other things instead of books. Exams have to always drive us on. Examinations make us efficient and careful.

These qualities mean very much in the world of work which we will face when we have left college. Now another advantage of examinations is that they make us feel self-assured. If we can pass a difficult test like others, it shows that we are not inferior; we are as good as others.

The world is a competitive world. We will have to compete for jobs, business, etc. Examinations are also a kind of competition.

All in all, let's hope we are not governed by our enemy—exams. Instead we should make good use of them and emerge as a better student.

New Words and Expressions

advantage	/əd'vɑːntidʒ/	n.	优势，有利条件
common	/'kɔmən/	adj.	共同的，公共的
compete	/kəm'piːt/	vi.	比赛，竞争
competition	/kɔmpi'tiʃən/	n.	竞争，竞赛
concern	/kən'səːn/	vt.	涉及，关系到
detest	/di'test/	vt.	厌恶，憎恨
diploma	/di'pləumə/	n.	文凭，毕业证书
dominate	/'dɔmineit/	v.	支配，占优势
efficient	/i'fiʃənt/	adj.	生效的，有效率的
emerge	/i'məːdʒ/	vi.	显现，浮现
govern	/'gʌvən/	v.	统治，支配
harm	/hɑːm/	vt.	伤害，损害
indulge	/in'dʌldʒ/	v.	纵情于，放任，迁就
inferior	/in'fiəriə/	adj.	差的，次的
nervous	/'nəːvəs/	adj.	神经紧张的，不安的
obtain	/əb'tein/	vt.	获得，得到
pale	/peil/	adj.	苍白的，暗淡的
self-assured	/selfə'ʃuəd/	adj.	有自信的

Exercise 7: Select the answer that best expresses the main idea of the paragraph reading B.

1) If we want to find a good job, we should _____ first.

　　A. address ourselves decently　　　　　B. get diplomas

　　C. pass the examinations　　　　　　　D. stay home waiting for the proper chance

2) What's the attitude of the students to the examination?

　　A. They like it very much.　　　　　　B. They have a compromising attitude.

　　C. They detest it.　　　　　　　　　　D. They are apathetic for it.

3) The examination does also well to us in _____.

　　A. driving us on　　　　　　　　　　B. making us efficient and careful

　　C. making us feel self-assured　　　　　D. all of above

4) Which expression is **NOT TRUE** according to this passage?

  A. Examinations have become a popular form of testing and can almost dominate one's future.

  B. Examination is also another kind of competition.

  C. Examination always makes us feel tortured, so we must abolish this kind of test.

  D. During the course of preparing examination, we can obtain a lot.

5) The author's attitude toward examination is _____.

  A. disgusting

  B. respectful

  C. making a good use of it, at the same time not being controlled by it

  D. relentless

Exercise 8: Fill in the blanks with words and expressions given below. Change the form where necessary.

obtain	detest	diploma	concern	indulge in	advantage
compete for		emerge	inferior	dominate	

1) Her teaching experience gave her a big _____ over the other applicants for the job.

2) She and her sister are always _____ attention.

3) This article _____ a man who was wrongly imprisoned.

4) She has a _____ in education.

5) The team has _____ international football for many years.

6) The sun _____ from behind the clouds.

7) I occasionally _____ a big fat cigar.

8) She's so clever, she makes me feel _____.

9) He said the police had _____ this information by illegal means.

10) She _____ having to talk to people at parties.

Exercise 9: Translate the following sentences.

1）她遇到的那个人是个医生。

2）他过去经常晚饭后在河边散步。

3）与汽车相比，自行车有很多优点。

4）她不但歌唱得好，而且舞跳得也好。

5）我父母一直鼓励我努力学习。

Grammar Focus: Form Words 实词

在英语中，有实义并可以在句子中独立担任成分的词，称为实词，实词一共有6类：①名词（noun）；②形容词（adjective）；③代词（pronoun）；④数词（numeral）；⑤动词（verb）；⑥副词（adverb）。在本单元中，我们重点学习名词的复数形式和所有格；形容词和副词比较级；人称、物主、反身代词的各种不同形式和数词的用法。

一、名词的数

名词可分为可数名词和不可数名词。其中，可数名词有单、复数形式。

（1）多数可数名词的复数形式是有规则的，如下表所示。

词　　尾	复数形式	例　　词	例　　外
绝大多数名词	在词尾加-s	book–books，bag–bags，day–days，map–maps	
以字母 s，sh，ch，x 和以辅音加 o 结尾	在词尾后加-es	bus-buses，dish-dishes，box-boxes，hero-heroes	photo–photos，piano–pianos，radio–radios
以字母 f 或 fe 结尾的名词	把 f 或 fe 改成 v，再加-es	life–lives，leaf–leaves，shelf–shelves	roof–roofs，chief–chiefs，proof–proofs
以辅音字母加 y 结尾的名词	把 y 改为 i，再加-es	baby–babies，factory–factories，country–countries	

（2）有些可数名词的复数形式是不规则的，请记住以下的特殊名词复数形式。

man – men　　　woman –women　　foot – feet　　tooth – teeth

child – two children　　　ox – oxen　　　mouse – mice

a Chinese – two Chinese　　　a Japanese – three Japanese

an American – four Americans　　　a German – five Germans

an Englishman – six Englishmen　　a Dutchman – seven Dutchmen

（3）不可数名词没有复数形式。较为常见的不可数名词有：

advice　　　baggage　　　bread　　cash　　equipment　　furniture　　information

knowledge　　luggage　　　money　　news　　traffic　　　trouble　　work

二、名词的格

在英语中名词有三个格：主格（作主语）、宾格（作宾语）和所有格（作定语）。其中只有所有格有形式变化。

类　　型	所有格形式	例　　词
表示有生命的东西的名词	一般在名词后加's	my sister's husband，Mr. Lin's telephone number
以-s 或-es 结尾的复数名词	只在名词后加'	the teachers' reading room，the workers' dinning-room
不以-s 结尾的复数名词	加's	people's needs，women's rights
复合名词	在后面的名词后加-s	Her son-in-law's photo，the editor-in-chief's office
两人共有的东西	只在后一个名词加-s	Jane and Helen's room
不是共有的	两个名词之后都要加-s	Bill's and Tom's cars
表示无生命东西的名词	与 of 构成词组，表示所有关系	the cover of the book，the title of the song the cover of the book，the title of the song

三、形容词和副词比较级和最高级

词　型	比　较　级	最　高　级	例　词
单音节	词尾加-er	词尾加-est	kind–kinder–kindest
三音节或三音节以上	在原级前加 more	在原级前加 most	difficult–more difficult–the most difficult
双音节	有时在词尾加-er；有时在原级前加 more	有时在词尾加-est；有时在原级前加 most	happy–happier–happiest， clever–more clever–most clever

四、代词

（1）人称代词有人称、性、数、格之分。英语中主要有下面这些人称代词。

数格　人称	单　数		复　数	
	主格	宾格	主格	宾格
第一人称	I	me	we	us
第二人称	you	you	you	you
第三人称	he	him	they	them
	she	her		
	it	it		

（2）表示所属关系的代词叫物主代词，可分为形容词性物主代词和名词性物主代词两大类。

人　称	形　容　词　性		名　词　性	
	单数	复数	单数	复数
第一人称	my	our	mine	ours
第二人称	your	your	yours	yours
第三人称	his	their	his	theirs

（3）表示"我自己"、"你自己"、"他自己"、"我们自己"、"你们自己"、"他们自己"的代词称为反身代词。

数　人称	单　数	复　数
第一人称	myself	ourselves
第二人称	yourself	yourselves
第三人称	himself, herself, itself	themselves

五、基数词和序数词的用法

（1）有些基数词可构成固定词组。

e.g. one by one——一个个　　　　　twos and threes——三三两两

如果这些词以复数形式出现时，则表示"数以百计"、"成千上万"等大概的数量。

e.g.(hundreds, thousands, millions)of people

当 hundred，thousand，million 前有具体数字或被 several 修饰时，后面不加-s。

e.g. three million readers.

（2）在表示"年、月、日"时，"年"用基数词，"日"用序数词。

e.g. 1949 年 10 月 1 日——Oct. the first, nineteen forty-nine

　　20 世纪 70 年代（1970s）——the seventies of twentieth century

（3）表达分数时，先用基数词读分子，再用序数词读分母。当分子大于一时，分母要用复数形式的序数词。

e.g. 1/3——one third　　　　5/6——five sixths

（4）编号的事物可用序数词或基数词加名词表示。

e.g. the Fourth Lesson = Lesson Four

　　the fifteenth page = page fifteen

但编号的事物数字较大时，一般用基数词。

e.g. Room 302　　　　page 215　　　the No. 101 middle school

（5）百分比用基数词＋percent 来表示。

e.g. 50%——fifty percent　　60%——sixty percent

（6）基数词可与表示度量衡单位的词连用。

e.g. twenty meters deep　　　ten-meter-long　　　one hundred yards

Exercise 10: Select the best choice for each sentence.

1) Mr. Brown has only ＿＿＿＿ son.

　A. a 18-year-old　　　　　　　　　B. a 18-years old

　C. an 18-year-old　　　　　　　　　D. an 18-years-old

2) I wonder if she knew it was a long ＿＿＿＿ from here to the supermarket.

　A. street　　　　B. road　　　　　C. way　　　　D. block

3) Living ＿＿＿＿ are usually higher in cities than in the country.

　A. costs　　　　B. charge　　　　C. price　　　　D. value

4) When they arrived at the traffic lights, they went the wrong _____.

   A. route   B. way   C. road   D. path

5) England and America are _____ in many ways.

   A. like   B. looked   C. likely   D. alike

6) I never saw Mary again, and I did not hear from her, _____.

   A. either   B. too   C. neither   D. also

7) The streets are wet because it has rained _____ all morning.

   A. strongly   B. thick   C. deep   D. hardly

8) The football match was televised _____ from the People's Stadium.

   A. live   B. lively   C. alive   D. living

9) The food tastes _____ and sells _____.

   A. well, well   B. good, good   C. good, well   D. well, good

10) He was so astonished that he _____ knew what to do.

   A. never   B. seldom   C. hardly   D. hard

11) We were so _____ to see the _____ open ceremony of the Olympic games in Beijing.

   A. exciting, exciting   B. exciting, excited

   C. excited, excited   D. excited, exciting

12) Food and _____ are very important to us all.

   A. clothes   B. cloth   C. clothing   D. dress

13) I don't know how to get used to living in Shanghai. Can you give me some _____?

   A. idea   B. advice   C. suggestion   D. answer

14) Everyone in the group had tried but _____ of them succeeded.

   A. none   B. each   C. neither   D. every

15) There is _____ waiting for you in the office. Hurry up.

   A. no one   B. everything

   C. someone   D. anybody

16) It is impossible for so _____ workers to do so _____ work in a single week.

   A. few, many   B. little, much

   C. few, much   D. little, many

17) The two boys often write to _____.

   A. another   B. other   C. each other   D. one

18) We can see _____ stars at night if it doesn't rain.

   A. a thousand of   B. many thousands

   C. thousand of   D. thousands of

19) What I want to tell you is _____ Mary is coming this afternoon.

   A. this   B. that   C. it   D. those

20) _____ of the money _____ run out.

   A. Three-fifth, has   B. Three-fifth, has been

   C. Three-fifths, has   D. Three-fifths, have

Exercise 11: Fill in with best choice.

What do you do at the weekend? Some ___1)___ like to stay at home, but ___2)___ like to go for a walk or play football, My friend Jack works ___3)___ a factory during the week. At the weekend he ___4)___ the same thing. On Saturday he ___5)___ his car and on Sunday he goes with his family to a village ___6)___ the country. His uncle and aunt have a farm there. It isn't ___7)___ but ___8)___ so much to do on a farm. The children help with the animals and give ___9)___ food. Jack and his wife help in the fields. At the end of the day, they ___10)___ hungry and Jack's aunt gives them a big meal.

1) A. one	B. ones	C. people	D. peoples
2) A. another	B. other	C. others	D. other ones
3) A. hard in	B. hardly in	C. hard on	D. hardly on
4) A. makes always	B. does always	C. always make	D. always does
5) A. wash	B. watch	C. washes	D. watches
6) A. into	B. on	C. in	D. at
7) A. a big	B. one big	C. big one	D. a big one
8) A. it's always	B. there's always	C. always it's	D. always there's
9) A. it his	B. it its	C. them its	D. them their
10) A. all were	B. were all	C. all are	D. are all

Unit 2 Environment & Conservation
Communicative Samples

Conversation 1

(Mr. Zhang is visiting his hometown where he spent his childhood. Now he is talking with Mr. Jackson.)

Zhang: We're nearly there. All of my past is coming back to me. Look, the old park, "People's Park" is still there. I used to walk through that park each day to get to school.

Jackson: Really? I thought you had lived in Xi'an all your life.

Zhang: No, actually I lived in this old city from the 1970s to the early 1980s.

Jackson: Have you ever been back here since you left?

Zhang: No. But I've always dreamed of visiting. I didn't ever have enough time, so I've never been back since.

Jackson: Are we in the city center now?

Zhang: Yes, we are. Wow! The busy road, the skyscrapers…and it seems that the old department store has disappeared.

Jackson: That's the department store, isn't it? *(pointing)*

Zhang: Oh yes, that's right! It has changed a lot. It is bigger and taller than ever; there was also no flyover here in 1980s.

Jackson: Look at those skyscrapers!

Zhang: Wonderful! In the past, there were only small shops. I used to buy candy from one of them in particular; its name was "Xiao Hong Shop".

Jackson: Twenty years have passed. Great changes have taken place; we have been getting older. As a saying goes, "Time waits for no one".

Zhang: I agree. Listen, let's find somewhere to park and then walk around the city. Ok?

Jackson: Sure. I'd be glad to.

Conversation 2

(Two people are talking about a kind of technology for pollution control.)

Bill: The more I learn about the world around me, the more aware I become of the problems facing us.

Kate: Do you mean the problems in China?

Bill:　Yes. Here and all over the world.

Kate: Well, there's one problem I'm certainly aware of and that is the pollution all around us.

Bill:　That's one of the great problems. Fortunately, in many parts of the world, as people become more aware and apply new technologies to solve the pollution problems. So there is hope for the future.

Kate: Could you give me an example of a technology that could help with pollution control?

Bill:　Well, there certain types of bacteria that we can use to help control some pollution problems.

Kate: How can that be? I thought bacteria just caused illness.

Bill:　That's not entirely true. Some certain kinds of bacteria can "eat" petroleum products.

Kate: That sounds very strange. Could they be used to clean up big oil spills?

Bill:　Yes, of course.

Kate: Wow! Maybe such bacteria which have worried us for so long will help us save the world!

New Words and Expressions

apply	/əˈplai/	vt.	申请，应用
childhood	/ˈtʃaildhud/	n.	孩童时期
disappear	/ˌdisəˈpiə/	vi.	消失，不见
dream	/driːm/	v.	梦见，梦想
illness	/ˈilnis/	n.	疾病，生病
skyscraper	/ˈskaiskreipə(r)/	n.	摩天楼
spill	/spil/	n.	溢出，溅出
technology	/tekˈnɔlədʒi/	n.	科技，技术

Exercise 1: Complete the following sentences.

A: _____ (每个人都意识到) the dangers of air pollution.

B: Yes, you're right. How can we solve this problem?

A: Governments _____ (正在采取一些措施) to solve it.

B: How do the governments do?

A: They limit the exhaust fumes coming from cars.

B: _____ (好主意).

Exercise 2: Fill in the missing letters.

childho_d　　　　d_eamed　　　　skyscrap_r　　　　_acteria　　　　d_sa_pear

lyover　　　　appl　　　　_llness　　　　sp_ll　　　　t_chnolog_

Paragraph Reading A: Pollution

Most Americans would find it's hard to think what life would look like without a car. However, some have become aware of the serious problems of air pollution caused by the car. The polluted air becomes poisonous and dangerous to health.

One way to get rid of the polluted air is to build a car that does not pollute air. That's what several of the large factories have been trying to do. But to build a clean car is easier said than done. Progress in this field has been slow down. Another way is replacing the current gasoline consuming car engine with another kind of engine. Now inventors are working on steam cars as well as electric cars. Many makers believe that it will take years to develop a useful model that pleases man.

To prevent the world from being further polluted by cars, we have to make some changes to the way many of us live. Americans for example, have to reduce the total number of their cars. They are encouraged to travel and go to work by bicycle. It is thought that such practice will help man to keep the air clean.

But this change will not come about easily. A large number of workers might find themselves without jobs if a car factory closed. Thus the problem of air pollution would become less important when put alongside that of unemployment. Although cars have led us to a better life, they have also brought us new problems.

New Words and Expressions

inventor	/in'ventə/	*n.*	发明家
alongside	/ə'lɔŋ'said/	*adv.*	在旁
aware	/ə'wεə/	*adj.*	意识到的
change	/tʃeindʒ/	*vt.*	改变，变革
consume	/kən'sjuːm/	*vt.*	消耗，消费
current	/'kʌrənt/	*adj*	当前的，通用的
dangerous	/'deindʒrəs/	*adj.*	危险的
develop	/di'veləp/	*vt.*	发展，进步
encourage	/in'kʌridʒ/	*vt.*	鼓励
engine	/'endʒin/	*n.*	发动机，机车
further	/'fəːðə/	*adj.*	更远的，更多的
gasoline	/'gæsəliːn/	*n.*	汽油

get rid of		v.	摆脱，除去
poisonous	/ˈpɔiznəs/	adj.	有毒的
pollution	/pəˈluːʃən/	n.	污染，玷污
practice	/ˈpræktis/	n.	实践，惯例
progress	/ˈprəugres/	vi.	前进，进步
replace	/ri(ː)ˈpleis/	vt.	取代，替换
serious	/ˈsiəriəs/	adj.	严肃的，认真的

Exercise 3: Select the answer that best expresses the main idea of the paragraph reading A.

1) What can we infer from the passage?

　　A. The cars caused much more traffic accidents nowadays.

　　B. It is impossible for us to replace the gas today.

　　C. More cars will make more serious pollution.

　　D.It isn't always easy to say which is more important, unemployment or pollution.

2) The most difficult thing to reduce the pollution caused by cars is _____.

　　A. to persuade the people to travel by bike

　　B. to develop a kind of new car to replace the traditional car as soon as possible

　　C. to reduce the total number of the cars

　　D. to discover a new type of engine

3) The phrase "such practice" in the third paragraph most probably refers to _____.

　　A. reduce the total number of the cars

　　B. change the ways of life

　　C. to travel and go to work by bicycle

　　D. both A and C

4) How many ways to reduce the car pollution are mentioned in the passage?

　　A. 3　　　　　　　　　　　　　　B. 1

　　C. 4　　　　　　　　　　　　　　D. 2

5) What is the author's attitude toward the relationship between the car and pollution?

　　A. negative　　　　　　　　　　　B. objective

　　C. optimistic　　　　　　　　　　D. pessimistic

Exercise 4: Fill in the blanks with words and expressions given below. Change the form where necessary.

| aware of | get rid of | replace | consume | practice | encourage | serious |
| progress | current | further | | | | |

1) The fire quickly _____ the wooden hut.

2) The word is no longer in _____ use.

3) It's in companies' interests to _____ union membership.

4) He said that the teacher was already _____ the problem.

5) I haven't played tennis for years, so I'm really out of _____.

6) Jane is still in hospital, but she's making _____.

7) We've _____ the old adding machine with a computer.

8) I've tried all sorts of medicines to _____ this cold.

9) The storm caused _____ damage.

10) He's too tired to walk any _____.

Exercise 5: Definitions of these words appear on the right. Put the letter of the appropriate definition next to each word.

1) _____ dangerous   a. a piece of machinery with moving parts which changes power from steam, oil into movement

2) _____ poisonous   b. a person who invents something new

3) _____ gasoline   c. likely to cause danger

4) _____ inventor   d. petrol

5) _____ change   e. to come or bring gradually to a larger, or more advanced state

6) _____ pollution   f. containing poison

7) _____ engine   g. close to and in line with the edge of something

8) _____ replace   h. the action of polluting or the state of being polluted

9) _____ develop   i. to make or become different form

10) _____ alongside   j. to take the place of

Exercise 6: Translate the following sentences.

1）昨天我们用了大约两个小时做完了那件工作。

2）孩子们学好英语和计算机是很重要的。

3）上学期他学习不努力，结果数学考试不及格。

4）学生们对报告人所讲的内容很感兴趣。

5）当他们到达电影院时，电影已经开始了。

Paragraph Reading B: Global Warming

The impact of global warming could be twice as severe as United Nations scientists had previously feared the world's largest climate-modeling experiment has shown.

Average temperature could rise by 11℃ (20℉) to reach highs that would change the face of the globe, which is said by researchers who have run 60,000 computer simulations of climate change.

The conclusions suggest that forecasts by the UN's Intergovernmental Panel on Climate Change (IPCC) may be much too conservative. In the worst case, the world would eventually heat up by almost double the maximum increase envisaged by the panel. The IPCC's latest report predicted that temperatures will rise by between 1.4℃ (2.5℉) and 5.8℃ (10.4℉) by 2100.

A world 11℃ warmer than it is today would be unrecognizable. While records show that the planet has been hotter than it is today for about 80 per cent of its history, there is no evidence that it has ever been more than about 7℃ warmer.

Although it would take hundreds of years for the full effects to be felt, the polar ice caps eventually would melt completely, causing sea levels to rise by 70m to 100m (230ft to 330ft). Coastal and low-lying cities such as London and New York would be submerged.

As the 11℃ figure is a global average, temperatures would be expected to climb even further in some regions. David Stainforth of the University of Oxford, the study's chief scientist, said: "When I start to look at these figures, I get very worried about them. An 11-degree warmed world would be a dramatically different world."

New Words and Expressions

average	/ˈævəridʒ/	adj.	一般的，通常的
chief	/tʃiːf/	n.	首领，领袖
climate	/ˈklaimit/	n.	气候，风土
conservative	/kənˈsəːvətiv/	adj.	保守的，守旧的
dramatically	/drəˈmætikəli/	adv.	戏剧地，引人注目地
eventually	/iˈventjuəli/	adv.	最后，终于
evidence	/ˈevidəns/	n.	明显，显著
figure	/ˈfigə/	n.	数字，形状
forecast	/ˈfɔːkɑːst/	n.	预测，预报
global	/ˈgləubəl/	adj.	球形的，全球的
impact	/ˈimpækt/	n.	冲击，影响
maximum	/ˈmæksiməm/	adj.	最高的，最多的
melt	/melt/	v.	（使）融化，（使）熔化
planet	/ˈplænit/	n.	行星
predict	/priˈdikt/	v.	预知，预言
previously	/ˈpriːvjuːsli/	adv.	先前，以前
researcher	/riˈsəːtʃə(r)/	n.	研究员
simulation	/ˌsimjuˈleiʃən/	n.	仿真，假装
submerge	/səbˈməːdʒ/	v.	浸没，淹没
temperature	/ˈtempritʃə(r)/	n.	温度

Exercise 7: Select the answer that best expresses the main idea of the paragraph reading B.

1) The author's purpose in this passage is _____.

A. to tell people to protect the surroundings

B. to make people understand how bad global warming is

C. to give some necessary explanations about global warming

D. to protect people against global warming

2) The word "submerged" in paragraph means "_____".

A. destroyed   B. ruined   C. flooded   D. conquered

3) Which of the following statements is TRUE ?

A. The globe will disappear 100 years later.

B. In every region the temperature will climb by 11℃.

C. If the temperature continues rising, some coastal cities will disappear.

D. The rising temperature will be of great influence on our lives today.

4) How severe is the global warming today?

A. It is more severe than the scientists had feared before.

B. It is as severe as the scientists had thought.

C. It is much better than the scientists had expected.

D. It is the less severe than the scientists had thought.

5) What's the tone of the author about the global warming?

A. Disappointed.   B. Optimistic.   C. Suspicious.   D. Worried.

Exercise 8: Fill in the blanks with words and expressions given below. Change the form where necessary.

previously	average	eventually	evidence	more than	melt
maximum	conservative	global	submerge		

1) The report found no _____ that the documents had been tampered with.

2) The sun _____ the snow.

3) At a _____ estimate, the holiday will cost $300.

4) This record was _____ held by Sebastian Coe.

5) _____ he tired of trying so hard.

6) _____ climatic changes may have been responsible for the extinction of the dinosaurs.

7) Business use computers a lot _____ they used to.

8) What's the _____ amount of wine you're allowed to take through customs duty-free?

9) At the first sign of danger the submarine will _____.

10) What is the _____ rainfall for July?

Exercise 9: Translate the following sentences.

1）北京是她游览过的最美丽的城市之一。

2）他们在北京生活了很多年，对这里的天气已经很习惯了。

3）我们深信如果我们勤奋工作，我们的愿望一定会实现。

4）老师告诉我们这本小说值得一读。

5）我的朋友问我是否我在工作中有困难。

Grammar Focus: Notional Words 虚词

冠词、介词、连词、感叹词这四种都不能在句子中独立担任任何成分，称为虚词。在本单元中，我们重点学习冠词和介词。

一、不定冠词的用法

（1）a, an 表示"一个"或表示泛指。

（2）a, an 用于固定搭配。

e.g. a bit of, a few, a little, a great deal of, a lot of

　　have a good time, have a word with, go out for a walk

　　once upon a time, many a time, a long time, a short time

　　as a result, as a whole, at a loss, at a time

　　in a hurry, in a moment, in a word

e.g. a bit of, a few, a little, a great deal of, a lot of

　　have a good time, have a word with, go out for a walk

　　once upon a time, many a time, a long time, a short time

　　as a result, as a whole, at a loss, at a time

　　in a hurry, in a moment, in a word

二、定冠词 the 的一般用法

（1）表示特指、前面已说过的，或说话人与听话人都知道的共同所指的事物。

（2）用于姓氏的复数名词之前，表示"一家人"。

e.g. The Greens have moved to the new house.

（3）在表示乐器名称的名词之前加 the（在表示体育项目的名词之前不加 the）。

（4）用于固定搭配。

e.g. at the moment、at the most、by the way、for the time being、in the distance、in the end、in the long run、on the average、on the contrary、on the whole

三、介词的主要分类

（1）表示"方向"。

e.g. to、for、towards、up、down、along、across、through、into、out、off、round、around、of、about、throughout、in

（2）表示"位置"。

e.g. at、in、on、by、over、beside、above、under、below、beneath

（3）表示"时间"。

e.g. at、in、on、over、for、through、throughout、from、during、since、till、by、until、
before、after

（4）表示"原因"。

e.g. of、from、with、for、through、because of、on account of、owing to、due to

（5）表示"方法"。

e.g. by、with

（6）表示"让步"。

e.g. in spite of、despite、for all、not with standing

（7）表示"关于"。

e.g. with regard to、with respect to、with reference to、as to、as for、regarding、in regard to、
concerning、on、about

（8）表示"除外"。

e.g. but、except、except for、with the exception of、besides

（9）表示"标准"、"比率"、"单位价格"。

e.g. by、at、for

四、某些介词短语应用非常广泛，应该掌握

（1）相同的动词与不同介词搭配时，有不同的意义。

e.g. Have you *heard form* your parents since they left?（收到来信）

　　Did you *hear about* the party?（听说）

　　The accident *resulted in* the death of two passengers.（导致）

　　His illness *resulted from* malnutrition.（由于）

（2）相同的形容词与不同的介词搭配，有不同的意义。

e.g. They are *favorable to* our plan.（赞成）

　　This kind of weather is *favorable for* swimming.（有利于）

　　His face is quite *familiar to* me.（为……熟悉）

　　I am still *familiar with* his face.（对……熟悉）

（3）有些形容词要求与介词搭配才具有一定的意义。

e.g. Are you *satisfied with* the result?

The students are *fond of* pop music.

These oranges are *inferior to* those I bought last week.

He is still not *accustomed to* the cold weather in Beijing.

（4）某些名词后要求用特定的介词。

e.g. There seems to be no *solution to* this problem.

There has been great *increase in* the production in the last twenty years.

The family background has great *influence on* the family members.

（5）某些名词之前要求用特定的介词。

e.g. *On my way* home, I met my old school classmates.

We sang and danced *to our heart's content*.

Exercise 10: Select the best choice for each sentence.

1) The suggestion _____ we go to Beijisng for a holiday was made by Julia.

    A. whether   B. if   C. when   D. that

2) My grandpa likes playing _____ table-tennis while my grandma likes playing _____ violin.

    A. /, the   B. a, a   C. /, /   D. the, the

3) Texas has _____ extensive coastline that runs along _____ Gulf of Mexico.

    A. an, the   B. the, the   C. a, the   D. an, /

4) Mr. Li was very busy _____ he still went to take part in Olympic activities.

    A. so   B. and   C. besides   D. but

5) I bought _____ coat yesterday. _____ coat was blue.

    A. a, A   B. the, A   C. the, The   D. a, The

6) Mr. Smith will learn to drive _____ next Monday.

    A. since   B. after   C. on   D. in

7) Do you think it is _____ useful dictionary?

    A. the   B. /   C. a   D. an

8) _____ the gate and you'll find the entrance to the park _____ the other side.

    A. Along, on   B. Through, on   C. Up, to   D. Across, on

9) The tables in that restaurant are so close together that there's hardly any room to move _____ .

    A. with   B. from   C. between   D. among

10) New York City is _____ exciting place to visit.

    A. /   B. a   C. the   D. an

11) It must be true. I heard it _____ the radio.

    A. above   B. over   C. in   D. from

12) January is _____ first month of the year.

    A. a   B. /   C. the   D. an

13) Are there any public holidays _____ Christmas and Easter?

    A. between   B. among   C. in   D. for

14) English is _____ language, and it is _____ important tool.

    A. a, an   B. /, an   C. the, the   D. a, /

15) Remember not to run _____ the road.

    A. on   B. at   C. across   D. through

16) _____ rich wish to be richer, and _____ poor fear to be poorer.

    A. The, a   B. A, a   C. A, the   D. The, the

17) Please give me a call _____ you arrive in Shanghai.

    A. as soon as   B. whether   C. while   D. until

18) We will stay at home _____ it snows tomorrow.

    A. though   B. if   C. as if   D. but

19) We are satisfied with the guesthouse _____ the price.

    A. except   B. except for   C. besides   D. beside

20) He looked in all direction, _____ he saw nobody. He had to solve the problem by himself.

    A. though   B. when   C. but   D. if

Exercise 11: Fill in with best choice.

Mrs. Jackson is an old woman who has a small room __1)__ an old house. She __2)__ there since 1974. That was the year when her husband __3)__ He had been ill __4)__ many years. After his death Mrs. Jackson had __5)__ money at all. She found work in a factory. Her job was to clean the offices. She __6)__ get up at 5 o'clock __7)__ the morning. Last year she was ill and her doctor said: "__8)__ work so hard." Now Mrs. Jackson sells newspapers __9)__ a big shop in the middle of town. She __10)__ doesn't have much money but she is happier now.

    1) A. in   B. on   C. from   D. of

    2) A. is living   B. lives   C. lived   D. has lived

    3) A. died   B. has died   C. dead   D. was dead

    4) A. since   B. for   C. in   D. during

    5) A. none   B. any   C. no   D. not

    6) A. must   B. must to   C. had to   D. has to

    7) A. of   B. at   C. in   D. on

    8) A. You haven't   B. Not   C. Don't   D. Better not

    9) A. outside   B. without   C. in front   D. out of

    10) A. always   B. still   C. yet   D. already

Unit 3   Web
Communicative Samples

Conversation 1

(Tom and Crystal, two college students, are discussing a computer craze.)

Tom:　　Crystal, have you found that computers have played a very important role in students' lives?

Crystal: Of course.

Tom:　　Now many students have computers. A computer craze has hit the campuses in many colleges of China.

Crystal: Yes, you are right. If you enter a dormitory, you will find one or two computers there.

Tom:　　It is true that computers have been used widely in students' studies. But some students often play computer games.

Crystal: That's true. According to the survey, computers greatly influence some students' studies.

Tom:　　In my university, many young video addicts could indulge themselves in games all night long.

Crystal: Yes. Fortunately, many universities and colleges are aware of such problems and are planning to carry out projects to correct this phenomenon.

Tom:　　The computers themselves are not the problem. It is the way they are used.

Crystal: I agree.

Tom:　　We're pretty sure that colleges and universities will find a good way to deal with these problems.

Crystal: I hope they will.

Conversation 2

(Two people are talking about computer viruses.)

Jane:　　Hi, what are you doing there?

Smith:　There is something wrong with my computer, but I don't know what's wrong with it.

Jane:　　Don't worry. Let me have a check.

Smith:　Is it serious?

Jane:　　Yes, there is the problem. There are viruses in your computer.

Smith: You're probably right. This often happens.

Jane: You have to know how to protect your computer against virus attacks. Otherwise they will destroy your beloved computer.

Smith: Do you have any good ideas?

Jane: Well, in actual fact, nothing can guarantee absolute computer security. But the latest anti-virus software can improve the security of computers and lower the possibility of infection.

Smith: Ok, I see.

Jane: Remember, in the absence of any security measures, to ensure safety from viruses or other problems encountered, prior periodic backup of important documents is essential.

Smith: You've given me a lot of good advice. Thank you very much.

New Words and Expressions

craze	/kreiz/	n.	狂热
deal	/diːl/	vi.	处理，应付
hit	/hit/	vt.	打击，碰撞
influence	/ˈinfluəns/	vt.	影响，改变
protect	/prəˈtekt/	vt.	保护
security	/siˈkjuəriti/	n.	安全
virus	/ˈvaiərəs/	n.	[微]病毒

Exercise 1: Complete the following sentences.

A: Hi, what are you doing there?

B: _____ (计算机出现点问题).

A: Don't worry. _____ (我查查看).

B: Is it serious?

A: Yes, _____ (你的计算机中病毒了). But I have removed them.

B: Thank you very much.

Exercise 2: Fill in the missing letters.

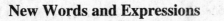

cr_ze   hi_   infl_ence   d_al   pr_tect

s_curity   _bsence   b_loved   viru_   _ddict

Paragraph Reading A: The Internet

The Internet is a loose network which enables PCs in most large organizations and many

homes and small businesses (using a standard connection to a telephone line) to communicate with each other around the world at a low cost. The Internet belongs to no one although the telecommunication which links it uses are owned and has no central authority; it is really a set of "communication protocols", more like a language than a physical network, which means that any computer, whatever its internal language, can communicate with any other. The Internet has existed for many years as an academic network, but took off as a mass application only in the mid 1990s. This was partly because of the invention of new software which made it easier to find useful information and move between different sites.

The Internet exhibits a characteristic crucial for all successful communication networks: that their value to each member increases with the number of other members. The same happened with telephones and, more recently, fax machines: neither would be useful—except as a status symbol—if no one else had one. Once enough other people were on the Web, it became worthwhile for yet more people. In reality, despite all the talk of Websites, "surfing" and cyber commerce, the main way most people use the Internet today is for e-mail—typed messages and documents sent from one PC to another. The e-mail population has reached "critical mass" since about 1995.

New Words and Expressions

academic	/ˌækəˈdemik/	adj.	学院的，理论的
authority	/ɔːˈθɔriti/	n.	权威，威信
characteristic	/ˌkæriktəˈristik/	adj.	特有的，典型的
communicate	/kəˈmjuːnikeit/	v.	沟通，通信
critical	/ˈkritikəl/	adj.	评论的，批评的
standard	/ˈstændəd/	n.	标准，规格
despite	/disˈpait/	prep.	不管，尽管
exhibit	/igˈzibit/	vt.	展出，陈列
loose	/luːs/	adj.	宽松的，自由的
mass	/mæs/	adj.	大规模的，集中的
network	/ˈnetwəːk/	n.	网络
organization	/ˌɔːgənaiˈzeiʃən/	n.	组织，机构
physical	/ˈfizikəl/	adj.	身体的，物质的
protocol	/ˈprəutəkɔl/	n.	草案，协议
reality	/ri(ː)ˈæliti/	n.	真实，事实
status	/ˈsteitəs/	n.	身份，地位
surf	/səːf/	vi.	冲浪

symbol	/'simbəl/	*n.*	符号，记号
telecommunication		*n.*	电信，无线电通信
worthwhile	/'wə:ð'(h)wail/	*adj.*	值得做的

Exercise 3: Select the answer that best expresses the main idea of the paragraph reading A.

1) Which of the following statements is TRUE?

   A. The Internet can make it cheaper for people in the USA to communicate with each other than the telephone.

   B. The Internet existed for many years as an academic network till the mid 1990s.

   C. The more people use the Internet，the more valuable it will become to them.

   D. The Internet was widely applied only because of the invention of new software.

2) Which do you think is the most proper as the headline of the passage?

   A. How the Internet works.

   B. The Internet is the most useful media in the world.

   C. More like a language than a physical network.

   D. Something about the Internet.

3) The Internet belongs to _____.

   A. Bill Gates   B. anyone who owns it

   C. not all people the world over   D. The passage doesn't tell us clearly.

4) The Internet can be used _____.

   A. in various fields   B. to communicate with each other

   C. as a language   D. for a lot of information or electronic mail

5) The Internet is _____.

   A. a combination of various kinds of computers

   B. a loose network where PCs can communicate with each other

   C. a kind of language

   D. an academic network

Exercise 4: Fill in the blanks with words and expressions given below. Change the form where necessary.

| loose | physical | communicate | symbol | critical | worthwhile |
| despite | surf | internal | exhibit | | |

1) They used carrier pigeons to _____ with the headquarters.

2) In the picture the tree is the _____ of life and the snake the _____ of evil.

3) The company insisted that he had a complete _____.

4) The doctor x-rayed her to see if there were any _____ injuries.

5) We had a long wait, but it was _____ because we got the tickets.

6) If the waves are big enough, we will go _____.

7) The radio wasn't working because of a _____ connection in the wires.

8) She _____ a curious lack of interest in fashion.

9) He came to the meeting _____ his illness.

10) We arrived at the _____ moment.

Exercise 5: Definitions of these words appear on the right. Put the letter of the appropriate definition next to each word.

1) _____ organization   a. to show (something) in public

2) _____ network   b. the ability, power or right to control and command

3) _____ authority   c. a group of people with a special purpose, such as a club or business

4) _____ academic   d. something or everything that in real

5) _____ mass   e. to gather together in large numbers

6) _____ exhibit   f. one's legal state position, or condition

7) _____ status   g. of teaching, studying, schools, colleges

8) _____ characteristic   h. (of) typical; representing a person's or thing's usual character

9) _____ reality   i. a large system of lines, tubes, wires, etc., that cross one another or are connected with one another

10) _____ protocol   j. first or original draft of a diplomatic agreement

Exercise 6: Translate the following sentences.

1）她告诉我她去过上海三次。

2）问题是我们如何才能准时到达那里。（on time）

3）我不知道他是否胜任这份工作。（be fit for）

4）我的自行车坏了，我可以用用你的吗？（may）

5）昨天在回家的路上，我遇到了我父亲的一位老朋友。

Paragraph Reading B: Americans' Use of the Internet

America Online is one of the largest American companies that provide links to the Internet. A recent report by AOL said the company provides service for more than 24 million people around the world. AOL is only one of many such companies.

AOL and other companies that provide links to the Internet also provide electronic mail and links to the World Wide Web. Most companies also provide information, electronic news, methods to research products and ways to buy almost anything. These companies have opened a small window through which to view the world.

Many Americans use the Internet for everyday communications. The Lebonette family in Virginia is a good example. Robert and Margaret Lebonette have three children. Their oldest son recently became a student at the

Ohio State University in Columbus. He now lives several hundred kilometers from home. Mrs. Lebonette says she communicates with her son more than when he was living at home. Both enjoy writing and receiving electronic mail. They sometimes send and receive electronic messages on an instant chat line. This permits them to answer each other immediately.

The youngest Lebonette's child is fifteen-year-old Jillian. She uses the computer to communicate with local friends and some who live many kilometers away. Using the computer to communicate costs very little. Jillian also uses the computer as a tool for schoolwork.

New Words and Expressions

chat	/tʃæt/	v.	聊天
electronic	/ilek'trɔnik/	adj.	电子的
immediately	/i'mi:djətli/	adv.	立即，马上
instant	/'instənt/	adj.	立即的，直接的
kilometer	/'kiləmi:tə/	n.	千米，公里
link	/liŋk/	vt.	连接，联合
method	/'meθəd/	n.	方法
online	/ɔnlain/	n.	联机，在线式
permit	/pə(:)'mit/	v.	许可，允许
product	/'prɔdʌkt/	n.	产品，产物
provide	/prə'vaid/	v.	供应，供给
research	/ri'sə:tʃ/	n./vi.	研究，调查
service	/'sə:vis/	n.	服务
tool	/tu:l/	n.	工具，用具
view	/vju:/	n.	景色，观点

Exercise 7: Select the answer that best expresses the main idea of the paragraph reading B.

1) What's the best title of the passage?

   A. Americans' Use of the personal computers.

   B. Americans' Use of the Internet.

   C. The Lebonette family's use of the network.

   D. America Online's use of the Internet.

2) Which of the following statements is **TRUE**?

   A. Only AOL provides links to the Internet.

   B. AOL only provides links to the Internet.

   C. AOL is just one of many such companies.

   D. AOL and other companies just provide links to the Internet.

3) Why do people like to use the Internet for communicating with each other?

   A. It is very convenient.　　　　　　　　B. It is very cheap.

   C. It is not limited by time and distance.　　D. All of the above.

4) What's the meaning of the word "view" here?

   A. Understand.　　　　　　　　　　　B. Know.

   C. Watch .　　　　　　　　　　　　　D. Touch.

5) From the passage we can infer that _____ .

   A. Men and women, old and young can all use the Internet to communicate

   B. University students can use the Internet to communicate

   C. America Online is the largest American companies that provide links to the Internet

   D. Only more than 24 million people around the world are using the Internet

Exercise 8: Fill in the blanks with words and expressions given below. Change the form where necessary.

online	provide	view	instant	chat	service	kilometer	link
research	permit						

1) I _____ his action as a breach of trust.

2) The two friends sat in a corner and _____ about the weather.

3) The bridge is almost 2 _____ long.

4) America _____ is one of the largest American companies that provide links to the Internet.

5) They are doing some _____ on the effects of brain damage.

6) The road _____ all the new towns.

7) The rules of the club do not _____ smoking.

8) This computer supplier provides very good after-sales _____.

9) The hotel _____ a shoe-cleaning service for its residents.

10) I will be back in an _____.

Exercise 9: Translate the following sentences.

1）如果我是你，我不会改变主意的。

2）这正是他们要找的磁带。（look for）

3）我进入房间时，他正在给朋友写信。

4）前天她因病未能去上班。（because of）

5）她宁愿呆在家里也不愿去看那无意义的电影。（prefer）

Grammar Focus:Tenses 时态（一）

英语的时态是英语语法的一个重要组成部分。在本单元中，我们来学习一般现在时、现在进行时、将来时、过去时和过去将来时。

一、一般现在时

（1）一般现在时通常用在以下几种情况：表示经常发生的或习惯性的动作或目前的状态；现状、性质、状态和经常的或习惯性的动作；不受时间限制的事实或普遍真理等。

（2）构成：大多以动词原形表示；主语为第三人称单数时，通常在动词后加-s 或-es（其变化规则同名词单数变复数的规则相同）。

e.g. work–works 　　learn–learns 　　come–comes

pass–passes 　　wash–washes 　　teach–teaches

fix–fixes 　　go–goes

二、现在进行时

（1）现在进行时表示以下几种情况：说话时正在发生或进行着的动作；现阶段正在进行而说话时不一定正在进行的动作；反复出现的或习惯性动作，含有说话人的赞扬、不满、讨厌、遗憾等情绪；事物发展的过程；按计划即将发生的动作等。

（2）构成：am / is / are＋现在分词（动词＋ing）。

一般情况下，现在分词的构成是在动词词尾加-ing。若动词词尾是 e，则去掉 e，再加-ing。

e.g. go – going 　　see – seeing 　　stay – staying

have – having 　　live –living 　　take – taking

cut – cutting 　　run – running 　　stop – stopping

die – dying 　　lie – lying 　　tie – tying

三、一般过去时

（1）一般过去时表示以下几种情况：过去时间里发生的动作或存在的状态；过去经常或反复发生的习惯性动作。

（2）构成。

1）规则动词的过去式是在动词原形后加-ed 或-d。若动词词尾是 y，则把 y 变成 i，再加-ed。

e.g. want – wanted 　　open – opened 　　play – played

live – lived 　　hope – hoped 　　move – moved

study – studied 　　cry – cried 　　try – tried 　　carry – carried

stop – stopped 　　beg – begged 　　permit – permitted

2）不规则动词的过去式有其特殊形式，须逐个记忆。

e.g. beat – beat 　　become – became 　　catch – caught 　　feel – felt

go – went 　　meet – met 　　sell – sold 　　tear – tore

grow – grew 　　hide – hid 　　see – saw

四、一般将来时

（1）一般将来时表示将来发生的动作或存在的状态。

（2）构成：由助动词 shall 或 will＋动词原形构成，其中 shall 多和第一人称搭配。

一般将来时除了上述形式外，还有 "be going to ＋动词原形"；"be to＋动词原形" 和 "be about to＋动词原形"，这些结构在用法上有差别，详见用法说明。

五、 过去将来时

（1）过去将来时表示从过去某一时间来看将要发生的动作或存在的状态；was / were going to＋动词原形，表示过去曾经打算或准备要做的动作。

（2）构成：由助动词 should 或 would＋动词原形构成，其中 should 多和第一人称搭配。

Exercise 10: Select the best choice for each sentence.

1) On Saturday afternoon, Mrs. Green went to the market, _____ some bananas and visited her cousin.

　　A. bought　　　　B. buying　　　　C. to buy　　　　D. buy

2) It never _____ here in winter.

　　A. snow　　　　B. snows　　　　C. has snows　　　　D. has snowed

3) That suit _____ over 60 dollars.

　　A. has costed　　　B. costed　　　　C. is costed　　　　D. costs

4) — I have bought an English-Chinese dictionary.

　　— When and where _____ you _____ it?

　　A. do, buy　　　　B. did, buy　　　　C. have, bought　　　　D. had, bought

5) We _____ with an old friend of ours the day before yesterday.

　　A. met　　　　B. meet　　　　C. was meeting　　　　D. have met

6) The accident _____ right here a week ago.

　　A. happens　　　B. happened　　　　C. was happening　　　　D. has happened

7) What _____ doing when you _____?

　　A. they were, got there　　　　　　B. were they, arrived there

　　C. were they, came there　　　　　　D. they were, reached there

8) John _____ Henry when they met at the airport.

　　A. shakes hand with　　　　　　　B. shakes hands with

　　C. shook hand with　　　　　　　D. shook hands with

9) The teacher said that the earth _____ round the sun in 365 days.

　　A. moves　　　　B. moved　　　　C. has moved　　　　D. is moving

10) According to the timetable, the train for Beijing _____ at seven o'clock in the evening.

　　A. leaves　　　　B. has left　　　　C. was left　　　　D. will leave

11) The war _____ in 1937.

　　A. was broken　　　B. was breaking　　　　C. had broken out　　　　D. broke out

12) It _____ Jack and Mary who helped the blind man the other day.

    A. was   B. is   C. are   D. were

13) There _____ a lot of new things last year.

    A. is   B. are   C. was   D. were

14) A mother who _____ her son will do everything for his happiness.

    A. is loving   B. loves   C. loved   D. has loved

15) Not every one _____ in for sports.

    A. goes   B. went to   C. has gone   D. had gone

16) I _____ when you called me.

    A. went out   B. am going out

    C. was going out   D. have gone out

17) There _____ a meeting to discuss the problem tomorrow.

    A. has   B. had   C. are to be   D. is to be

18) They told us that they _____ us to overcome the difficulties in English.

    A. helped   B. help   C. will help   D. were going to help

19) If it rains tomorrow, I _____ stay at school.

    A. would   B. will   C. will be   D. would be

20) I first met Lisa 3 years ago. She _____ at a bookshop at the time.

    A. has worked   B. was working

    C. had been working   D. had worked

Exercise 11: Fill in with best choice.

Brickton is a little village __1)__ from Manchester. When people __2)__ to go to Manchester, they usually go __3)__ train. It takes about __4)__ . A lot of people live in Brickton but __5)__ jobs are in Manchester. In Manchester there are __6)__ cinemas than in Brickton. People there are not very __7)__ cinemas but if they want to see films, they can often see __8)__ on television. Brickton is __9)__ Manchester and so the people there __10)__ use their cars so often.

   1) A. not far   B. not long   C. not near   D. not away

   2) A. went   B. want   C. wanted   D. wants

   3) A. by   B. in   C. on   D. with

   4) A. an half hour   B. half an hour   C. half hour   D. half a hour

   5) A. its   B. their   C. it's   D. the

   6) A. many   B. more   C. much   D. most

   7) A. interested on B. interesting on   C. interested in   D. interesting in

   8) A. some old   B. olds   C. old one   D. old ones

   9) A. more small that B. more small than C. smaller that   D. smaller than

  10) A. don't need to   B. aren't   C. don't must   D. mustn't

Unit 4 Climate & Weather
Communicative Samples

Conversation 1

(Yang Ming asks his teacher some questions about climate.)

Yang: Good morning, Mr. Zhang. Could you tell me the difference between the climate of Beijing and Kunming?

Zhang: Of course. Beijing is situated in the North and Kunming is in the Southwest.

Yang: Is the climate related to the latitude?

Zhang: Yes, Beijing is in the high latitudes while Kunming is in the low latitudes.

Yang: Does the latitude influence the temperature?

Zhang: Certainly, it's generally colder in Beijing than in Kunming. The weather in Beijing is very bad in the autumn.

Yang: Why? Can you explain?

Zhang: It's cloudy and windy. Throughout the whole year, the wind blows very hard. The dirt carried in the air can make people dirty. It can even get through the window and fall on your furniture.

Yang: But the strong wind offers a good chance to fly kites. What about Kunming? What is the weather like there?

Zhang: It's warm and sunny. The weather is agreeable, comfortable and humid. The range of temperatures across the year isn't that wide.

Yang: So it's like spring throughout the year?

Zhang: That's right.

Yang: Thank you very much.

Conversation 2

(Wang Lin and Alice are drinking coffee.)

Wang: Hi, Alice. It's a sunny day today, isn't it?

Alice: Yeah, I like sitting in the sun, drinking coffee and listening to light music.

Wang: You really know how to enjoy yourself and make yourself comfortable.

Alice: I'm afraid I've got a piece of bad news. It is forecast that it will be cloudy tomorrow.

Wang: It's so changeable! Maybe the day after tomorrow it will be snowy.

Alice: How smart you are! It is predicted to snow.

Wang: Really? That's great! If so, we can buy a roll of film to take photos, and invite our friends Amy, Martin and Sally to play with snowballs.

Alice: And we can also build a snowman on our playground!

Wang: That's great! I really like building snowmen. So the upcoming forecast isn't such bad news at all.

Alice: Let's hope it's correct!

Wang: Yes, let's.

New Words and Expressions

autumn	/ˈɔːtəm/	n.	秋天
changeable	/ˈtʃeɪndʒəbl/	adj	可改变的
dirt	/dəːt/	n.	污垢，泥土
humid	/ˈhjuːmid/	adj.	充满潮湿的，湿润的
latitude	/ˈlætitjuːd/	n.	纬度，范围
snowball	/ˈsnəubɔːl/	n.	雪球
throughout	/θru(ː)ˈaut/	prep.	遍及，贯穿

Exercise 1: Complete the following sentences.

A: Hi, Alice. _____ (今天阳光明媚), isn't it?

B: Yeah, I like sitting in the sun, drinking coffee and listening to light music.

A: _____ (你真会享受生活).

B: Yes, of course. Life is lovely.

A: Maybe you're right. _____ (我可以加入你们吗)?

B: Welcome!

Exercise 2: Fill in the missing letters.

l_titud_   a_tumn   t_mperat_re   sno_ball   ch_ngeable

pr_dict   thr_ughout   dir_   _greeable   h_mid

Paragraph Reading A: Predicting Weather

To find out what the weather is going to be, many people go straight to the radio, television or newspaper to get an expert weather forecast. But if you know what to look for, you can use your own senses to know your weather.

There are many signs that can help you. For example, in fair weather, the air pressure is generally high. The air is still and often full of dust. Far away objects may look misty. But when a storm is gathering, the pressure falls and you are often able to see things more clearly. Sailors took note of this long ago and came up with a saying "The farther the sight, the nearer the rain."

Your senses of smell can also help you detect weather changes. Just before it rains, odors become stronger. This is because odors are suppressed in a fair, high-pressure center. In other words, when a bad weather low moves in, air pressure lowers and smells are released.

You can also hear an approaching storm. Sounds bounce off heavy storm clouds and return to earth with force. An old saying describes it in this way: "Sound traveling far and wide, a stormy say will come." And don't laugh if your grandmother says she can feel a storm coming. It is commonly known that most of the old people probably feel pains in their bones when the humidity rises and the pressure drops, and the bad weather is on the way.

New Words and Expressions

approaching	/əˈprəʊtʃ/	n.	接近，逼近
bounce	/baʊns/	v.	（使）反跳，弹起
describe	/disˈkraib/	vt.	描写，记述
detect	/diˈtekt/	vt.	察觉，侦查
drop	/drɔp/	v.	滴下，落下
expert	/ˈekspəːt/	n.	专家，行家
generally	/ˈdʒenərəli/	adv.	一般，通常
humidity	/hjuːˈmiditi/	n.	湿气，潮湿
misty	/ˈmisti/	adj.	有薄雾的
object	/ˈɔbdʒikt/	n.	物体，目标
odor	/ˈəʊdə/	n.	气味，名声
pressure	/ˈpreʃə(r)/	n.	强制，紧迫
release	/riˈliːs/	vt.	释放，解放
sailor	/ˈseilə/	n.	海员，水手
senses	/sens/	n.	感觉，判断力
sign	/sain/	n.	标记，符号
straight	/streit/	adj.	直的，诚实的
suppress	/səˈpres/	vt.	镇压，抑制

Exercise 3: Select the answer that best expresses the main idea of the paragraph reading A.

    1) What is the passage mainly about _____?

        A. how to find out the weather

        B. how to use your sense to know the weather

        C. what the weather is about

        D. how to deal with the bad weather

    2) If you can see the thing clearly, what will the weather most probably be?

        A. The weather will be fair.

        B. The weather will be hot.

        C. A storm is coming.

        D. It will be windy soon.

    3) What will happen if a storm comes?

        A. The old feel pains in their bones.

        B. The odors become strong.

        C. Sound travels far and wide.

        D. All of the above.

    4) "The farther the sight, the nearer the rain." most probably comes from _____.

        A. a astronomer   B. a report

        C. a scientist   D. a sailor

    5) This passage is written in _____.

        A. the objective tone   B. the subjective tone

        C. the sarcastic tone   D. all of the above

Exercise 4: Fill in the blanks with words and expressions given below. Change the form where necessary.

sign	pressure	generally	senses of	bounce	release	suppressed
detect	come up	describe				

    1) She _____ the rabbit from the trap.

    2) The ball hit the wall and _____ off it.

    3) I'll tell let you know if anything _____.

    4) The _____ of the water turns this wheel, and this is used to make electric power.

    5) Try to _____ exactly how it happened.

    6) I _____ a note of annoyance in his voice.

    7) It is _____ agreed that smoking is bad for you.

    8) I could see no _____ of life in the deserted town.

    9) I'm afraid I haven't got a very good _____ direction.

    10) Opposition to the government was quickly _____.

Exercise 5: Definitions of these words appear on the right. Put the letter of the appropriate definition next to each word.

1) _____ straight   a. full of, covered with, or hidden by mist

2) _____ expert   b. to come near

3) _____ forecast   c. a person with a job on a ship

4) _____ misty   d. (a person) with special skill or knowledge which comes from experience or training

5) _____ sailor   e. the (amount of) water vapour contained in the air

6) _____ object   f. not bent or curved

7) _____ approaching   g. to say, esp. with the help of some kind of knowledge (what is going to happen at some future time)

8) _____ humidity   h. a smell, esp. an unpleasant one

9) _____ drop   i. to fall or let fall, esp. suddenly

10) _____ odor   j. a thing that can be seen or felt

Exercise 6: Translate the following sentences.

1）他们已决定将会议推迟到下周三。（put off）

2）事实上，大多数事故是可以避免的。（in fact）

3）到上学期期末，他们已经学了二十个单元。

4）学生们总是把教室保持的干干净净。（keep）

5）当今人们掌握一两门外语是十分必要的。

Paragraph Reading B: "Road Rage" Behavior

While cloudy days have been known to bring on an occasional bout of the blues in some, new study findings suggest that sunless days may actually play a role in "road rage" —the highway phenomenon of aggressive driving marked by verbal or physical abuse.

In the new study, college students experienced more symptoms of anxiety and irritability on a

cloudy day compared with on a sunny day. Additionally, students were more likely to report observing aggressive driving, engaging in aggressive driving themselves, or having more feelings of anger and hostility on cloudy days than on sunny days.

Lead investigator, Dr. Mark Wagner, an associate professor of psychology at Wagner College in Staten Island, New York, presented the findings last month at the annual meeting of the American Psychological Society in

New Orleans.

"I think that when a person is on the road, in a crowded urban area in particular, many things can cause them to feel stress because there is the constant threat from other drivers," Wagner explained. "Weather doesn't really cause (a person) to have road rage, but it can be a 'last straw' when other things have already caused them to feel irritable," he added.

People may want to pay more attention to keep their own emotions in check, especially on cloudier days, and they should "watch out" for road rage from other people when the weather isn't sunny, Wagner said.

New Words and Expressions

abuse	/əˈbjuːz/	v.	滥用，虐待
additionally	/əˈdiʃənlli/	adv.	加之，又
aggressive	/əˈgresiv/	adj.	好斗的，侵略性的
annual	/ˈænjuəl/	adj.	一年一次的
anxiety	/æŋˈzaiəti/	n.	忧虑，焦急
associate	/əˈsəuʃieit/	vi.	交往，结交
attention	/əˈtenʃən/	n.	注意，关心
behavior	/biˈheivjə/	n.	举止，行为
compare	/kəmˈpɛə/	v.	比较，相比
emotion	/iˈməuʃən/	n.	情绪，情感
engage	/inˈgeidʒ/	vi.	答应，从事
irritable	/ˈiritəbl/	adj.	易怒的，急躁的
observe	/əbˈzəːv/	vt.	观察，遵守
occasional	/əˈkeiʒnəl/	adj.	偶然的，非经常的
particular	/pəˈtikjulə/	adj.	特殊的，特别的
phenomenon	/fiˈnɔminən/	n.	现象
rage	/reidʒ/	n.	愤怒，情绪激动
sunny	/ˈsʌni/	adj.	阳光充足的
symptom	/ˈsimptəm/	n.	症状，征兆
urban	/ˈəːbən/	adj.	城市的，市内的

Exercise 7: Select the answer that best expresses the main idea of the paragraph reading B.

1) What is road rage?

    A. The road is rough.

    B. The highway phenomenon of getting rage is on the road.

    C. The highway phenomenon of aggressive driving marked by verbal or physical abuse.

    D. The highway phenomenon of quarrelling is on the road.

2) What is the role of weather in road rage?

　　A. Important.　　　　　　　　　　B. Not so important.

　　C. Last straw.　　　　　　　　　　D. All of the above.

3) When the weather isn't sunny, what do people need to pay attention to?

　　A. Don't lose way.　　　　　　　　B. Drive carefully.

　　C. Watch out for road rage.　　　　D. Don't get angry.

4) This passage may come from _____.

　　A. the newspaper　　　　　　　　B. the scientist report

　　C. the TV report　　　　　　　　　D. the psychology magazine

5) Which one is not right in the symptoms of road rage?

　　A. Anger.　　　　　　　　　　　　B. Hostility.

　　C. Stress.　　　　　　　　　　　　D. Tired.

Exercise 8: Fill in the blanks with words and expressions given below. Change the form where necessary.

occasional	play a very important role	additionally	annual	sunny
aggressive	compare with	irritable	attention	emotion

1) Computers _____ in our daily lives.

2) It is a _____ day today, isn't it?

3) Our staff turnover is low _____ other companies.

4) I'm not a heavy drinker, but I like the _____ glass of wine.

5) His speech has an effect on our _____ rather than on our reason.

6) He likes to be the centre of _____.

7) What's your _____ salary?

8) A successful businessman must be _____.

9) An _____ charge is made for heavy bags.

10) He gets _____ when he's got toothache.

Exercise 9: Translate the following sentences.

1）她讲英语太快，很多同学都听不懂。（so … that）

2）请记住离开教室时一定要关灯。（turn off）

3）今天，计算机已被广泛的应用到人们的日常生活中。

4）我认为大学生每天花一两个小时做体育锻炼是很重要的。

5）请讲话慢一点，以便大家都能理解你。（so that）

Grammar Focus:Tenses 时态（二）

六、过去进行时

（1）定义：过去进行时主要表示过去某一时间或某一段时间内正在进行的动作。

（2）构成：由 was / were + 现在分词构成。

（3）用法。

1）过去进行时的动词主要表示在过去某一时刻或某一段时间内正在进行或持续进行的动作，这一特定的过去时间可用时间状语表示。

　　e.g. We were having an English lesson this time yesterday.

　　　　A year ago we were living in Shanghai.

　　　　He was reading a novel in the library this morning.

2）在没有表示过去时间的状语时，需要通过上下文来看出这是过去某时正在进行的动作。在这种情况下，过去进行时常和一般过去时配合使用，过去进行时表示过去时的时间背景，也可以互为时间背景。

　　e.g. He was watching TV when I came in.

　　　　While we were having supper, all the lights went out.

　　　　While I was reading, my sister was playing.

3）过去进行时动词常与 always、continually、frequently 等词连用，表示过去经常发生的行为，通常带有赞美、厌烦等情绪。

　　e.g. The old man was always mislaying his keys.

　　　　The two brothers were frequently quarreling.

4）表示动作的动词 go、come、start、stay、leave 等的过去进行时，可以表示过去将来即将发生的动作。

　　e.g. She asked whether he was leaving the next day.

　　　　They wanted to know when we were coming to see them.

（4）一般过去时与过去进行时的用法比较。

　　一般过去时通常表示过去发生的一个单纯的事实，是一个已经完成的动作；而过去进行时则表示在过去某一时刻或某一时间段正在进行的动作。

　　e.g. I was reading a novel last night.昨晚我在看小说。（可能没看完）

　　　　I read a novel last night. 昨晚我看了一本小说。（已经看完了）

　　　　I was quickly getting used to that kind of life.
　　　　我正在迅速变得习惯于这种生活。（还在适应过程中）
　　　　I quickly got used to that kind of life.
　　　　我很快就习惯于这种生活了。（已经适应）

七、将来进行时

（1）定义：将来进行时表示将来某一时刻或某一时间段正在进行的动作。

（2）构成：由 shall / will be + 现在分词构成。

（3）用法。

1）表示在将来某一时刻或某段时间正在进行的动作，常常带有时间状语短语与或时间状语从句。

e.g. When you get to the station at nine tomorrow, you uncle will be waiting for you there.

I will be busy this evening, I will be writing an article.

What will you be doing this time tomorrow?

2）表示按计划将要发生的动作。

e.g. They will be having their holiday in June.

He will be taking his exams next week.

Will you be telephoning him tomorrow?

Exercise 10: Select the best choice for each sentence.

1) He _____ his leg when he _____ in a football match against another school.

   A. broke, played   B. was breaking, was playing

   C. broke, was playing   D. was breaking, played

2) When I came to see him yesterday evening, he _____ his dinner.

   A. has eaten   B. was eaten   C. eats   D. was eating

3) — What were you doing when he arrived at your house?

   — I had just put on my coat and _____ to visit my sister.

   A. was left   B. was leaving   C. left   D. went

4) When I _____ on the street, I met Sue.

   A. walked   B. had walked   C. walk   D. was walking

5) Mrs. White _____ early in the morning when she was young.

   A. was used to get up   B. used to getting up

   C. was used to getting up   D. is used to getting up

6) They _____ a meeting from 2 to 4 yesterday afternoon.

   A. were having   B. had   C. would have   D. have

7) I hope you _____ her over soon.

   A. sent   B. would be sending

   C. were sending   D. will be sending

8) It started to rain while I _____ for a bus.

   A. waited   B. am waiting   C. wait   D. was waiting

9) When the telephone rang, I _____ the evening news.

   A. have watched   B. was watching   C. am watching   D. would watch

10) Good night. I _____ you tomorrow.

   A. shall be seeing   B. shall see   C. are seeing   D. were seeing

11) When he got home, the wind _____ heavily.
    A. is blowing   B. was blowing
    C. blow   D. had blown

12) What _____ at ten last night?
    A. were you doing   B. do you do
    C. had you done   D. have you done

13) I _____ my breakfast when the milkman came.
    A. had   B. had been having
    C. have been having   D. was having

14) You can have my typewriter. I _____ it.
    A. am not going to use   B. won't use
    C. won't be using   D. won't have used

15) I won't be free in Friday morning. I _____ a friend off.
    A. shall be seeing   B. shall be seen
    C. shall have seen   D. am seeing

16) Come on. They _____ supper in a minute.
    A. were having   B. will be having
    C. will have   D. would have had

17) Be sure to come. We _____ you.
    A. shall have expecting   B. shall be expecting
    C. shall expecting   D. should be expecting

18) What _____ you _____ at eight tomorrow evening?
    A. do … do   B. will … do
    C. are … going to do   D. will … be doing

19) Lily _____ for you in the hall at seven. Is that all right?
    A. is waiting   B. will have waited
    C. waits   D. will be waiting

20) When the fire broke out last night, 200 workers _____ in the building.
    A. are working   B. have worked
    C. had worked   D. were working

Exercise 11: Fill in with best choice.

Dear Sally,

Thank you very much for your letter. I am ___1)___ that you've had such bad weather. Perhaps it'll be better when the spring ___2)___. We have had good weather. ___3)___ week it was very hot and on Sunday I ___4)___ the garden all day. Now it is 8 o'clock ___5)___ but I ___6)___ outside to write this letter.

Yesterday I went to the cinema. The film ___7)___ "Red River". It was about a place in the south of England ___8)___ the river became red, but ___9)___ was able to explain it. Then a journalist came and found that a company ___10)___ some chemicals into the river. The film wasn't very good.

I hope you are very well.

Yours,
Jimmy

1) A. sadly   B. sorry   C. unpleasant   D. unhappily
2) A. is coming   B. will come   C. is going to come   D. comes round
3) A. The last   B. In the last   C. On the last   D. Last
4) A. was in   B. have been in   C. was on   D. have been on
5) A. in the afternoon B. in the evening C. on the afternoon   D. on the evening
6) A. am sitting still B. am still sitting C. sit still   D. still sit
7) A. was calling   B. has called   C. called   D. was called
8) A. where   B. there   C. in that   D. from which
9) A. none   B. no people   C. nobody   D. no person
10) A. had thrown   B. was thrown   C. did throw   D. throwing

Unit 5　Culture
Communicative Samples

Conversation 1

(Jane and David are talking about their summer holiday plans.)

Jane:　Hi, David. Have you decided how you're going to spend your summer holiday?

David: Yes. I'm going hiking and climbing to the top of Mount Huashan in Sichuan with my family. Have you been there?

Jane:　I went there with my friends when I was studying in Xi'an Foreign Language Institute. Are you going to climb it by the old route or the new route?

David: What's the difference?

Jane:　Well. The old route is harder and rougher. The steps are narrower and steeper. The newly-built road is wider and flatter. The views are different too.

David: Then I'll climb up by the old route at night and walk down by the new route.

Jane:　That's a good idea. And if you don't want to climb, you can take a cable car.

David: I hear that people say it is cold and windy on the top, especially before daybreak. Should I bring some warmer clothes?

Jane:　You may if you like. There are coats that can be rented.

David: Thanks. I'm very grateful for the information. Have a nice holiday!

Jane:　You too.

Conversation 2

(Lisa and Wang Fang are talking about holidays.)

Lisa:　Christmas is coming. Wang Fang, may I ask you some questions?

Wang: Of course, go ahead.

Lisa:　Do you celebrate Christmas in China?

Wang: No, we only have Chinese New Year celebrations with feasts and fireworks.

Lisa:　But Christmas is the biggest holiday of the year. People are busy shopping and wrapping

presents for relatives and friends before Christmas Eve.

Wang: That sounds exciting.

Lisa: The kids hang their stockings over the fireplace.

Wang: Why do children do that?

Lisa: Because Santa Claus can fill them with some candy and toys.

Wang: What will they do if they don't have a fireplace?

Lisa: No problem. They always find someplace to hang them. By the way, what are you going to do on Christmas?

Wang: My tutor, Prof. Marker, and his wife have invited me to a Christmas dinner.

Lisa: That sounds great.

New Words and Expressions

fireplace	/ˈfaiəpleis/	n.	壁炉
hang	/hæŋ/	vt.	悬挂，附着
hiking	/haikiŋ/	n.	徒步旅行
relative	/relətiv/	adj.	有关系的，相对的
rent	/rent/	v.	租，租借
route	/ruːt/	n.	路线，路程
stocking	/stɔkiŋ/	n.	长袜

Exercise 1: Complete the following sentences.

A: Lisa, ＿＿＿＿＿＿＿＿＿＿ (复活节马上到了). May I ask you some questions?

B: Of course, ＿＿＿＿＿＿＿＿＿＿ (请讲).

A: Do you know why Easter is celebrated?

B: Sorry, I don't know. ＿＿＿＿＿＿＿＿＿＿ (能给我讲讲吗)?

A: Because it is celebrated to remind us that Christ rose from the dead some 2,000 years ago.

B: I got it. Thank you very much.

Exercise 2: Fill in the missing letters.

| _iking | roughe_ | s_ocking | r_lative | _rapping |
| rout_ | r_nt | h_ng | fire_lace | daybre_k |

Paragraph Reading A: The Cultures

People from different cultures sometimes do things that make each other uncomfortable without meaning to or sometimes without even realizing it. Most Americans have never been out of the country and have very little experience with foreigners. But they are usually friendly and open, and enjoy meeting new people, having guests and bringing people together formally or informally. They tend to use first names in most situations and speak freely about themselves. So if your American hosts do something that makes you uncomfortable, try to let them know how you feel. Most people will appreciate your honesty and try not to make you uncomfortable again. And you'll all learn something about another culture.

Many travelers find it easier to meet people in the U.S. than in other countries. They may just come up and introduce themselves or even invite you in before they really know you. Sometimes Americans are said to be superficially friendly. Perhaps it seems so, but they are probably just having a good time. Just like anywhere else, it takes time to become real friends with people in the U.S.

If and when you stay with American friends, they will probably enjoy introducing you to their friends and family, and if they seem proud of knowing you, it's probably because they are. Relax and enjoy it.

New Words and Expressions

appreciate	/ə'priːʃieit/	vt.	鉴赏，感激
culture	/'kʌltʃə/	n.	文化，文明
experience	/iks'piəriəns/	vt.	经验，体验
foreigner	/'fɔrinə/	n.	外国人，外地人
formally	/'fɔːməli/	adv.	正式地，形式上
freely	/'friːli/	adv.	自由地，直率地
guest	/gest/	n.	客人，来宾
honesty	/'ɔnisti/	n.	诚实，正直
host	/həust/	n.	主人
informally	/in'fɔːməli/	adv.	非正式地
introduce	/ˌintrə'djuːs/	vt.	介绍，传入
invite	/in'vait/	vt.	邀请，引起
perhaps	/pə'hæps/	adv.	或许，多半
probably	/'prɔbəb(ə)li/	adv.	大概，或许
realize	/'riəlaiz/	vt.	了解，实现
relax	/ri'læks/	vi.	放松，休息
superficially	/sjuːpə'fiʃəli/	adv.	浅薄地
uncomfortable	/ʌn'kʌmfətəbl/	adj.	不舒服的，不安的

Exercise 3: Select the answer that best expresses the main idea of the paragraph reading A.

1) People from different cultures sometimes make each other uncomfortable _____.

　　A. on purpose

　　B. by understanding

　　C. without understanding or being conscious of

　　D. because of different cultures

2) If American hosts do something that makes you uncomfortable, _____.

　　A. don't make friends with them

　　B. go back to visit them another day

　　C. tell them that you feel unhappy

　　D. try to let them know you feel happy

3) American will become your friend _____.

　　A. after they really know people

　　B. when they meet each other in the first time

　　C. after people are introduced to them

　　D. when they invite people

4) The word "superficially" means _____.

　　A. very deep　　　　　　　　　　　B. on the surface

　　C. complete　　　　　　　　　　　D. extremely good

5) The passage is mainly about _____.

　　A. the different cultures of different countries

　　B. the American friends

　　C. the American customs

　　D. the American cultures

Exercise 4: Fill in the blanks with words and expressions given below. Change the form where necessary.

uncomfortable	realize	appreciate	introduce	formally	honesty
invite	relax	culture	experience		

1) I _____ John to my friends last year.

2) They've _____ us to stay for the weekend.

3) He felt _____ when his parents started arguing in front of him.

4) The music will help to _____ you.

5) Our country has _____ great changes in the last 30 years.

6) Different countries have different _____.

7) She spoke English so well that I never _____ she was a German.

8) We've never doubted her _____.

9) At the police station he was _____ charged with murder.

10) His abilities were not _____ in his job.

Exercise 5: Definitions of these words appear on the right. Put the letter of the appropriate definition next to each word.

1) _____	foreigner	a. to make or become less active and worried
2) _____	guest	b. a person who receives guests and provides food, drink, and amusement for them
3) _____	introduce	c. a person who is in someone's home by invitation, either for a short time or to stay
4) _____	perhaps	d. not formally
5) _____	informally	e. a person belongs to a foreign race or country
6) _____	host	f. on the surface, not deep
7) _____	freely	g. possibly, maybe
8) _____	relax	h. to make know for the first time to each other or someone else
9) _____	superficially	i. without any limitation on movement or action
10) _____	probably	j. almost certain; according to what is likely

Exercise 6: Translate the following sentences.

1）我们希望你将来成为一名教师。（in the future）
2）她比她妹妹大三岁。
3）我现在无暇去看电影。（afford）
4）昨天我去看她时，她正在忙于做作业。
5）你相信他说的是真实的吗？

Paragraph Reading B: Manners

Good manners do not come naturally, they have to be learnt. If children were not told and shown how to behave politely, they would grow up rough and rude like savages.

Good manners are not the same in all countries. However, while different kinds of good manners may exist in different places, the principle of good manners is always the same everywhere. It is consideration for the feelings of others. Good manners are the mark of a gentleman, and a real gentleman always tries to consider other people's feelings. They will not say things that will hurt them; they will not speak in a rude way to offend them. When they are with others, they know what they do not like. So good manners are really a form of unselfishness. No one can have really good manners if he is selfish and conceited, and always wants his own way, and seeks his own comfort. They may be outwardly polite, but they will not have the spirit

of good manners.

Good manners are necessary for success in life. Rough, rude, selfish and vain people are always disliked, and can never be popular. A rude businessman or shopkeeper soon loses his customers.

New Words and Expressions

behave	/bi'heiv/	vi.	举动，举止
comfort	/'kʌmfət/	n.	安慰，舒适
conceited	/kən'si:tid/	adj.	自以为是的
consideration	/kənsidə'reiʃən/	n.	体谅，考虑
dislike	/dis'laik/	vt.	讨厌，不喜欢
exist	/ig'zist/	vi.	存在，生存
manner	/'mænə/	n.	礼貌，风格
mark	/ma:k/	vi.	作记号
naturally	/'nætʃərəli/	adv.	自然地
offend	/ə'fend/	v.	犯罪，冒犯
politely	/pə'laitli/	adv.	客气地，斯文地
principle	/'prinsəpl/	n.	法则，原则
rough	/rʌf/	adj.	粗糙的，粗略的
rude	/ru:d/	adj.	粗鲁的，无礼的
savage	/'sævidʒ/	adj.	野蛮的，未开化的
seek	/si:k/	v.	寻找，探索
selfish	/'selfiʃ/	adj.	自私的
spirit	/'spirit/	n.	精神，勇气
vain	/vein/	adj.	徒然的，无益的

Exercise 7: Select the answer that best expresses the main idea of the paragraph reading B.

1) Children can have good manners _____.

    A. when they were born

    B. when they are taught

    C. when they learn by themselves

    D. when they grow up naturally

2) Different countries have different manners, but _____.

    A. the principle of good manners are different everywhere

    B. the principle of good manners is always the same everywhere

    C. the different kinds of good manners may exist in the same place

    D. the different kinds of bad manners may exist in the same place

3) The mark of good manners is _____.

    A. to consider others' feeling   B. not to hurt others

    C. not to speak in a rude way   D. all of the above

4) A person won't be really good manners unless he is _____.

    A. rough   B. rude

    C. unselfish   D. vain

5) It can be inferred from the passage that _____.

    A. a person with bad manners can't succeed

    B. a person with bad manners is to be successful

    C. a rude businessman will own more customers than a polite businessman

    D. an impolite businessman will be popular

Exercise 8: Fill in the blanks with words and expressions given below. Change the form where necessary.

manner	grow up	behave	principle	offend	exist in	selfish
dislike	conceited	comfort				

1) I was very _____ that you forgot my birthday.

2) The technology for performing these operations already _____.

3) I _____ having to get up early.

4) I don't want to sound _____, but I think my new book might be a best-seller.

5) I agree it had to be done, but not in such an offensive _____.

6) She has been _____ rather oddly.

7) The priest spoke a few words of _____ to the dying man.

8) She acted from purely _____ motives.

9) What do you want to be when you _____?

10) Make it a _____ to save some money each week.

Exercise 9: Translate the following sentences.

1）你一定要小心，不然，你会弄伤你自己的。

2）不要认为上课迟到是理所应当的。（take … for granted）

3）张同志总是乐于帮助别人，他从不先考虑自己。（be ready to do）

4）这就是我们昨天谈起的那个男孩。

5）我不知道她没有来出席会议的真正原因。

Grammar Focus:Tenses 时态（三）

八、现在完成时

（1）定义：现在完成时表示在现在以前发生的动作或情况。

（2）构成：由助动词 have / has + 过去分词构成。

（3）用法。

1）表示过去发生的某一动作对现在造成的影响或结果，常与非延续性动词连用，并常带有不确定的时间状语，如 already、yet、once、twice、just、ever、never 等。这一用法强调动作到现在为止已经完成或刚完成，汉语常用"了"或者"过"来表示。

e.g. Have you ever considered moving to the south?

They have just joined our computer to the Internet.

注意：have been to 和 have gone to 在意义上有区别。

e.g. He has gong to Shanghai.

Where have you been?

2）表示从过去某时开始一直延续到现在的动作和状态（也许还会继续进行下去），常用延续性的动词，并多于 since 和 for 引导的时间状语连用，也可以表示到目前为止的时间状语，如 so far、up to now、until now 等连用。

e.g. I have studied English since 2000.

He has lived here for two years.

The weather has been cold so far this winter.

注意：非延续性的动词不能使用现在完成时这一用法。

如：他已经离开这儿两个月了。

不能说成 He has left here for two months. 而应是 He has been away from here for two months.

（4）现在完成时和一般过去时的区别。

1）现在完成时和一般过去时都表示过去完成的动作，但现在完成时强调这一动作与现在的关系，如对现在产生的结果或影响等；而一般过去时则表示动作发生在过去，不一定表示和现在的关系。试比较：

I have lost my pen. （笔还没找到，现在我没有笔用）

I lost my pen yesterday. （笔是昨天丢的，现在找到与否，没有说明）

2）现在完成时说明的是现在的情况，是现在时态，因此不能和表示过去的时间状语，如 yesterday、last month、three years ago、in 1991 等连用。这些时间状语只能和过去时态连用。

e.g. The War of Liberation began in 1946.

I wrote to him last night.

We had a get-together in the Chaoyang Park two weeks ago.

注意：现在完成时却可以和表示过去时间的副词 just 和 before 连用。

e.g. He has just come.

We have seen the film before.

3）现在完成时常和表示不确定的时间副词 already、often、never、ever、always、yet、not yet 等连用。也可以和包括"现在"在内的时间状语连用，如 now、today、this month、this year 等。

e.g. The new books have not arrived yet.

Many westerners have never seen a giant panda.

We have planted many trees this year.

4）现在完成时可和疑问副词 where、why、how 连用，但通常不和疑问副词 when 连用，when 一般只与过去时态连用。

e.g. Why have you powered the computer up?（强调和现在的关系，即电脑开着）

When did you get to know it? （只问时间）

九、现在完成进行时

（1）定义：现在完成进行时主要表示在现在以前这段时间里一直进行的动作。

（2）构成：由 have / has been + 现在分词构成。

（3）用法。

1）表示发生在过去一直持续到现在的动作。常带有由 since、for 引导的时间的状语。

e.g. It has been raining for hours.

We have been living here since 1995.

这个动作很可能仍然在进行，也可能刚刚结束，通常根据上下文来判断。

e.g. We've just been talking about you.

Tom has been working hard since the new term began.

Where have you been living these years?

How long have you been waiting for me?

2）某些不能用于进行时的动词也不能用于现在完成进行时。如表示知觉的动词 see、hear、smell、taste、notice、feel 等；表示态度和情感的动词 believe、agree、like、hate、want、think 等；表示某种抽象关系或概念的动词 have、depend、seem、belong to、consist of、possess 等。

Exercise 10: Select the best choice for each sentence.

1) You'd better stay at home until your homework _____.

A. finishes   B. will finish   C. was finished   D. has been finished

2) I won't leave until I _____ my work.

    A. do   B. did   C. am doing   D. have done

3) Every means _____ tried to improve teaching and learning.

    A. has   B. has been   C. have   D. are

4) Don't get off the bus until it _____.

    A. has stopped   B. stopped   C. will stop   D. shall stop

5) His friend _____ the club for two years.

    A. has joined   B. joined   C. has been in   D. had joined

6) I wonder if they _____ yet.

    A. start   B. had started

    C. have started   D. started

7) The weather _____ cold for many days this month.

    A. is   B. was   C. has been   D. had been

8) Since last century, his family _____ teachers.

    A. are   B. were   C. have been   D. had been

9) There _____ a lot of changes here in the last twenty years.

    A. have been   B. have had   C. had been   D. will have

10) You can't go home until you _____ your exercises.

    A. have done   B. did   C. will be   D. had done

11) Our team _____ every match so far this year, but we still have three more games to play.

    A. was winning   B. has won   C. had won   D. wins

12) The evening party _____. You are a little late.

    A. just begun   B. just has begun

    C. has just begun   D. has begun just now

13) He _____ home for nearly three weeks.

    A. has gone away   B. has left

    C. has been away from   D. went away from

14) He _____ an engineer for more than a year.

    A. became   B. have become

    C. was   D. has been

15) They _____ good friends since they met in New York.

    A. have made   B. have become

    C. have been   D. have turned

16) — Do you know our city at all?

    — No, this is the first time I _____ here.

    A. was   B. have been   C. came   D. am coming

17) His sister _____ in New York for the last three years.

    A. should be living   B. would be

    C. has been living   D. should live

18) _____ English?

    A. How long time are you studying

    B. How long do you study

    C. How long have you been studying

    D. How long time have you studied

19) I _____ for him for over five years and he never once _____ "Good morning" to me.

    A. have been working, has said   B. have been working, said

    C. have worked, have been saying   D. had working, have said

20) The driver _____. I think someone else ought to drive.

    A. is drinking   B. have drunk

    C. had been drunk   D. has been drinking

Exercise 11: Fill in with best choice.

I am 30 years old. I ___1)___ born in 1960 in a town in the west of England. I ___2)___ there all my life. But I usually ___3)___ my holidays in London. My town is not ___4)___ it was in 1960 or 1965. In those days we ___5)___ walk from one side to ___6)___ in about fifteen minutes. There ___7)___ two schools but ___8)___ big factories. Then in 1968 they built two factories and a lot of new people came to our town. ___9)___ factories are very big and I now have a job in one of ___10)___.

   1) A. am   B. have   C. was   D. were

   2) A. am living   B. have lived   C. lived   D. live

   3) A. am spending   B. spend   C. am passing   D. pass

   4) A. same as   B. same that   C. the same as   D. the same that ...

   5) A. can   B. could   C. was able to   D. were able

   6) A. another   B. the other   C. other   D. one other

   7) A. have been   B. has been   C. was   D. were

   8) A. no   B. not any   C. none   D. not

   9) A. All the   B. The all   C. Both the   D. The both

 10) A. they   B. them   C. their   D. this

Unit 6　Sports & Games
Communicative Samples

Conversation 1

(Max and Tom are in the sports shop.)

Max: Look at this equipment! I think there's something for every sport here.

Tom: I'll say. Wait, there are no parachutes! Have you ever tried parachuting?

Max: Parachuting? No, I've never done that. Have you?

Tom: I've done it three times.

Max: You're kidding. When?

Tom: The summer after high school.

Max: What was it like? Were you scared?

Tom: Oh, yeah. I was terrified! But it was really exciting.

Max: What other things have you tried?

Tom: I used to ride motorcycles before I was married. Have you ever done that?

Max: Lots of times. I still do it every chance I get. I love it. Why did you stop?

Tom: My wife says I might get hurt. So…you're still single, aren't you?

Max: No. I'm married, but my wife has a very interesting hobby. She goes bungee jumping whenever she can.

Tom: Incredible!

Conversation 2

(George and White are talking about an experience of playing golf.)

George: Hello, White. Have you ever played golf?

White: Yeah. There were a few times when I was a teenager. Then I played once more about five years ago.

George: Did you like it?

White: Well, I'll tell you about my last golf game.

You can decide if I liked it.

George: Ok, I'm listening.

White: Max and Nick invited me and my sister to spend a day at their country club. When we got there, the guys decided we should play golf. Of course, my sister and I don't have golf shoes.

George: So, what did you do?

White: We had to play golf in our sandals.

George: In your sandals? How was the game?

White: The first four holes were OK, but after that, it was terrible.

George: Why? What happened?

White: We were starting to play the last hole when it started raining. My sandals got really wet and slippery, so I fell over. Then everyone started laughing. I was really mad and embarrassed!

George: So, what did you do?

White: I promised myself never to go golfing again!

New Words and Expressions

embarrass	/im'bærəs/	vt.	使困窘，使局促不安
equipment	/i'kwipmənt/	n.	装置，设备
hole	/həul/	n.	洞，孔
motorcycle	/'məutəsaikl/	n.	摩托车，机车
promise	/'prɔmis/	vt.	允诺，答应
sandal	/'sændl/	n.	凉鞋
scare	/skɛə/	v.	惊吓，受惊
teenager	/'ti:neidʒə/	n.	十几岁的青少年

Exercise 1: Complete the following sentences.

A: More and more people today are realizing the importance of physical exercise.

B: _____ (体育锻炼能增强体质).

A: Do you like doing exercise?

B: Yes, of course. _____ (我喜欢打高尔夫).

A: Really. I like it to. Shall we play golf together this afternoon?

B: _____ (走吧).

Exercise 2: Fill in the missing letters.

_quipment   pro_ise   san_al   s_are   h_le

parach_te   m_torcycl_   t_enager   e_barrassed   bun_ee

Paragraph Reading A: Sports and Games

Sports and games do a lot of good to our health. They can make us strong, prevent us from

getting too fat, and keep us healthy and fit. They can especially be of great value to people who work with their brains most of the day; for sports and games give people valuable practice in exercising the body.

What's more, they make our life richer and more colorful. If we do not have a strong body, we will find it hard to do whatever we want. So persons of all ages enjoy watching and taking part in various kinds of sports – track and field, swimming, skating, football, volleyball and basketball, etc..

Sports and games are also very useful in character-training. They demand not only physical skill and strength but also courage, endurance, discipline and usually teamwork. For boys and girls, what is learned in the playground often has a deep effect on their character. If each of them learns to work for his team and not for himself on the football field, he will later find it natural to work for the good of his country instead of only for his own benefit. A healthy citizenry makes for a strong country, let's all take part in sports and games.

New Words and Expressions

character	/ˈkærɪktə/	n.	特性，性质
courage	/ˈkʌrɪdʒ/	n.	勇气，精神
demand	/dɪˈmɑːnd/	n.	要求，需求
discipline	/ˈdɪsɪplɪn/	n.	纪律，学科
effect	/ɪˈfekt/	n.	作用，影响
endurance	/ɪnˈdjurəns/	n.	忍耐（力），持久（力）
especially	/ɪsˈpeʃəli/	adv.	特别，尤其
fit	/fɪt/	adj.	合适的，恰当的
health	/helθ/	n.	健康，健康状态
instead	/ɪnˈsted/	adv.	代替，改为
prevent	/prɪˈvent/	v.	防止，预防
skating	/ˈskeitiŋ/	n.	溜冰
strength	/streŋθ/	n.	力量，力气
teamwork	/ˈtiːmwəːk/	n.	联合作业，协力
track	/træk/	n.	跟踪，足迹
valuable	/ˈvæljuəbl/	adj.	贵重的，有价值的
value	/ˈvæljuː/	n.	价值，估价
various	/ˈvɛərɪəs/	adj.	不同的，各种各样的
volleyball	/ˈvɒlibɔːl/	n.	排球

Exercise 3: Select the answer that best expresses the main idea of the paragraph reading A.

1) To our health, sports and games do the following good physically except _____.

   A. making our bodies stronger and stranger

   B. making us fit in doing our works

   C. making us healthier than before

   D. getting too fat

2) From the whole passage, we can find sports and games can give people influences, for example, _____.

   A. making us richer

   B. training our personality

   C. contributing for our country less

   D. making us selfish

3) If your friend is weak and has some time to exercise, what is a practical suggestion of you?

   A. Do some sports and games.

   B. See a doctor at once.

   C. Make friends with sportsman.

   D. Surf on the internet all day.

4) On the football field, the spirit of _____ can't be cultivated.

   A. helping others   B. team efforts

   C. cooperating with each other   D. complaining others' poor skill

5) Sports and games demand our many parts but not _____.

   A. physical skill and strength   B. endurance

   C. discipline   D. discourage

Exercise 4: Fill in the blanks with words and expressions given below. Change the form where necessary.

prevent …from	valuable	take part in	demand	various
not only…but also	what's more	courage	endurance	instead of

1) Guests may deposit their _____ in the hotel safe.

2) Shakespeare was _____ a writer _____ an actor.

3) Long-distance races are won by the runners with the greatest _____.

4) The new system is cheaper, and _____, it's better.

5) More and more people _____ Olympics games.

6) She showed remarkable _____ when she heard the bad news.

7) Unless we get more funding we'll be _____ finishing our experimental programs.

8) _____ being a doctor, he became an successful writer.

9) There has been snow today in _____ parts of the country.

10) The manager has refused to agree to our _____ for a 6% pay rise.

Exercise 5: Definitions of these words appear on the right. Put the letter of the appropriate definition next to each word.

1) _____ fit　　　　　　a. the combination of qualities which make a particular person, thing, place, etc, different from others; nature

2) _____ value　　　　　b. the power of enduring

3) _____ strength　　　　c. the usefulness, helpfulness, or importance of something

4) _____ teamwork　　　 d. the quality or degree of being strong or powerful

5) _____ track　　　　　 e. a team game in which a large ball is struck by hand backwards and forwards across a high net without being allowed to touch the ground

6) _____ character　　　　f. the course or line taken by something as it moves or travels

7) _____ effect　　　　　 g.(a method of) training to produce obedience and self-control

8) _____ endurance　　　 h. a result or condition produced by a cause

9) _____ volleyball　　　 i. physically healthy and strong

10) _____ discipline　　　 j. the ability of a group of people to work together effectively

Exercise 6: Translate the following sentences.

1）要求他现在来是没有用的，因为他很忙。（be no use + V-ing）

2）在睡觉前别忘记锁好门。

3）我们认为仅仅学习理论是没有用的，他们必须与实践相结合。

4）科学家们正在尽最大努力防止大气污染。（prevent … from）

5）他宁可呆在家里也不去游泳。（would rather … than）

Paragraph Reading B: The Sporting Spirit

I am always amazed when I hear people saying that sport creates goodwill between the nations, and that if only the common people of the world could meet one another at football or cricket, they would have no inclination to meet on the battlefield. Even if one didn't know from concrete examples that international sporting contests lead to orgies of hatred, one could deduce it from general principles.

Nearly all the sports practiced nowadays are competitive. You play to win, and the game has little meaning unless you do your utmost to win. On the village green, where you pick sides and no feeling of local patriotism is involved, it is possible to play simply for the fun and exercise. But as soon as the question of prestige arises, as soon as you feel that you and some larger unit will be disgraced if you lose, the most savage combative instincts are aroused. Anyone who has played even in a school football match knows this. At the international level sports is frankly mimic warfare. But the significant thing is not the behavior of the players but the attitude of the spectators; and, behind the spectators, the nations who work themselves into furies over these absurd contests, and seriously believe—at any rate for short periods—that running, jumping and kicking a ball are tests of national virtue.

New Words and Expressions

absurd	/əbˈsəːd/	adj.	荒谬的，可笑的
amaze	/əˈmeiz/	vt.	使吃惊
arise	/əˈraiz/	vi.	出现，发生
battlefield	/ˈbæt(ə)lfiːld/	n.	战场，沙场
concrete	/ˈkɔnkriːt/	n.	混凝土
contest	/ˈkɔntest/	n.	论争，竞赛
create	/kriˈeit/	vt.	创造，创作
cricket	/ˈkrikit/	n.	板球
deduce	/diˈdjuːs/	vt.	推论，演绎出
disgrace	/disˈgreis/	n.	耻辱，丢脸的人、事
frankly	/ˈfræŋkli/	adv.	坦白地，真诚地
goodwill	/gudˈwil/	n.	善意，亲切
hatred	/ˈheitrid/	n.	憎恨，乱意
inclination	/ˌinkliˈneiʃən/	n.	倾向，爱好
involve	/inˈvɔlv/	vt.	包括，笼罩
significant	/sigˈnifikənt/	adj.	有意义的，重大的
spectator	/spekˈteitəː/	n.	观众
virtue	/ˈvəːtjuː/	n.	德行，美德
warfare	/ˈwɔːfɛə/	n.	战争，竞争

Exercise 7: Select the answer that best expresses the main idea of the paragraph reading B.

1) In some persons' mind, sport can create _____ between the nations.

　　A. friendships　　　　　　　　　B. self-confidence

　　C. assurance　　　　　　　　　　D. selfish personality

2) From the whole passage, we can find the main idea is base on the sport's _____.

　　A. competitive features　　　　　　B. warmhearted characters

　　C. making-friend feature　　　　　D. communicative characters

3) Playing simply for the fun and exercise to arousing savage combative instincts, _____ is the most important cause.

　　A. you find that you and some friends can communicate and make friends

　　B. you find that you and some larger unit will help each other

　　C. you find that you and some larger unit will be disgraced if you lose

　　D. you find that you are interested in the sports and can lose it

4) In the sentence "Anyone who has played even in a school football match knows this", "this" refers to _____.

    A. the question of self-respect arises

    B. as soon as the question of prestige arises and you feel that you and some larger unit will be disgraced if you lose, the most savage combative instincts are aroused

    C. sport creates goodwill between the nations

    D. I am always amazed

5) We can get a conclusion that the following action is the test of national virtue like _____.

    A. long running   B. jumping

    C. playing a ball   D. all of above

Exercise 8: Fill in the blanks with words and expressions given below. Change the form where necessary.

goodwill	amaze	inclination to	at any rate	mimic	contest
spectator	lead to	absurd	disgrace		

1) We may miss the next bus, but _____ we'll be there before midday.

2) He has an _____ see everything in political terns.

3) The big match attracted 24,000 _____.

4) This will _____ trouble in the future.

5) Given sufficient _____ on both sides, there's no reason why this dispute shouldn't be resolved.

6) You _____ yourself last night by drinking too much.

7) How many people are _____ the seat on the council?

8) He looks _____ in that hat.

9) The _____ coloring of this moth protects them form predators.

10) It _____ us to hear that you were leaving.

Exercise 9: Translate the following sentences.

1）尽管下着大雨，他们仍不停地工作。（in spite of）

2）医生建议这个病人尽快戒烟。（give up）

3）瞧着睡着的小孩，玛丽不由得想起了她自己的童年。（can't help + v-ing）

4）老师进教室时发现学生们在读英文。（find）

5）他们已下定决心一定要在月底前完成这项工作。

Grammar Focus:Tenses 时态（四）

十、过去完成时

（1）定义：过去完成时表示在过去某一时间或动作前已经完成了的动作。过去完成时所表示的时间就是"过去的过去"。

（2）构成：由 had + 过去分词构成。

（3）用法。

1）表示动作或状态从过去某一时间之前开始并一直延续到这一时间，常与延续性动词连用，并常有 for、since、by、when、until 等表示一段时间或表示起讫的时间状语。

e.g. I had stayed in Beijing for three years by then.

The boy told his mother that he had been ill since he came back from the school.

2）表示动作在过去某一时间之前已经结束，通常与非延续性动词连用。

e.g. When they got to the field, the football match had already started.

He had learned 1000 English words by the end of last term.

注意：过去完成时动词可以表示过去某一时刻或某一动作之前完成的动作或呈现的状态。在强调过去某一动作发生在另一动作之前时（有时两者相距很近），往往用这种时态。

e.g. When I came in he had finished his homework.

With their help I realized that I had been wrong.

They fulfilled the plan earlier than they had expected.

但在含有 before、after 等引导的状语从句的复合句中，由于这类词本身的意义能够明确表示动作的先后顺序，因此过去完成时往往由一般过去时取代。

e.g. We had breakfast after we did morning exercises.

The train left just before he reached the platform.

3）表示过去未曾实现的希望、打算或意图，常与 hope、intend、mean、expect、think、want、suppose 等词连用。

e.g. We had hoped to catch the 9:30 train, but found it was gone.

十一、将来完成时

（1）定义：将来完成时表示在将来某一时间之前所完成的动作。

（2）构成：由 shall / will have + 过去分词构成。

（3）用法。

1）表示动作或状态延续到将来某一时间，常用延续性动词，多于表示将来某一时间的状语或状语从句连用。

e.g. He will have been in the army for 10 years by next June.

We shall have walked a long way before we reach the village.

2）表示动作或状态在将来某一时间以前结束，但其影响却延续到那一时间，常用非延续性动词。

e.g. I shall have finished my homework by ten o'clock.

When the old man comes next week, his son will have left for Hong Kong.

Exercise 10: Select the best choice for each sentence.

1) By the time we got to the theater the play _____ for half an hour.

　　A. has begun　　　　　B. began　　　　　C. has been on　　　　　D. had been on

2) No sooner _____ the thief _____ the policeman than he took to his heels.

　　A. had, seem　　　　B. did, see　　　　C. have, seen　　　　D. does, see

3) After she _____ told the news, she ran home to tell her mother.

　　A. would have　　　　　　　　　B. would have been
　　C. had been　　　　　　　　　　D. should have

4) They sang a song which they _____ before.

　　A. did not sing　　　B. had not sung　　C. sang　　　　　　D. would have sung

5) He _____ his homework before I came.

　　A. had done　　　　B. has done　　　　C. has been doing　　　D. would have done

6) We were glad that by the time we got there the play _____ yet.

　　A. had begun　　　B. hadn't begun　　C. has begun　　　　D. hasn't begun

7) The old man thanked me for what my son _____.

　　A. did　　　　　　B. has done　　　　C. does　　　　　　D. had done

8) By the end of last term we _____ English for two years.

　　A. have studied　　　　　　　　B. have been studied
　　C. would studied　　　　　　　　D. had studied

9) When we arrived, the party _____.

　　A. already began　　　　　　　　B. has already begun
　　C. had already begun　　　　　　D. was just begun

10) By this time next year, you _____ from college.

　　A. will have graduated　　　　　B. shall have graduated
　　C. would graduate　　　　　　　D. will graduate

11) I felt so bad. I was sure that I _____ a cold.

　　A. has caught　　　　　　　　　B. had caught
　　C. is caught　　　　　　　　　　D. had been caught

12) He told me that Teresa _____ shopping.

　　A. had gone　　　　B. has gone　　　　C. went　　　　　　D. is going

13) It was a good novel, but I _____ it before.

　　A. has read　　　　　　　　　　B. is reading
　　C. had read　　　　　　　　　　D. has been read

14) I didn't go to the film because I _____ it before.

　　A. would have seen　　　　　　　B. would have been seen
　　C. has seen　　　　　　　　　　D. had seen

15) She wishes she _____ him.

A. had not married

B. would not have married

C. would not marry

D. have married

16) He _____ this one before lunch.

A. will finish

B. will have finished

C. will have been finishing

D. would have finished

17) How many words _____ we _____ by the end of the term?

A. should … learned

B. shall … learned

C. shall … have learned

D. should … have learned

18) When we get there they _____ probably _____.

A. will … leave

B. would … leave

C. would … have left

D. will … have left

19) I hope we _____ the jobs ready before you come tomorrow.

A. would complete

B. would have competed

C. will complete

D. will have completed

20) By this time next year they _____ the school.

A. will have built

B. would have built

C. will build

D. would have been built

Exercise 11: Fill in with best choice.

Have you ever had to stay __1)__ a long time? About six months ago I __2)__ very weak and so I went __3)__ a doctor. He looked at me and asked a lot of questions: "Have you been working __4)__ ?" "Have you __5)__ anything special?" And so on. Finally he __6)__ that it was not very serious but that I __7)__ not to meet other people. I had to stay in bed for two weeks and take some medicine __8)__ It wasn't so bad because my friends came and talked to me __9)__ the window. I'm glad my bedroom is on the __10)__ .

1) A. in the bed for	B. in the bed since	C. in bed for	D. in the bed since
2) A. felt	B. filled	C. fell	D. feel
3) A. and see	B. to see	C. for see	D. for to see
4) A. too hard	B. too hardly	C. too much hard	D. too much hardly
5) A. ate or drank	B. ate or drunk	C. eaten or drunk	D. eat or drank
6) A. told	B. said me	C. told to me	D. told me
7) A. ought	B. would	C. should	D. must
8) A. all the days	B. every days	C. all days	D. every day
9) A. through	B. along	C. though	D. across
10) A. flat ground	B. ground flat	C. floor ground	D. ground floor

Unit 7　People's Life
Communicative Samples

Conversation 1

(Daisy shows a photo of her family to Mary.)

Mary: Hi, Daisy. How many members are there in your family?

Daisy: There are five. Here, I've got some photos. The old couple standing in the back are my parents.

Mary: Oh, your parents! They are smiling a lot. They look really happy.

Daisy: Yeah. My father was an English teacher in a middle school, and my mother was a doctor. Now both of them are retired.

Mary: I guess your fluent English must be inherited from your father.

Daisy: Maybe. When I was little, he liked to teach me English.

Mary: What a wise father! Who is the man on the left?

Daisy: He's my younger brother.

Mary: Is that you?

Daisy: I was studying in Los Angeles then.

Mary: You are still as lovely as you were.

Daisy: Thank you, by the way, I'm planning to see my parents this weekend. Would you like to go with me? My mother is preparing my favorite dishes. Come and have a taste, OK?

Mary: Oh, I'd love to. I'll be glad to meet your parents. It seems you really have a happy family.

Conversation 2

(Two friends are going on a trip.)

David: Hey, Robert, would you like to get away from the city and come to Lake Benjamin with my family next week?

Robert: I'd love to. Do I need anything?

David: Well, the first thing you'll need is a sleeping bag.

Robert: I don't get it. What do I need a sleeping bag for?

David: For sleeping in, of course. You can share our tent.

Robert: Do you mean this is a camping trip?

David: That's right, so insect repellent is a good idea.

Robert: Why do I need that?

David: Oh! You should use insect repellent there, or you'll get eaten alive!

Robert: What else will I need?

David: You might need an extra set of warmer clothes.

Robert: Why do I need those? It's the middle of summer!

David: Just in case it rains or suddenly turns cold.

Robert: Good thinking.

New Words and Expressions

alive	/əˈlaiv/	*adj.*	活着的，活泼的
couple	/ˈkʌpl/	*n.*	（一）双，夫妇
extra	/ˈekstrə/	*adj*	额外的
favorite	/ˈfeivərit/	*adj.*	喜爱的，宠爱的
insect	/ˈinsekt/	*n.*	昆虫
retire	/riˈtaiə/	*vi.*	退休，引退
taste	/teist/	*v.*	品尝，体验

Exercise 1: Complete the following sentences.

A: Hi, Maria, _____ (你想看看相片吗)?

B: Yes, I'd love to. Oh, how nice! Now, _____ (这是谁)?

A: This is Judy, my daughter.

B: _____ (她真是个可爱的女孩). Who is this?

A: This is my wife.

B: Well, you certainly have a lovely-looking family.

Exercise 2: Fill in the missing letters.

coupl_	r_pellent	ex_ra	fav_rite	war_er
_etired	tast_	i_sect	_live	ten_

Paragraph Reading A: Making Good Use of Time

A man's life occupies, at best, but a limited space of time. The magnitude of a man's success in life depends largely upon how he makes use of his time. Those who achieve greatness in different channels of success are, as a whole, the hardest working people. Our famous scholar Yao

and Shun wasted not a single minute while Da Yu, our great emperor, valued even the briefest space of time. They were our great men; their accomplishments stand out in our history in bold relief.

If we wish to do something useful, the sure way to success is to use every minute that we may have at our disposal. The odd hours which we have after our daily work are the best time for reading. There is a great deal of wisdom locked up in books. Nowadays we can find such a rich spring of knowledge for quenching our thirst.

Of course, different people follow different occupations. They do not need the same sort of information. Here they must make their own choice to get the books best suited to their particular needs. The time spent on such reading will add greatly to their stock of knowledge and prepare then for greater work in their respective fields of activity. Once the reading habit is formed, they will enjoy reading far more than they enjoy doing anything else.

New Words and Expressions

accomplishment	/əˈkɔmpliʃmənt/	n.	成就，完成
achieve	/əˈtʃiːv/	vt.	完成，达到
bold	/bəuld/	adj.	大胆的
channel	/ˈtʃænl/	n.	路线
daily	/ˈdeili/	adj.	每日的，日常的
depend	/diˈpend/	vi.	依靠，依赖
disposal	/disˈpəuzəl/	n.	处理，布置
emperor	/ˈempərə/	n.	皇帝，君主
famous	/ˈfeiməs/	adj.	著名的，出名的
limit	/ˈlimit/	vt.	限制，限定
magnitude	/ˈmægnitjuːd/	n.	数量，巨大
occupy	/ˈɔkjupai/	vt.	占用，占领
quench	/kwentʃ/	vt.	结束，熄灭
respective	/risˈpektiv/	adj.	分别的，各自的
scholar	/ˈskɔlə/	n.	学者
success	/səkˈses/	n.	成功，成就
thirst	/θəːst/	n.	口渴，渴望
waste	/weist/	vt.	浪费，消耗

Exercise 3: Select the answer that best expresses the main idea of the paragraph reading A.

1) From the whole passage, we can find the theme is _____.

   A. urging we should read useful books as much as possible

   B. we should find precious life for a person

   C. we have limited space of time

   D. we should devote ourselves into our jobs

2) According the passage, a man's success in life depends largely upon _____.

   A. personality   B. good hobbies

   C. making use of his time   D. talents

3) The sure way to success is _____.

   A. to value every minute at our disposal

   B. to spend the best time reading

   C. to spend the best time communicating with friends

   D. surfing on the internet

4) What is the relation between reading and jobs?

   A. Reading is only for killing time.

   B. Reading will let persons find suitable jobs' position in a company.

   C. Some persons like reading and it has nothing to do with their jobs.

   D. Reading will prepare for greater work in their respective fields of activity.

5) From the passage, when the habit is once formed, they will enjoy _____ far more than they do anything else.

   A. drinking with friends   B. gambling with relatives

   C. watching TV and know the outer world D. finding knowledge from books

Exercise 4: Fill in the blanks with words and expressions given below. Change the form where necessary.

occupy	depend...on	at best	make use of	success	respective
thirst	particular	accomplishment		as a whole	

1) Reading _____ most of my free time.

2) She _____ her time there by learning English language.

3) He lost his way in the desert and died of _____.

4) Is there any _____ colour you would prefer?

5) Being able to play the piano well is one of her many _____.

6) Lucy has just started up a new company; I hope she makes a _____ of it.

7) There are some areas of poverty, but the country _____ is fairly prosperous.

8) This is, _____, only a temporary solution.

9) After the party we all went off to our _____ rooms.

10) We're _____ you to finishing the job by Monday.

Exercise 5: Definitions of these words appear on the right. Put the letter of the appropriate definition next to each word.

1) _____ magnitude   a. the act of disposing; control, management

2) _____ bold   b. any way by which news, ideas, etc may travel

3) _____ thirst   c. feeling caused by a desire or need to drink

4) _____ achieve   d. ruler of an empire

5) _____ disposal   e. (degree of) importance

6) _____ channel   f. for a short time; in a few words

7) _____ scholar   g. satisfy (sth) by drinking

8) _____ briefest   h. without fear; well marked

9) _____ emperor   i. complete; accomplish, get (sth) done

10) _____ quench   j. person who studies an academic subject deeply

Exercise 6: Translate the following sentences.

1）医生说饮酒过多会对健康有害。（do harm to）

2）最后她终于明白了她为什么受到了批评。

3）今天早晨她起床晚了，只好不吃早餐就去上班了。（without）

4）我的朋友不喜欢足球，但他特别爱好游泳。（be fond of）

5）明天晚上我父亲要去车站为他的朋友送行。（see sb.off）

Paragraph Reading B: Surviving in a Forest

If you get into the forest with your friends, stay with them always. If you don't, you may get lost. If you really get lost, this is what you should do. Sit down and stay where you are. Don't try to find your friends—let them find you by staying in one place.

There is another way to help your friends find you. Give them a signal by shouting or whistling three times. Any signal given three times is a call for help. Keep on shouting or whistling; always three times together. When people hear you, they will know that you are not just making noise for fun. They will let you know that they have heard your signal. They will give you two shouts, two whistles, or two gun-shots. When someone gives you a signal, it is an answer to a call for help.

If you don't think that you will get help before night comes, try to make a little house—cover up the holes with branches and with lots of leaves. Make yourself a soft bed with leaves and grass.

What should you do if you get hungry or need drinking water? You would have to leave your little house to look for a river. Don't just walk away. Pick off small branches and drop them as you walk so that you can find your way back. The most important thing to do when you are lost is—stay in one place.

New Words and Expressions

branch	/brɑːntʃ/	n.	分支，分部
forest	/ˈfɔrist/	n.	森林，林木
hungry	/ˈhʌŋgri/	adj.	饥饿的，渴望的
leaf	/liːf/	n.	叶，树叶
noise	/nɔiz/	n.	喧闹声，噪声
shout	/ʃaut/	v.	呼喊，呼叫
signal	/ˈsignl/	n.	信号
soft	/sɔft/	adj.	柔软的，温和的
whistle	/(h)wisl/	n.	口哨，汽笛

Exercise 7: Select the answer that best expresses the main idea of the paragraph reading B.

1) _____ is the good suggestion to get into the forest with your friends.

A. Staying with your friends always in order not to get lost

B. Exploring by yourself

C. The experiences to find the short-up

D. The advanced equipment

2) If you really get lost in forest, _____ is the best choice.

A. calling for help with telephone

B. trying to find your friends

C. staying where you are

D. being hurried and worried

3) From the passage, we can find a way to call for help, it is _____.

A. making vivid color to let others find you

B. shouting or whistling always three times together

C. making out some noises

D. climbing a tall tree to find others

4) In order to let you know that they have heard your signal, they will _____.

A. make louder noises

B. sing a song

C. let someone tell you from airplane

D. give you two shouts, two whistles, or two gun-shots, etc.

5) Which will be the passage's main idea?

A. How to pass through the forest.

B. What to do when you are lost in forest.

C. How to shout or whistle three times together.

D. The importance to stay in one place.

Exercise 8: Fill in the blanks with words and expressions given below. Change the form where necessary.

get into	forest	shout	keep on	noise	signal	branch
cover up	whistle	leaf				

1) The government is trying to _____ the scandal.

2) Jim's making those strange _____.

3) These shoes are too small; I can't _____ them.

4) We had to _____ because the music was so loud.

5) A red light is usually a _____ for dangers.

6) We must do a lot of things to preserve _____.

7) The _____ of the tree were turning yellow.

8) The train _____.

9) Don't climb up the tree. The _____ are not strong enough.

10) She _____ working although she was tired.

Exercise 9: Translate the following sentences.

1）你能检查一下我的作文，看我还需要做什么改动吗？

2）明年我哥哥即将大学毕业。

3）这个小女孩儿比那个男孩子聪明。

4）据说这座大桥下周就要完工。

5）昨天晚上直到十点她才做完了作业。

Grammar Focus: Passive Voice 被动语态

一、被动语态的构成

被动语态的句子是由"助动词 be+过去分词"的形式表示过程的，过去分词保持不变，而所有的变化，即人称、数、时态的变化，都体现在助动词 be 的变化上。

（1）主动语态转换成被动语态。

如果想熟练地掌握被动语态，必须首先了解主动句的结构，清楚句子的成分。变换时，请遵循下列步骤。

步骤1：把原主动句中的宾语转换为被动语态的主语。

步骤2：把动词改为被动形式即"be+过去分词"，这一步很容易出错，要特别注意：这时动词的人称和数要随着新的主语（原来主动句中的宾语）而变，同时 be 动词的时态要跟原来主动语态的时态保持不变，be 动词后面的过去分词就是原来主动语态句子中的动词的过去分词。

步骤3：原来主动语态句子中的主语，如果需要，就放在 by 后面，以它的宾格形式出现（因为 by 是介词，后面需跟宾格作介词的宾语），以指明做事的人或物。如果没有必要，可以省略。

步骤 4：其他的成分（定语、状语）不变。

（2）被动语态的时态。

主动语态与被动语态皆指动词的形式而言。主动语态变为被动语态时，谓语成分要作相应的变化。请特别注意，将来进行时转换成被动语态时，以一般将来时表示；各种完成进行时转成被动语态结构时，以一般完成时表示。主动语态与被动语态的时态比较请参见下面的表格。

时　态	主　动　语　态	被　动　语　态
现在	现在时动词	am are is +过去分词
过去	过去时动词	was were +过去分词
将来	shall will +动词原形	shall will be +过去分词
现在进行	am are is +现在分词	am are is being + 过去分词
过去进行	was were +现在分词	was were being +过去分词
现在完成	have has +过去分词	have has been+过去分词
过去完成	had	had been+过去分词
将来完成	shall will have+过去分词	shall will have been+过去分词
过去将来	should would +动词原形	should would +be+过去分词
过去将来完成	should would have + 过去分词	should would have been+过去分词
将来进行	shall will be+现在分词	—

　　注意：被动语态没有完成进行时态，一般也没有将来进行时态，如果有用这种时态的主动结构要变为被动结构，（由主动语态变为被动语态）可以用完成时态或一般时态。

　　1）完成进行时变为被动语态时，要用完成时表示。

e.g. 主动句 The builders have been building this skyscraper for two months. (现在完成进行时)

　　　被动句 This skyscraper has been built for two months. (现在完成时)

　　2）将来进行时变为被动语态时，要用一般将来时表示。

e.g. 主动句 You will be doing the experiment here at this time next Monday. (将来进行时)

　　　被动句 The experiment will be done here at this time next Monday. (一般将来时)

　　（3）情态动词的被动语态。

e.g. 主动句 You must hand in your homework this afternoon.

　　　被动句

　　　[肯定句]Your homework must be handed in this afternoon.

　　　[否定句]Your homework mustn't be handed in this afternoon.

二、被动语态的使用场合
（1）动作执行者不明显，不重要或不愿说出时。

1）汉语中无主语的句子。

e.g. Teachers are needed everywhere in China.

（无主语的固定句式：It must be pointed out that… It is reported… It is believed that… It has been decided that… It is thought that… It is taken for granted that… It is said… It is known that…）

2）汉语中当主语泛指某些人时。

e.g. When he was asked to have a rest, he always smiled and said, "Thank you, but I'm not tired."

（2）需要突出或强调动作的承受者时。

汉语句子中常常出现"被；为…所；受…"等表示被动的词语。

e.g. A bit of important information was stolen.

三、注意事项
（1）主动语态不能变为被动语态的情况。

1）当宾语是反身代词或相互代词时。

e.g. The girl found herself in the valley.

　　They help each other.

2）当谓语是表示状态的及物动词时。

e.g. The salary can last him only a week.

3）当宾语是不定式或动名词时。

e.g. We all want to be teachers.

They enjoy playing basketball in the evening.

4）当感官动词表示结果时。

e.g. The new comer smiled his thanks.

（注意这类动词有：smile、smell、sound、taste、look、seem、remain、prove、appear、fall、turn）

5）当宾语作状语，表示数量、重量、大小、程度时。

e.g. The jade weighs one ton.

（注意这类动词有：cost、weigh、number、keep、wash、drink、sell）

6）句型"主语+have/get+宾语+过去分词"也不能变为被动语态，它本身就具有被动含义。

e.g. I had my tooth pulled yesterday.

（2）主动语态表示被动含义的情况。

1）主动语态表示被动含义的几个固定句型。

① be worth doing sth.

e.g. The novel is well worth reading twice.

② have/get sth./sb.+过去分词

e.g. I had my bike repaired.

③ 主语+want/need/repair doing(=to be done)

e.g. The room needs (wants, repairs) cleaning/to be cleaned.

④ be +under/in +抽象名词（表达被动含义）

e.g. The car is under/in repair.

2）用主动语态形式表示被动含义的常用动词。

常见的可以这样用的动词有 clean、sell、lock、translate、read、write、wash、wear、cook、tear、cut、keep、burn、strike、pull、act、last、feel 等。

e.g. The door doesn't lock.

Potatoes cook slowly.

3）表示被动的一些不定式。

① There be 句型。

e.g. There is a lot of work to do.

② 不定式修饰 have 等动词的宾语，而句子的主语是不定式的逻辑主语时。

e.g. I have many things to do.

③ easy, hard, difficult 等性质形容词+不定式时。

e.g. The maths problem is difficult to work out.

④ 当不定式修饰 buy, get, give 等动词的直接宾语，而间接宾语是不定式的逻辑主语时。

e.g. His mother bought him a bike to ride.

4）少数动词的进行时，有时有被动的含义。

e.g. Our new school house is building.

注意：并非所有的及物动词都可用于被动语态，有些则是不可以的。如 meet、become、suit、fit、last、catch、hold、lack、kill(time)、take place、break one's word 等。

Exercise 10: Select the best choice for each sentence.

1) A great many buildings _____ in our hometown in the last few years.

 A. was built   B. were built

 C. has been built   D. have been built

2) Football _____ all over the world.

 A. plays   B. is played

 C. is playing   D. are played

3) No permission has _____ for anybody to enter the building.

 A. been given   B. given

 C. to give   D. be giving

4) The book _____ to the library on time.

 A. must return   B. returning

 C. must be returned   D. returned

5) The first man-made spacecraft in China _____ into space on Oct. 15, 2003.

 A. was launched   B. has been launched

 C. launched   D. is launched

6) _____ that tennis is a match invented by an Englishman.

 A. That is said   B. This is said   C. It said   D. It is said

7) The task _____ in 3weeks.

 A. will be finished   B. has been finished

 C. is finished   D. was finished

8) Do you know when the Chinese Communist Party _____?

 A. was found   B. was founded   C. found   D. had found

9) A new bridge _____ in the city at present.

 A. is built   B. is being built

 C. is being build   D. was being built

10) The Great Wall _____ all over the world.

    A. know   B. knew

    C. is knowing   D. was known

11) The classroom _____ the happy voice of the students last night.

    A. filled with   B. was filled with

    C. full of   D. was full with

12) You can see the house _____ for years.

    A. isn't painted   B. hasn't painted

    C. hasn't been painted   D. hadn't been painted

13) The question asked by Tom is hard _____.

    A. to answer   B. to be answered

    C. to be answering   D. for answer

14) The TV set _____ by my uncle last Sunday.

    A. has been mended   B. was mended

    C. mended   D. had mended

15) Rebecca told her mother that her homework _____.

    A. has been finished   B. has finished

    C. had been finished   D. had finished

16) The novel seems to _____ into English.

    A. have translated   B. has been translated

    C. have been translated   D. has translated

17) A new shopping center _____ in this area next year.

    A. will build   B. will be built

    C. is going to build   D. has built

18) This museum _____ by thousands of people every month.

    A. is visited   B. visit   C. visits   D. is visiting

19) The magazine _____ for two weeks.

    A. may have   B. may keep   C. may be kept   D. may borrow

20) The key _____ on the desk when I went out.

    A. will be left   B. is left   C. was leave   D. was left

Exercise 11: Fill in with best choice.

Why do people drink? Often because they __1)__ but this can't be the __2)__ reason; there __3)__ be other reasons, too. In many countries, when friends see __4)__, they often have a drink while they sit and talk. Many English people don't need __5)__; they drink tea several times __6)__ day even if they are alone! In most countries people say __7)__ when they drink together. They English __8)__ cheers. In all countries there are many places (coffee, bars, etc.) __9)__ main purpose is to sell drinks. Since there are so many of these places, it seems that many people drink more often than they really __10)__.

1) A. have thirsty　　　B. have thirst　　　C. are thirsty　　　D. are thirst

2) A. lonely　　　B. single　　　C. only　　　D. alone

3) A. shall　　　B. must　　　C. should　　　D. ought

4) A. each other　　　B. themselves　　　C. them　　　D. another

5) A. another　　　B any other　　　C. anyone else　　　D. other persons.

6) A. a　　　B. during　　　C. the　　　D. by

7) A. something specially　　　　　B. something special

　　C. anything specially　　　　　D. anything special

8) A. often say　　　B. often says　　　C. say often　　　D. says often

9) A. of which　　　B. where the　　　C. what's　　　D. that the

10) A. need to　　　B. need it　　　C. must　　　D. must it

Unit 8　Studying Online
Communicative Samples

Conversation 1

(Two college students talk about a new reading technique.)

Sam:　I heard there's a very effective technique for reading English.

Harry: Do you refer to SQ3R?

Sam:　Yes. Do you know much about this method?

Harry: Well, I have read about it.

Sam:　What is SQ3R then?

Harry: SQ3R stands for *Survey, Question, Read, Recite* and *Review*.

Sam:　I see. Could you tell me a bit about one may follow this technique?

Harry: OK. Perhaps I can give you an example.

Sam:　Go ahead.

Harry: Let's say for example that you read a science report. You first do a survey of the report by reading only the title and the subtitles, then you form a few questions about the article and with these questions in mind start reading the report more carefully.

Sam:　So far you've done the S, the Q and the R. What is the second R? Is it to recite the whole report?

Harry: No. *Recite* means to memorize the main idea and the important points of the report, such as the findings of the report.

Sam:　I see. Now how about the last R?

Harry: It means to review the important parts of the report.

Sam:　Thanks for explaining that to me.

Harry: Not at all. It's my pleasure.

Conversation 2

(Victor is trying to get some information from Tim about the Internet.)

Victor: I'm quite a devoted "net worm". I do think that the Internet is truly marvelous.

Tim:　Do you mind telling me something about it?

Victor: No, of course not. I think one can learn the latest news by visiting different websites.

Tim: I can't understand how that makes much difference. We can be well informed by reading newspapers.

Victor: What newspapers tell us would always be the happenings of several hours ago. The Internet can tell us what's going on the moment it is happening.

Tim: Wow, that's quick. What else can you tell me about the internet?

Victor: One can come across a lot of people on the net through online chat rooms, and even make friends on the other side of the Earth.

Tim: That's interesting. I was told it even helps some people to find their childhood friends. What else?

Victor: The Internet helps me with my English study.

Tim: Oh, you're exaggerating!

Victor: When I try to search for information using Yahoo and other search engines, the English language on the Internet works to further encourage my study of the language.

Tim: I see. It seems each coin has two sides.

Victor: That's right.

New Words and Expressions

ahead	/əˈhed/	*adj.*	在前，向前
article	/ˈɑːtikl/	n.	文章，物品
exaggerate	/igˈzædʒəreit/	v.	夸大，夸张
subtitle	/ˈsʌbtaitl/	n.	副题（书本中的）
survey	/səˈvei/	n.	测量，调查
website	/ˈweb‚sait/	n.	网站

Exercise 1: Complete the following sentences.

A: Hi, Jim. _____ (CAI 是什么意思)?

B: It means Computer Assisted Instruction.

A: _____ (你知道计算机辅助教学的优点是什么吗)?

B: Yes, of course.

A: Can you tell me some details about it?

B: Ok. It can give a student _____ (即时信息反馈).

A: Sounds interesting.

Exercise 2: Fill in the missing letters.

_head   w_bsite   a_ticle   sur_ey   on_ine   techniq_e

engin_   e_agger_te   su_title   h_ppenings

Paragraph Reading A: The Distance Learning

The concept of distance learning or learning at home is not new. Educational institutions have been offering correspondence degrees for decades. Lately, IT in general and the Web in particular expanded the opportunities for distance learning. The concept of open universities or virtual universities is expanding rapidly and hundreds of thousands of students in dozens of countries from Great Britain to Israel to Thailand are studying in such institutions. Some universities, such as California State University, offer hundreds of courses, and degrees to students in dozens of countries. Other universities are offering more limited courses and degrees but use innovative teaching methods and multimedia support.

The virtual university concept allows universities to offer classes worldwide. Moreover, we may soon have integrated degrees, where students, customizing a degree that will best fit their needs, will be able to take courses at different universities. Students can take just-in-time, on-the-job education, and continue with lifelong learning if they like.

A unique program integrates two technologies—the Web and interactive television. The objective of the program is to provide participants with a hi-tech based, innovative and interactive learning experience to improve their managerial and professional competence. The students choose what lecture to watch and when they want to watch it. In addition to the lectures, all supporting material, exercises, and so on are provided on the Web. The students can interact electronically with the instructors and with each other, by using E-mail and chat rooms.

New Words and Expressions

addition	/əˈdiʃ ən/	*n.*	增加，加法
concept	/ˈkɔnsept/	*n.*	观念，概念
correspondence	/ˌkɔrisˈpɔndəns/	*n.*	函授，信件
customize	/kʌstəmaiz/	*v.*	[计]定制，用户化
decade	/ˈdekeid/	*n.*	十年，十
distance	/ˈdistəns/	*n.*	距离，远离
dozen	/ˈdʌzn/	*n.*	一打，十二个
expand	/iksˈpænd/	*vt.*	使膨胀，扩张
innovative	/ˈinəuveitiv/	*adj.*	创新的
institution	/ˌinstiˈtjuːʃ ən/	*n.*	协会，制度

instructor	/in'strʌktə/	n.	教师，讲师
integrated	/'intigreitid/	adj.	综合的，完整的
interact	/ˌintər'ækt/	vi.	互相作用，互相影响
interactive	/ˌintər'æktiv/	adj.	交互式的
multimedia	/'mʌlti'miːdjə/	n.	多媒体的采用
opportunity	/ˌɔpə'tjuːniti/	n.	机会，时机
participant	/pɑː'tisipənt/	n.	参与者，共享者
professional	/prə'feʃənl/	adj.	专业的，职业的
rapidly	/'ræpidli/	adv.	迅速地
support	/sə'pɔːt/	vt.	支持，支援
unique	/juː'niːk/	adj.	唯一的，独特的
virtual	/'vəːtjuəl/	adj.	虚的，实质的

Exercise 3: Select the answer that best expresses the main idea of the paragraph reading A.

1) What is the main feature of the distance learning?

　　A. That IT technology and the Web in particular offer the chances.

　　B. There is no limitation of space and time.

　　C. Both A and B.

　　D. There is no difference compared with traditional classroom.

2) ＿＿＿＿ lets online students interact with their classmates.

　　A. Telephone 　　　　　　　　　　B. Writing letters

　　C. Meeting or interviewing 　　　　D. E-mail and chat rooms

3) There are no limitations for the students to learn online courses except ＿＿＿＿.

　　A. learning time 　　　　　　　　B. learning location

　　C. learning courses to a degree 　　D. learning school

4) What are the distance Universities activities now?

　　A. Offering classes worldwide.

　　B. Customizing a degree that will best fit their needs.

　　C. Helping students can take just-in-time, on-the-job education, even lifelong learning.

　　D. All of above.

5) Compared with traditional classroom teaching, virtual teaching becomes ＿＿＿＿.

　　A. more vividly 　　　　　　　　　B. more convenient

　　C. more courses to learn 　　　　　D. more limitation

Exercise 4: Fill in the blanks with words and expressions given below. Change the form where necessary.

| concept of | allow to | dozen of | professional | so on | in addition to |
| interact | unique | expand | in general | | |

1) You need a ＿＿＿＿ to sort out your finances.

2) I can't grasp the basic ＿＿＿＿ mathematics.

3) The two ideas _____.

4) _____ her work has been good, but this essay is dreadful.

5) I can't tell whether he or she is to blame—it's six of one and half a _____ the other.

6) Our foreign trade has _____ greatly in recent years.

7) _____ Jim, there is six other applicants.

8) This diet _____ you _____ drink one glass of wine a day.

9) The town is _____ in the wide range of leisure facilities it offers.

10) Our courses include English, math, Chinese, and _____.

Exercise 5: Definitions of these words appear on the right. Put the letter of the appropriate definition next to each word.

1) _____ institution   a. showing a pleasing mixture of qualities, groups

2) _____ decade   b. a person who teaches

3) _____ innovative   c. a period of ten years

4) _____ managerial   d. a habit or custom which has been in existence for a long time

5) _____ instructor   e. separation in space or time

6) _____ virtual   f. a group of twelve

7) _____ distance   g. a person who takes part or has a share in an activity or event

8) _____ dozen   h. almost what is stated

9) _____ integrated   i. newly invented or introduced

10) _____ participant   j. concerning a manager or management

Exercise 6: Translate the following sentences.

1）老师问学生是否在学习中遇到过困难。

2）除去这些，你还需要填入你的电话号码和地址。

3）如果她得到这份工作，她每天得干八小时的工作。

4）请你告诉她不要再迟到了。

5）今天是新学期的第一天，老师和学生们在互相做介绍。

Paragraph Reading B: The E-mail

Free E-mail means that you needn't pay for their services. You can get one or more free E-mail accounts if you wish.

How can free E-mail be Free?

Most free E-mail providers make their money by showing you advertisements. They may be graphical banners that you see as you collect your mail from their site, small text messages that appear at the end of your E-mail message or even advertisements that are sent directly to your E-mail inbox. Some smaller providers offer free E-mail as a community service, without any advertising whatsoever. Finally, some large sites offer free E-mail as an attempt to lure visitors back to the site again and again.

Although you are not paying for free E-mail, you will be indirectly paying in other ways. In general, companies offering free E-mail services are not doing so out of kindness…they expect to gain something in return, either tangible benefits (i.e. cash) or intangible benefits (name recognition, happier customers etc.).

Other free E-mail services, such as POP mail services, make their living by reselling or reusing you E-mail information. For instance, they might send you an ad message a week, or sell your name to companies in certain fields (some free E-mail services require you to complete a personal profile when you sign up; this is to better target the advertising they offer you).

New Words and Expressions

account	/əˈkaunt/	n.	计算，账目
advertisement	/ədˈvəːtismənt/	n.	广告，做广告
appear	/əˈpiə/	vi.	出现，看来
attempt	/əˈtempt/	vt.	尝试，企图
banner	/ˈbænə/	n.	旗帜，横幅
benefit	/ˈbenifit/	vt.	有益于，有助于
collect	/kəˈlekt/	v.	收集，聚集
gain	/gein/	vt.	得到，增进
graphical	/ˈgræfikəl/	adj.	绘画的
indirectly	/ˌindiˈrektli/	adv.	间接地，拐弯抹角地
instance	/ˈinstəns/	n.	实例，建议
personal	/ˈpəːsənl/	adj.	私人的，个人的
profile	/ˈprəufail/	n.	侧面，外形
provider	/prəˈvaidə/	n.	供给者，供应者
site	/sait/	n.	地点，场所
tangible	/ˈtændʒəbl/	adj.	切实的
whatsoever	/wɔtsəuˈevə/	pron.	无论什么

Exercise 7: Select the answer that best expresses the main idea of the paragraph reading B.

1) To Free E-mail services, we can find _____ in our common days.
   A. we have to pay for them   B. we can get one or more free E-mail accounts
   C. we have no freedom in use   D. we lose our all secrets

2) What is the mail idea of the passage?
   A. What is the Free E-mail.   B. The general introduction to Free E-mail.
   C. Appealing us to use Free E-mail.   D. Free E-mail is loved by use in the current society.

3) Companies offers free E-mail in order to get _____.

    A. nothing

    B. tangible cash benefits

    C. intangible name recognition, happier customers' benefits

    D. both B and C

4) Depending on _____ free E-mail services can make their living.

    A. sending you a free E-mail to greet you a week

    B. selling your name to companies in certain fields

    C. sending you on ad message a week or selling your name to companies in certain fields

    D. sending you a free E-mail written by manager

5) From the passage, we can infer _____.

    A. to most E-mails, there is no meal without cost

    B. we can't live without E-mails

    C. E-mails are the only way to communicate with others

    D. we all really share free E-mails

Exercise 8: Fill in the blanks with words and expressions given below. Change the form where necessary.

provider	advertisement	banner	at the end of	site	for instance
in return	profile	attempt	personal		

1) The marchers waved _____ saying "We want work".

2) I've been looking after four young children all day and I really am _____ my tether.

3) In _____ she is very like her mother.

4) Her _____ life is a mystery to his colleagues.

5) He will _____ to beat the world record.

6) You can't rely on her: _____, she arrived an hour late for an important meeting yesterday.

7) They are letting us use their computer, and _____ we are giving them the results of our research.

8) If you want to look for a job, why not put an _____ in the local paper?

9) I picked a sheltered _____ for the tent.

10) Most free E-mail _____ make their money by showing you advertisements.

Exercise 9: Translate the following sentences.

1）她工作中一遇到麻烦就去找她的朋友。

2）我的朋友打算在北京的一家外国公司求职。

3）她不喜欢跳舞，我也不喜欢跳舞。

4）由于他们努力工作，他们用了八天而不是十天就完成了计划。

5）她在这家工厂干了很多年，她有很多实践经验。

Grammar Focus:Infinitive 动词不定式

一、不定式的概述

动词不定式与动词的-ing 形式、过去分词形式一样是动词的一种非谓语形式。它与动词原形同形，但它的前面一般要带有一个不定式的符号"to"，我们为了把它与介词的 to 区别开来，也叫它小品词。它只是一个符号，没有词性，但动词不定式也存在不带 to 的情况。

二、不定式作名词的用法

动词不定式在句中的作用有时和名词相同，在句子中可以作主语、表语或宾语。

e.g. He likes to play ping-pong ball.（作宾语）

　　　For him to draw such a picture is not easy.（作主语）

　　　His job is to clean all the windows.（作表语）

注意：动词不定式可以有自己的宾语。

　　　　中的 ping-pong ball 作不定式 to play 的宾语

　　　　中的 such a picture 作不定式 to draw 的宾语

　　　　中的 all the windows 作不定式 to clean 的宾语

（1）不定式作主语。

e.g. To see is to believe.

　　　To obey the laws is important.

1）当作主语的不定式短语较长时，常用 it 组形式主语而将真正的主语（即不定时短语）放在谓语之后。

句型一：It is easy (difficult、hard、important、right、wrong、possible、impossible、necessary、unnecessary、foolish、wise、kind、cruel、nice…)to do…

句型二：It is a pleasure (pity、pleasant thing、crime、an honour…) to do sth.

句型三：It takes (sb.)+时间+to do sth.

2）"句型一"中我们常用 for sb.或 of sb.来作不定式的逻辑上的主语，但是什么情况下用 for 或 of，主要是从以下两方面来进行区别。

① for sb.的句型通常使用表示客观情况的形容词。

e.g. It is important for us to express our opinions.

注意：表示客观情况的形容词有 difficult、easy、hard、important、impossible、Interesting、necessary、unnecessary、possible。

② of sb.的句型通常使用表示主观感情或态度的形容词。

e.g. It is clever of him to leave that country.

注意：表示主观感情或态度的形容词有 careful、clever、impolite、nice、polite、right、 wise、wrong。

（2）不定式作表语。

1）不定式作表语，一般紧跟在系动词如 be、seem、remain、appear、get 等后面，用来说明主语的内容。

2）当用 one's dream、business、with、idea、plan、job、work、task、duty 及 what one wants to do 等作主语时，常用不定式作表语。

句型一：主语（事物）+be+ 不定式（作表语），表示主语的具体内容

e.g. His plan is to clean the room.

句型二：主语（人）+be+不定式（作表语），表示时态将来时，为即将之意

e.g. He is to clean the room.

（3）不定式作动词宾语：不定式用在及物动词后担当宾语，常见的及物动词有：agree、aim、appear、arrange、ask、attempt、beg、choose、decide、demand、desire、expect、fail、happen、hope、manage、offer、plan、prepare、pretend、promise、prove、refuse、seem、want、wish。

e.g. He decided to incite all of his classmates to attend the holiday at the beach.

　　The theory proved to be correct at last.

（4）不定式作介词宾语。

1）当介词 but、expect、besides 前面是其他动词时，介词后接带 to 的不定式；若前面有实义动词 do 及其各种形式时，介词后面的不定式可以省去 to。

句型：but、expect、besides+（to）do sth.

e.g. What do you like to do besides play balls?

　　There was nothing for the students to do except read the books aloud.

2）另外，介词 instead of 前后两个成分必须对等，如果前面一个成分是一个不定式，后面的不定式就可以省去 to。

e.g. We want to watch TV instead of do our homework.

3）除 but、expect、besides 外，个别介词可用"连接代词（副词）+不定式"作宾语。

e.g. The boy has his own ides of how to finish it.

三、不定式作形容词的用法

不定式有时起形容词的作用，用来修饰名词或代词，在句子中担任定语。

（1）动宾关系和主谓关系。

1）名词或代词+不定式（to+不及物动词+介词）

e.g. He is looking for a room to live in.

2）名词或代词（地点、工具等）+不定式（to+动作性动词）+介词。

e.g. Please pass me some paper to write on.

　　Please lend me something to write with.

3）主谓关系：不定式所修饰的名词或代词是它的逻辑主语。

e.g. The factory to produce electricity will be set up next year.

4）主谓关系的特殊情况：在主谓关系还包括当不定式所修饰的是序数词或是形容词最高级所修饰的名词时，或者这个名词被省略时，这个名词和不定式之间也是逻辑上的主谓关系。

e.g. She is always the last (person) to speak at the meetings.

（2）不定式修饰 something、anything、nothing。

当不定式修饰 something、anything、nothing 时，当然也要放在这些词后面做后置定语；如果有形容词修饰上述三个词时，应该放在它们的后面；如果既有形容词又有不定式修饰上述三个词时，词序应为：

something/anything/ nothing+形容词+不定式

e.g. Do you have anything to read?

四、不定式作副词的用法

（1）原因。

1）修饰表示感情的形容词。常用形容词有 angry、anxious、clever、delighted、disappointed、eager、foolish、fortunate、frightened、glad、happy、lucky、pleased、proud、ready、sorry、willing、worthy、unfortunate、surprised。

e.g. He is lucky to get here on time.

2）修饰表示感情以外的形容词。下列形容词常用这类结构中，且这类句子的主语可以是人，也可以是物：comfortable、difficult、easy、good、hard、pleasant。

e.g. The house is very comfortable to live in.

（2）目的。

1）放在句首，加强语气。

e.g. To serve the people well, I study hard.

2）在不定式前加上 in order to 或 so as 加强语气。

e.g. In order to serve the people well, I study hard.

　　I study hard so as to serve the people well.

（3）结果。

e.g. I hurried to get there only to find him out.

（4）其他用法。

句型　too+ adj./adv. +(for sb.)+to do sth.

e.g. The book is too hard for the boy to read.

不定式修饰副词 enough 的用法

e.g. He is old enough to go to school.

不定式在句中做独立成分

e.g. To tell you the truth, I didn't think the film is good.

五、不定式作宾语补足语的用法

不定式作宾语补足语的情况很多，常用的动词有 advice、allow、ask、beg、command、cause、expect、encourage、force、get、hate、intend、invite、instruct、like、order、oblige、prefer、persuade、permit、promise、press、request、tell、want、wish、remind、warn 等，在这些动词之后，不定式常作宾语补足语。

（1）省略 to 的用法。

1）不定式在某些感觉动词（fell、hear、listen to、watch、look at、notice、observe）和使役动词（let、have、make）后做宾语补足语时，省去 to,但在被动语态中 to 不可省。

e.g. Let me hear anyone say anything about it?

2）在动词 help 后，to 可以省，也可以不省。

e.g. I will help him (to) clean the room.

（2）to be 结构的用法。

动词 think、consider、find、believe、suppose、know、understand、take 后，不定式作宾语补足语时常用 to be 结构。

e.g. I consider him to be an honest man.

Exercise 10: Select the best choice for each sentence.

1) You'd better _____ where you are.

 A. remain   B. to remain   C. remaining   D. remained

2) Is it necessary _____ the dictionary immediately?

 A. of me to return   B. for me to return

 C. that I return   D. my returning

3) He told me that he would rather _____ with me.

 A. not go   B. to go   C. not to go   D. to not go

4) Her mother didn't allow her _____ the mountain on such a rainy day.

 A. to risk climbing   B. risking to climb

 C. for risk to climb   D. risk climbing

5) You had better _____ your father's advice.

  A. to follow　　　　B. followed　　　　C. follow　　　　D. following

6) In those days his family didn't have enough room _____.

  A. living in　　　　B. living　　　　C. to live　　　　D. to live in

7) Why not _____ Bill to answer this question.

  A. going to ask　　　　　　　　B. go and ask

  C. went to ask　　　　　　　　D. goes and ask

8) They knew him very well. They had seen him _____ up from childhood.

  A. to grow　　　　B. grow　　　　C. growing　　　　D. was growing

9) The doctor made me _____ at hospital for weeks.

  A. stayed　　　　B. to stay　　　　C. stay　　　　D. staying

10) The doctor did everything he could _____ the patient.

  A. saved　　　　B. saving　　　　C. save　　　　D. to save

11) Why not _____ doing it in some other way?

  A. try　　　　B. trying　　　　C. tried　　　　D. to try

12) — Have you decided when _____?

  — Yes, the day after tomorrow.

  A. will be leaving　　　　　　　　B. to be leaving

  C. are you leaving　　　　　　　　D. to leave

13) She is always pleased _____ at the party.

  A. to be invited to sing　　　　　　B. to invite to sing

  C. to be invited singing　　　　　　D. to invite singing

14) Her daughter promised _____ in the bedroom until the baby stopped crying.

  A. stay　　　　　　　　　　B. to stay

  C. staying　　　　　　　　　D. to staying

15) He preferred _____ rather than _____ by others.

  A. driving, being driven　　　　　　B. drive, be driven

  C. driving, driving　　　　　　　　D. driving, to drive

16) How _____ the problem will be discussed at tomorrow's meeting.

  A. to solve　　　　　　　　　　B. to be solved

  C. being solved　　　　　　　　　D. solving

17) In order to get to Peter's house early I had his secretary _____ a map for me.

  A. to draw　　　　B. draw　　　　C. drawn　　　　D. drawing

18) Your teeth are not in good condition. _____ your milk without sugar?

  A. Why you have not　　　　　　B. Why have you not

  C. Why have not　　　　　　　　D. Why not have

19) A lot of people find modern art very hard _____.

  A. understand　　　　　　　　B. understanding

  C. to understand　　　　　　　　D. being understood

20) Mr. Li often warns his son _____ alone.

    A. never to swim   B. not to swimming

    C. never swim   D. not swim

Exercise 11: Fill in with best choice.

Dear Fred,

    Thanks for you letter. It was ___1)___ from you. Your new job sounds very interesting and you ___2)___ with it. I am still with the same firm that I joined five years ago when we ___3)___. ___4)___ I am happy there, I must say that I sometimes feel that I ___5)___ to move, but here in Bakewell there are only ___6)___ companies.

    I like this town. What I like ___7)___ living here is that it is quiet. Perhaps I should say it was quiet ___8)___ these big lorries started coming through the town. Anyway, they only come through during the day, never ___9)___ night. If you have time before the end of the summer, why don't you come and ___10)___ with us for one weekend? That would be very pleasant.

    I hope you are still well. Write again soon.

    Yours,

    Terry

    1) A. well to listen   B. well to hear

        C. good to listen   D. good to hear

    2) A. look pleased   B. seem pleased

        C. look pleasing   D. seem pleasing

    3) A. left school   B. left the school

        C. have left school   D. have left the school

    4) A. Although   B. Already

        C. Because   D. Through

    5) A. ought   B. should   C. would   D. must

    6) A. some   B. any   C. few   D. a few

    7) A. more about   B. most about

        C. more of   D. most of

    8) A. as long as   B. as far as   C. when   D. until

    9) A. during   B. at the   C. in   D. at

    10) A. live   B. pass   C. stay   D. rest

Unit 9　Traffic & Transmission
Communicative Samples

Conversation 1

(Peter is waiting in a bus station for a long-distance bus, and needs some help. He approaches Jane sitting next to him.)

Peter:　Excuse me. I was wondering if you could help me.

Jane:　Sure. I'll be glad to try. What do you need?

Peter:　Can you tell me when the next bus leaves for Chicago? I'm not sure how to read this timetable.

Jane:　Hmm. It looks like one leaves at 12:15.

Peter:　Thank you very much. I couldn't figure it out. What's the time now?

Jane:　Eleven twenty. You've got plenty of time.

Peter: Good. Do you know where I could get a cup of coffee?

Jane:　There's a machine over there.

Peter: I'm sorry to keep bothering you, but can you show me how it works?

Jane: Of course. Put one of these plastic cups under the spout. Put your money here at the top. Select the kind of coffee you want and push the button next to it. The coffee will automatically be poured into your cup.

Peter: Thank you. Oh, it only takes quarters. Do you have change for a dollar?

Jane:　Let me see. Here you are.

Peter: Thanks.

Jane:　You're welcome.

Conversation 2

(Susan is asking the way to Waterfront Park.)

Susan:　　　Excuse me.

Policeman: Yes? Is there anything I can help you with, Ma'am?

Susan:　　　Could you tell me what's the best way to get to Waterfront Park from here? Can I take the subway?

Policeman: No. You can catch the No. 34 bus in front of that hotel. Get off at Harbor Street. Actually, it's just a short walk from here.

Susan: Really? How far is it?

Policeman: About ten or fifteen minutes. You know, there
              are guided tours of the city you can take.

Susan: Oh? What does the city tour include?

Policeman: They take you by all the major points of interest.
              You can get a good idea of where everything is.

Susan: Hmm. How much is it?

Policeman: It's one dollar per person for an hour-long tour.
              If you're interested, I can arrange it for you.

Susan: That sounds like a good idea. Thanks a lot.

Policeman: Don't mention it.

New Words and Expressions

approach	/ə'prəutʃ/	n.	逼近，走进
automatically	/ɔːtə'mætikli/	adv.	自动地，机械地
include	/in'kluːd/	vt.	包括，包含
memorize	/meməraiz/	v.	记住，记忆
pour	/pɔː/	v.	灌注，倾泻
technique	/tek'niːk/	n.	技术，技巧
tour	/tuə/	v.	旅行，游历

Exercise 1: Complete the following sentences.

A: Excuse me ,Sir?

B: Yes? _____ (有什么可以帮助您的), Ma'am?

A: Could you tell me the way to People's park?

B: _____ (你可以乘坐 9 号地铁).

A: Thank you very much.

B: _____ (不用客气).

Exercise 2: Fill in the missing letters.

app_oaches	d_llar	tou_	a_tomatically	_lastic
time_able	sub_ay	in_lude	gui_e	po_r

Paragraph Reading A: Traffic Safety

Traffic safety is one of the most important issues of every modern city. Due to the invention of the motor car and all sorts of other motor vehicles, we now read news in the paper about traffic accidents nearly every day. We cannot help sympathizing with the victims. Of course, if we could do away with those modern vehicles, no such things would happen. But it is

against the progress of civilization. We cannot return to the backward past ages.

But if we cannot entirely prevent the traffic accidents from happening, at least we can lessen their chances of occurrence. We can lessen them by educating pedestrians and car drivers of the ways of traffic safety. For example, a pedestrian, when walking next to the road, should always stay on the sidewalk or pavement. All this will enable him to lessen his chances of meeting with danger. But the car driver needs to be particularly responsible in maintaining road safety. For if an accident happens, he really is the killer, doing the deed on behalf of Death. So if a driver, when driving a car is always on the alert, he will seldom commit the act of killing another person. In short, traffic safety can be achieved only through the cooperation of both the driver and the pedestrian.

New Words and Expressions

alert	/əˈləːt/	adj.	提防的，警惕的
backward	/ˈbækwəd/	adv.	向后地，退步
civilization	/ˌsivilaɪˈzeiʃən/	n.	文明，文化
cooperation	/kəuˌɔpəˈreiʃən/	n.	合作，协作
deed	/diːd/	n.	行为，事实
due to		adv.	由于，应归于
enable	/iˈneibl/	vt.	使能够
entirely	/inˈtaiəli/	adv.	完全地，全然地
invention	/inˈvenʃən/	n.	发明，创造
issue	/ˈisjuː/	n.	问题，结果
maintain	/menˈtein/	vt.	维持，维修
modern	/ˈmɔdən/	adj.	近代的，现代的
occurrence	/əˈkʌrəns/	n.	发生，出现
pavement	/ˈpeivmənt/	n.	人行道，公路
pedestrian	/peˈdestriən/	n.	步行者
responsible	/risˈpɔnsəbl/	adj.	有责任的，可靠的
sidewalk	/ˈsaidwɔːk/	n.	人行道
sympathize	/ˈsimpəθaiz/	vi.	同情，共鸣
vehicle	/ˈviːikl/	n.	交通工具，车辆
victim	/ˈviktim/	n.	受害人，牺牲者

Exercise 3: Select the answer that best expresses the main idea of the paragraph reading A.

1) To traffic safety description, the passage reflects the point _____.

   A. it is one of the most important problems of every modern city

   B. it is the most important problems of every modern city

   C. it has relation with air pollution

   D. it was ignored by us in past time

2) To those modern vehicles, which is the right attitude implied in the article?

   A. They are against the progress of civilization.

   B. Doing away with them.

   C. We will return to the past ages.

   D. Using them while paying more attention to solving their backwards.

3) The responsibility of road safety is particularly on the part of _____.

   A. friendship   B. car driver

   C. safety attention   D. traffic lights

4) _____makes a driver become the killer?

   A. Accident happening

   B. Lessening traffic accident's chances of occurrence

   C. Obeying the rules

   D. Educating a pedestrian

5) According to the passage, we can find traffic safety depended on _____.

   A. passengers and teachers

   B. drivers and governments

   C. the cooperation of both the driver and the pedestrian

   D. authority and rules

Exercise 4: Fill in the blanks with words and expressions given below. Change the form where necessary.

due to	issue	deed	on behalf of	cannot help	do away with
lessen	pavement	maintain	achieve		

1) I brought the new stamp the day of its _____.

2) The government _____ free school meals.

3) The pain was already _____.

4) The team's success was largely _____ her efforts.

5) I've _____ only half of what I'd hoped to do.

6) I hope you will _____ your recent improvement.

7) He _____ having big ears.

8) Don't ride your bicycle on the _____.

9) _____ are better than words when people need help.

10) _____ my colleagues and myself I thank you.

Exercise 5: Definitions of these words appear on the right. Put the letter of the appropriate definition next to each word.

1) _____ vehicle   a. warning to be ready for danger

2) _____ sympathize   b. directed towards the back

3) _____ sidewalk   c. something that moves on wheels, such as a car, bus, etc.

4) _____ victim   d. the people or countries that have reached an advanced stage of human development

5) _____ backward   e. completely; in every way

6) _____ entirely   f. dull

7) _____ occurrence   g. pavement

8) _____ pedestrian   h. to feel or show approval

9) _____ civilization   i. an event

10) _____ alert   j. a person or thing that suffers pain, death

Exercise 6: Translate the following sentences.

1）首先知道这两种语言的差异对于我们来讲是非常重要的。

2）我想知道我们为什么要做这件工作。

3）我们盼望着尽快见到我们的新老师。

4）很抱歉，让你等了这么长时间。

5）她看上去像是病了，请叫个医生来。（send for）

Paragraph Reading B: The Public Transport

Transportation may prove to be a sticky question for most cities in the world. It depends entirely on where you happen to end up. The public transport system in China mainly consists of trains, the underground, coaches and buses. Among its modern means of transportation, China has a vast network of airports and air lines within easy reach of almost every big city. With civil airports and scheduled flights, travel both within and outside China can be an exhilarating experience.

Nothing can match airplanes for speed and comfort. They get you to your destination quickly and smoothly.

Trains are usually comfortable, frequent and fast, thought some of them are very crowded. They are usually quicker than coaches especially on direct routes. For long distance journeys between major cities, the best way is to take an express train. They are more expensive than coaches but cheaper than planes.

Buses are generally extremely noisy, dirty and unsafe, especially during morning and evening rush hours. There are two types of buses in China—single-deck buses and double-deck buses. Usually each bus has two conductors who collect fares. The functioning of minibuses – which stop anywhere upon a person's request have brought much convenience to passengers.

Nowadays taxis are easy to get in major cities. You can find taxis at taxi ranks, at airports, railway stations and in town centers. You can also telephone for a taxi or stop one on the street. Taxis are much more expensive than buses though they are more convenient and faster.

New Words and Expressions

coach	/kəutʃ/	n.	四轮大马车，教练
conductor	/kən'dʌktə/	n.	领导者，售票员
consist	/kən'sist/	vi.	由…组成
convenience	/kən'viːnjəns/	n.	便利，方便
crowded	/'kraudid/	adj.	拥挤的，塞满的
destination	/ˌdesti'neiʃən/	n.	目的地
exhilarating	/ig'ziləreitiŋ/	adj.	令人喜欢的
express	/iks'pres/	vt.	表达，表示
extremely	/iks'triːmli/	adv.	极端地，非常地
frequent	/'friːkwənt/	adj.	频繁的
journey	/'dʒəːni/	n.	旅行，旅程
match	/mætʃ/	n.	相配，比赛
public	/'pʌblik/	n.	公众，公共场所
rush	/rʌʃ/	vi.	冲，奔
schedule	/'ʃedjuːl/	n.	时间表，进度表
speed	/spiːd/	n.	迅速，速度
sticky	/'stiki/	adj.	黏的，黏性的
system	/'sistəm/	n.	系统，体系
transportation	/ˌtrænspɔː'teiʃən/	n.	运输，运送
underground	/'ʌndəgraund/	n.	地铁
vast	/vɑːst/	adj.	巨大的，辽阔的

Exercise 7: Select the answer that best expresses the main idea of the paragraph reading B.

1) How many kinds of Chinese transportation are mentioned in the passage?

A. 3   B. 4   C. 5   D. 6

2) Which kind of transportation is the most comfortable?

A. Airplane.   B. Trains.

C. Buses.   D. Taxis.

3) Compared with airplanes, buses and taxis, the train has main _____.

A. more expensive than taxis   B. more crowded than airplanes

C. more comfortable than buses   D. noisier than airplanes

4) Generally, the features of buses are that _____.

    A. noisy, but clean

    B. safer, especially during morning and evening rush hours

    C. minibuses have brought much convenience to passengers

    D. none of above

5) Taxis are much more expensive than buses, why do many persons take taxis?

    A. More convenient.   B. Faster.

    C. More comfortable.   D. More convenient and faster.

Exercise 8: Fill in the blanks with words and expressions given below. Change the form where necessary.

sticky	consist of	end up	match	crowded	extremely
convenience	journey	rush	express		

1) The new curtains are a perfect _____ for the carpet.

2) I am in a dreadful _____ so I can't stop.

3) Did you have a good _____?

4) His dismissal was rather a _____ business for all concerned.

5) The letter was sent _____.

6) I had a very _____ schedule on the trip.

7) After much discussion about holidays abroad we _____ in England.

8) It was a great _____ to have the doctor living near us.

9) I'm _____ sorry for the delay.

10) The committee _____ 15 members.

Exercise 9: Translate the following sentences.

1）老师问谁负责班里的清洁工作。（in charge of）

2）我建议她用不同的方法做这件工作。（suggest）

3）据说我们学校明年将有更多的学生。

4）老师在会议开始时讲的话很重要。

5）如果你不能来出席会议，请提前告知我们。

Grammar Focus: Gerund 动名词

一、动词-ing 的概述

动词-ing 形式是三种非谓语动词中的一种，它由动词原形加-ing 构成。有的动词-ing 形式在句中起名词作用，有的则起形容词或副词作用。所以在句中，动词-ing 形式可以担当除了谓语外的任何成分，即主语、表语、宾语（介词宾语和动词宾语）、定语、状语和宾语补足语。动词-ing 形式仍具有动词的若干特点，所以它又可以有自己的宾语和状语等。

（1）动词-ing 作主语。

1）基本用法：动词-ing 作主语通常表示事物化、抽象化的概念，而且谓语动词一律用单数。

e.g. Seeing is believing.

Having done the work is an experience you'll never forget.

2）it 作形式主语。

e.g. It is no use talking too much.

It's no good crying.

句型 It is no use/good +V-ing

或 It is of no use/useless +V-ing 意思为 "…是没有用"

（2）动词-ing 作表语。

基本用法：动词-ing 作表语时，一般表示比较抽象的习惯性动作。

e.g. His hobby is painting.

What he likes best is making jokes.

The day is so charming!

（此例句中，动词-ing 作表语，表述的是主语的特征，相当于形容词。）

注意：起形容词作用的动词-ing 作表语时，一般表示主动或主语的性质和特征。含有 "令人……" 的意思。主语多数情况下是物，而动词-ing 是由能够表示人们某种感情或情绪的动词变化而来的。常见的举例如下。

| amusing | astonishing | boring | encouraging | exciting | inspiring |
| interesting | missing | moving | promising | puzzling | surprising |

e.g. The news sounds encouraging.

（3）动词-ing 作宾语。

1）动词-ing 作动词的宾语。

下列动词和词组只能用动词-ing 作宾语。

admit	advise	allow	appreciate	avoid	can't help doing sth.	consider
delay	deny	enjoy	escape	excuse	forbid	forgive	give up
imagine	mind	keep	keep(on)	permit	practise	prevent	put off
resist	risk	suggest	understand

e.g. I can't imagine doing that with them.

She denied making a mistake.

2）动词-ing 作介词的宾语。

动词-ing 还可以作介词的宾语，常见的以介词结尾的固定词组如下所示。

| insist on | be sick of | excuse…for | hear of | think of | be ashamed of |
| devote… to | prevent…from | look forward to | add to | know of | keep…from |

be/get used to	lead to	set about	stop…from	be proud of	get to
spend…in	be engaged in	be succeed in	come to	spend…(in)	doing sth.
depend on	be fond of	stick to	be busy (in) doing (sth.)		thank…for
be good at	be sentenced to	be afraid of	feel like	be interested in	
carry on	be tired of	contribute to	dream of	save…from	

e.g. I'm proud of being a Chinese.

Our teacher has devoted her life to her teaching.

（4）动词-ing 作定语。

1）起名词作用的动词-ing 作定语时，表示所修饰词的用途，它的位置一般是放在它所修饰的词的前面。

e.g. a sleeping car   dancing teacher   drinking water   exciting news

     reading room   smoking room   walking stick   writing desk

2）起形容词作用的动词-ing 作定语时，还含有进行和主动的意思。

① 动词-ing 作定语时一般表示现在正发生的动作。

e.g. The man running over there is our chairman.

I know the young man sleeping on the bench.

②有时动词-ing 所表示的动作与谓语动词的动作同时发生。

e.g. The road joining the two villages is very wide.

They lived in a room facing the north thirty years ago.

③如果动词-ing 作定语时是单个词，往往放在它所修饰的词的前面；但如果是动词-ing 短语作定语时，则要放在它所修饰的词的后面。

e.g. The swimming boy is my younger brother.

This is the path leading to the school.

（5）动词-ing 作宾语补足语。

动词-ing 经常用在动词 feel、hear、leave、keep、listen、listen to、look at、notice、see、watch 等后作宾语补足语，其中宾语和宾语补足语存在着逻辑上的主谓关系，且表示动作正在进行，状态正在持续。

e.g. The parents can hear their daughter playing the piano.

He kept me waiting for a almost an hour.

（6）动词-ing 作状语。

1）动词-ing 作时间状语。

e.g. Hearing the bad news, they couldn't help crying.

While playing the piano, she got very excited.

Having turned off the radio, he began to go over his lessons.

2）动词-ing 作原因状语。

① 动词-ing 所表示的动作和谓语动词所表示的动作同时发生或几乎同时发生时，用动词-ing 的一般形式。

e.g. Not recognizing the voice, he refused to give the person his address.

Being so angry, he couldn't go to sleep.

② 动词-ing 所表示的动作在谓语动词所表示的动作之前发生，用动词-ing 的完成式。

e.g. Having been to the Great Wall many times, he didn't to (there) last week.

Not having received his father's letter, he decided to make a call to him.

3）动词-ing 作让步状语。有时，动词-ing 前可带有连词 although、whether、even if、even though。

e.g. Although working from morning till night his father didn't get enough food.

4）动词-ing 作方式或伴随状语。

e.g. They came into the classroom, singing and laughing.

5）动词-ing 作结果状语。动词-ing 作结果状语时，不经常被使用，通常放在句末，中间有逗号。有时为了突出结果，分词前带有 thus。

e.g. The bus was held up by the snowstorm, thus causing the delay.

（7）动词-ing 的否定式和动词-ing 短语。

1）动词-ing 的否定式：not+动词-ing。

e.g. His not getting to the station on time makes everyone worried.

Not knowing received a reply, he decided to write again.

2）动词-ing 短语为：物主代词/名词所有格+动词-ing，此时物主代词和名词的所有格是这个 -ing 的逻辑主语，动词-ing 短语可以作主语、表语和宾语。

e.g. Li Ming's being late made his teacher very angry.

I think the biggest problem is their not having enough time.

注意：虽然有时动词-ing 和动词-ing 短语在句子中的意思有较大的不同，但大多数情况下，它们的区别并不大，只不过动词-ing 短语表示的内容更具体些。

e.g. Do you mind opening the door?

Do you mind my/me opening the door?

Exercise 10: Select the best choice for each sentence.

1) It's necessary to be prepared for a job interview. _____ the answers ready will be of great help.

   A. To have had   B. Having had   C. Have   D. Having

2) — What's made Tom so upset?

   — _____ the game. It shocked him so much.

   A. For losing   B. Lost

   C. Losing   D. Because of losing

3) What worried the child most was _____ to visit his mother in the hospital.

   A. his not allowing   B. his not being allowed

   C. his being not allowed   D. having not been allowed

4) As I will be away for at least a year, I'd appreciate _____ from you now and then so that I can know how everyone is getting along.

   A. having heard   B. to hear   C. hearing   D. being heard

5) We should prevent such a silly mistake _____ again.

   A. occurring   B. to occur

   C. to be occurred   D. from being occurred

6) He is an experienced driver and he is used _____ on all kinds of roads.

   A. to drive   B. to have driven   C. for driving   D. to driving

7) It is time to listen to the new. Would you mind _____ the radio?

   A. me to open   B. me opening   C. my opening   D. my turning on

8) I object _____ loud music playing while I eat.

   A. have   B. to have   C. having   D. to having

9) It is very cold outside. I feel like _____ something hot.

   A. to drink   B. a little   C. drinking   D. to have

10) I can never get used _____ this kind of food.

   A. to eat   B. to eating   C. for eating   D. with eating

11) Tom now rides his bike to work instead of _____ by bus.

   A. travel   B. travels   C. traveling   D. to travel

12) Mary enjoys _____ TV while she's having supper.

   A. watching   B. to watch   C. being watched   D. watch

13) _____ in the garden on Saturday afternoons isn't Ted's idea of fun.

   A. Worked   B. Working   C. Being worked   D. The working

14) Can you imagine these fat men _____ the mountain?

   A. to climb   B. climbing   C. climb   D. had climbed

15) Peter is looking forward _____ his new job in the bank on Monday.

   A. starting   B. to starting   C. to start   D. start

16) It's no good _____ about your age.

   A. to worry   B. worried   C. worrying   D. worry

17) Is there any use _____ the matter further?

    A. to discuss   B. to discussing   C. discussing   D. with discussing

18) She is a very-known writer and speaker. She devoted all her life _____.

    A. to write and lecturing   B. writing and lecturing

    C. to write and lecture   D. to writing and lecturing

19) — Does your car need _____?

    — I certainly need _____ mine.

    A. washing, to wash   B. to wash, washing

    C. washing, washing   D. to wash, to wash

20) Serving the people whole-heartedly makes life worth _____.

    A. to live   B. living   C. being lived   D. of living

Exercise 11: Fill in with best choice.

I have a brother who is ___1)___ me. We ___2)___. Yesterday was an important day ___3)___ and our friends. In the morning ___4)___ of us had a big exam at the technical college. Then ___5)___ there was a big meeting at the youth club at 9 o'clock. (That's where we usually go when we want to ___6)___ ourselves.) A rich woman had given us some money and yesterday we ___7)___ decide what to do ___8)___. Many people wanted to buy something new for our club, but my brother and I wanted to give the money to another club that has ___9)___. In the end we decided to give half the money to the poor club and ___10)___ half for ourselves.

1) A. so old as	B. so old that	C. the same age that	D. the same age as
2) A. both are 16	B. are both 16	C. are 16 both	D. are 16 the both
3) A. to us	B. for us	C. with us	D. on us
4) A. most	B. much	C. more	D. few
5) A. last night	B. the last night	C. last evening	D. the last evening
6) A. enjoy	B. meet	C. like	D. divert
7) A. had to	B. must	C. should	D. would
8) A. with it	B. with them	C. for it	D. for them
9) A. something	B. any thing	C. nothing	D. everything
10) A. keep another	B. keep the other	C. hold another	D. hold the other

Unit 10 Letters
Communicative Samples

Conversation 1

(Tang walks out of the Post Office with a small parcel under her arm, which she forgets to mail.)

Clerk: Excuse me, Madam. Can I help you?

Tang: Yes. I forgot to mail this parcel.

Clerk: Ok. Let me weigh it. … It's two and a half pounds. Airmail? Insured?

Tang: Can it go by UPS?

Clerk: No, United Parcel Service only provides parcel delivery within the U.S. Yours is mailed to China.

Tang: Yes, I see. Airmail please. What are the insurance rates? Is it worth it?

Clerk: Well, that all depends on the value. Insurance rates are relatively low and worth the small extra expense.

Tang: Then insure it please. Will fifteen dollars cover everything?

Clerk: Oh yes, it will.

Tang: By the way, can I include this letter in the package?

Clerk: No, that's against the regulations. If you want the letter to arrive with the parcel, you can put it in an ordinary envelope with the proper first class stamp, and then fasten the envelope to the parcel with glue, and write clearly on it: "Letter Inside."

Tang: Thank you very much.

Conversation 2

(Clara is at the Post Office.)

Clerk: Good morning. What can I do for you?

Clara: I'd like to send a telegram to someone in Los Angeles.

Clerk: May I have the name and address?

Clara: Her name is Kate Bill. She lives at 381 Pine Street, Los Angeles.

Clerk: Can you spell the name, please?

Clara: The last name is Bill, B-I-L-L. Her first name is Kate, K-A-T-E.

Clerk: Thank you. What is the message?

Clara: Could you first tell me the rate?

Clerk: Two dollars and thirty-eight cents for the first seven words and thirty-four cents for each additional word.

Clara: I see. And how much is it to send a letter telegram?

Clerk: It's three dollars and seventy-four cents for the first twenty- two words and seventeen cents for each additional word.

Clara: I'll send a letter telegram then. The message is "CONGR-ATULATIONS ON YOUR WEDDING DAY. THINKING OF YOU. HOPE TO SEE YOU SOON. CLARA."

Clerk: All right. This will arrive tomorrow morning.

Clara: Thank you.

New Words and Expressions

insured	/inˈʃuəd/	n.	被保险者，保户
message	/ˈmesidʒ/	n.	消息，通信
package	/ˈpækidʒ/	n.	包裹，包
rate	/reit/	n.	速度，价格
regulation	/regjuˈleiʃ ən/	n.	规则，规章
spell	/spel/	vt.	拼写，拼成

Exercise 1: Complete the following sentences.

A: Good morning. What can I do for you?

B: Yes. Could you tell me _____ (发一封电报多少钱)?

A: _____ (寄到哪里)?

B: Los Angeles.

A: It's three dollars for _____ (前 20 个字) and seventeen cents for each additional word.

B: Thank you.

Exercise 2: Fill in the missing letters.

_arcel	in_ured	r_gulation	m_ssage	e_pense
add_tional	telegra_	rat_	s_ell	packa_e

Paragraph Reading A: The President's Letters

Do you want to say what you think in a letter to the President of the United States? You will get a reply from him—written in ink, not typed—after only a few days.

The President gets about 4,000 letters every week. He answers everyone who writes to him on

special White House paper. But he doesn't need a lot of time for it. In fact, he only spends 20 minutes a week looking at his personal correspondence. He has the most modern secretary in the world to help him.

It's computer, worth $ 800,000, which has its own rooms on the first floor of the White House. It has a bank of electronic pens which write like the President writes, in his favorite light blue ink. Each letter the President receives gets a number, according to the type of answer it needs. The pens then write the correct reply for it, according to the number. Each letter takes less than a second to write. A White House official said: "it is not important that the letters come from a computer. Each letter says what the President wants to say."

New Words and Expressions

correct	/kəˈrekt/	*adj.*	正确的，恰当的
official	/əˈfiʃəl/	*n.*	官员，公务员
own	/əun/	*adj.*	自己的，特有的
president	/ˈprezidənt/	*n.*	总统，会长
reply	/riˈplai/	*n.*	答复，报复
secretary	/ˈsekrətri/	*n.*	秘书，书记
special	/ˈspeʃəl/	*adj.*	特别的，特殊的
type	/taip/	*n.*	类型，典型
worth	/wə:θ/	*adj.*	值钱的

Exercise 3: Select the answer that best expresses the main idea of the paragraph reading A.

1) _____ for a reply from the President.

    A. You have to wait a long time

    B. You have to wait at least one month

    C. You only have to wait several days

    D. You only have to wait a few weeks

2) The reply from the President _____.

    A. is always printed

    B. is always written in ink

    C. is always typed

    D. is always writer by himself

3) It takes the computer _____ to write ten letters.

    A. no more than ten seconds   B. less than ten seconds

    C. a little more than ten seconds   D. at least one second

4) The computer can be described as _____.

    A. expensive but efficient

    B. heavy and inefficient

    C. possessing a beautiful handwriting

    D. the President's most reliable secretary

5) It can be inferred from the passage that _____.

    A. the President never reads any letters written to him by ordinary people

    B. the President hires a very efficient secretary to deal with his correspondence

    C. the President does not really care about the letters he receives every week

    D. the President is assured that the computer expresses his views in the letters

Exercise 4: Fill in the blanks with words and expressions given below. Change the form where necessary.

reply	correspondence	according to	receive	electronic	less than
own	favorite	special	official		

1) She gave me a _____ gift last Sunday.

2) I _____ a car but rarely drive it.

3) I have sent her a letter, but she made no _____.

4) I have _____ a lot of complains about the new radio program.

5) My _____ sport is playing basketball.

6) _____ Marry you were in Shanghai last week.

7) I don't understand all this _____ mails he sent me.

8) She has a lot of _____ to deal with.

9) The news is almost certainly true although it is not _____.

10) I read much _____ I did at school.

Exercise 5: Definitions of these words appear on the right. Put the letter of the appropriate definition next to each word.

1) _____ type		a. private
2) _____ President		b. right
3) _____ modern		c. a particular kind, class, or group
4) _____ secretary		d. a person who holds an office
5) _____ correct		e. a person with the job of preparing letters, keeping records, arranging meetings
6) _____ electronic		f. the head of government in many modern states that do not have a king or queen
7) _____ ink		g. to answer; an act of replying
8) _____ reply		h. of the present time, or of the not far distant past
9) _____ personal		i. of electron
10) _____ official		j. coloured liquid used for writing, printing, or drawing

Exercise 6: Translate the following sentences.

1) 我们应避免犯同样的错误。（avoid）
2) 这是一个很幸福的家庭，他们去过许多国家。
3) 如果他们早一点儿离开学校，就不会赶不上汽车了。（miss）
4) 汤姆因迟到向同学们和老师道歉。（apologize to ... for）
5) 老师说作业必须在次日早晨交上。

Paragraph Reading B： Applicants and Employers

Young people often wonder at the large number of employers who do not respond to their applications for jobs. They say that despite enclosing return envelopes they hear nothing at all or, at best, an impersonal note is sent declaring that the post for which they applied has been filled. Applicants often developed the suspicion that vacancies are earmarked for friends and relatives and that advertisements are only put out to avert this accusation. Many of them are tired of writing around and feel that if only they could obtain an interview with the right person their application would meet with success.

Not to acknowledge applicants' letters is impolite and there seems little excuse for this. Yet even sending brief replies to the people who apply takes much time and money. That so-called return envelope may not have been stamped by the sender, and a hard-pressed office manager may be reluctant to send off long letters of explanation to disappointed job-hunters. A brief note is all that can be managed and even that depends on the policy of the firm. But this difficulty is reasonably easy to remove with a little goodwill.

New Words and Expressions

acknowledge	/ək'nɔlidʒ/	vt.	承认，答谢
avert	/ə'və:t/	v.	转移
brief	/bri:f/	adj.	简短的，短暂的
declare	/di'klɛə/	vt.	断言，宣称
disappoint	/ˌdisə'pɔint/	vt.	使失望
employer	/im'plɔiə/	n.	雇主，老板
enclose	/in'kləuz/	vt.	放入封套，装入
envelope	/'enviləup/	n.	信封，封套

explanation	/ˌeksplə'neiʃən/	n.	解释，解说
impersonal	/im'pə:sənl/	adj.	非个人的
impolite	/impə'lait/	adj.	无礼的，粗鲁的
job-hunter	/dʒɔb-'hʌntə/	n.	求职的人，找工作的人
manager	/'mænidʒə/	n.	经理，管理人员
policy	/'pɔlisi/	n.	政策，方针
reasonably	/'ri:zənəbli/	adv.	适度地，相当地
reluctant	/ri'lʌktənt/	adj.	不顾的，勉强的
remove	/ri'mu:v/	vt.	移动，开除
respond	/ris'pɔnd/	v.	回答，响应
suspicion	/səs'piʃən/	n.	猜疑，怀疑
vacancy	/'veikənsi/	n.	空白，空缺
wonder	/'wʌndə/	vt.	对…感到惊讶，惊奇

Exercise 7: Select the answer that best expresses the main idea of the paragraph reading B.

1) The passage is primarily about _____.

   A. applicants and employers

   B. impolite managers

   C. vacancies and advertisements

   D. writing an application letter

2) Many job-hunters think that they can get a job if _____.

   A. their application is acknowledged

   B. the return envelope is stamped

   C. they can get an interview

   D. there is really a vacancy

3) The author thinks that a letter to decline an applicant should be _____.

   A. a long letter of explanation

   B. a brief letter with a little goodwill

   C. a brief letter to avert accusation

   D. an impersonal note in a stamped envelope

4) What is the chief reason for a manager not to acknowledge applicants' letters?

   A. Sending letters of acknowledgement takes much time and money.

   B. He finds the return envelopes unstamped.

   C. He does not want to disappoint the applicants.

   D. He is acting on the policy of the firm.

5) What is the major complaint of job-hunters?

   A. Their letters of application often get no response.

   B. Letters of acknowledgement carry no explanation.

   C. Letters of acknowledgement sound impersonal.

   D. Vacancies are set aside for friends by employers.

Exercise 8: Fill in the blanks with words and expressions given below. Change the form where necessary.

wonder	respond	application	impersonal	suspicion	acknowledge
remove	send off	if only	reluctant to		

1) I have a _____ that he is not telling me the truth.

2) I have _____ for those flowers I saw advertised in the paper.

3) He refused to _____ defeat.

4) She asked where he'd been, but he didn't _____.

5) _____ he wouldn't eat so noisily.

6) He _____ the mud form his shoes.

7) Giving people time to get to know one another will make the meeting less _____.

8) They were _____ move because they could not get a good price for their old house.

9) We received 300 _____ for the job.

10) I _____ what really happened.

Exercise 9: Translate the following sentences.

1）如果没有你们的帮助，我们是不会取得那么大进步的。（without）

2）学校为学生们提供了教室和阅览室。（provide）

3）她和她的朋友都不会用英文打字。（neither … nor）

4）我们刚一到校天就开始下起雨来。（hardly … when; no sooner … than）

5）她很后悔昨天没有去参加晚会。（regret）

Grammar Focus: Participle 分词

一、过去分词的概述

过去分词也是非谓语动词之一。规则动词的过去分词由动词原形加-ed 构成，不规则动词的过去分词没有统一的构成规则，需要逐一记忆。过去分词一般表示完成的和被动的动作，它在句子中起形容词或副词作用。它在句中可担任表语、定语、宾语补足语和状语。同时，它和动词-ing 形式、动词不定式一样，它在句子中不能担任谓语。但还保留一部分动词性质，即它可以带自己的状语和宾语。

（1）过去分词作表语。

1）基本用法：过去分词作表语一般表示被动或主语所处的状态，含有"感到…"的意思。主语多数情况下是人。而作表语用的过去分词有许多是由能够表示人们某种感情或情绪的动词变化而来的。

e.g. amused、astonished、broken、crowded、delighted、discouraged、dressed、excited、finished、frightened、injured、inspired、interested、known、lost、married、pleased、satisfied、shut、tired、worried、wounded/hurt。

e.g. How did the audience receive the new play?

They got very excited.

2）作表语的过去分词与被动语态中的过去分词的区别。

这两种不同语法功能的句子在形式上是一样的，都是由 "be 动词+过去分词" 构成，有时很容易混淆。它们的具体区别如下。

①从表示的含义上来区分。

作表语的过去分词，表示主语所处的状态。

被动语态中的过去分词，表示的是主语承受的动作。

e.g. The blackboard is broken.

（系表结构，表示主语 the blackboard 所出的状态 broken。）

The blackboard was broken by Li Ming.

（被动语态，表示 the blackboard 承受的动作。）

②从时态上区分。

作表语的过去分词，只用于一般现在时、一般过去时、现在完成时和过去完成时。

被动语态中的过去分词，被动语态除了不能用于完成进行时和将来进行时外，可用其他任何时态。

③从时态的一致性上区分。

作表语的过去分词，其时态不需用保持一致。

被动语态中的过去分词，其时态要与相应主动时态的时态保持一致。

e.g. The blackboard was broken by Li Ming.

或 Li Ming broke the blackboard.

注意：有一些形容词就能够说明状态，此时不用过去分词，而用形容词。

e.g. The window is open.

④ "be+不及物动词的过去分词"，一般是系表结构，而不是被动语态。常用来组表语的不及物动词有下列这些单词。

| arrived | come | educated | fallen | gone | known | learned |
| retired | mistaken | returned | risen | | | |

e.g. My watch is gone.

It's not my fault. You are mistaken.

（2）过去分词作定语。

1）分词作定语时的位置。

①当单个过去分词作定语时，一般位于所修饰的名词之前，但有时为了强调动作，也可放在它所修饰词的后面。

e.g. Look at the broken glasses.

What is the language spoken in Japan?

②当过去分词短语作定语时，位于被修饰名词的后面。

e.g. I have a radio made in China.

The little girl dressed in white is Mary.

注意：一般来讲，及物动词的动词-ing 形式修饰事物，过去分词形式修饰人。

e.g. When they heard the exciting news, they got excited.

The excited people shouted loudly and cheered.

2）使用过去分词的场合。

①过去分词表示的动作在谓语动词表示的动作之前发生

e.g. This is a picture painted by my father.

The letter mailed last night will reach him tomorrow.

②过去分词表示的动作是没有一定时间性的

e.g. People like the Great Wall built about two thousand years ago.

Is it a letter written in pencil?

（3）过去分词作宾语补足语。

1）基本用法。

宾语补足语，又简称为宾补，跟在宾语后面，是用来补充说明宾语意义的成分，与宾语存在逻辑上的主谓关系。过去分词可以作宾补，但它通常用在一些感觉动词或使役动词的宾语后面，强调它的动作性，因此翻译时，一般将过去分词译成动词。

感觉动词：hear、see、notice、watch、feel、find、leave...

使役动词：make、let、have、get、keep...

e.g. I had a decayed tooth pulled off.

2）"have/get+过去分词"的用法。

①过去分词在动词 have、get 两个词后面作宾补时，常常表示这个动作不是由主语完成的，而是由别人完成的。

e.g. You'd better have/get the dangerous building pulled down.

How often do you have/get your hair cut?

②"have/get+过去分词"，可以表示这是主语的一种经历。

e.g. I had my left arm broken yesterday.

Li Ming had his bike stolen.

3）"make oneself+过去分词"的用法。

e.g. I can't make myself understood because of my broken English.

A liar cannot make himself believed.

I didn't make myself heard because a lot of people cried in the hall.

（4）过去分词作状语。

1）基本用法：过去分词和过去分词短语也可以在句子中作状语，用来修饰谓语动词或整个句子，表示动作发生的时间、原因、条件、结果、让步或伴随等情况。但该状语一般表示一个次要的动作。

e.g. Once seen, it can never be forgotten.

Given more water, the fish couldn't die.

Seen from a spaceship, the earth looks like a blue green white ball.

2）过去分词或动词-ing 作状语时，它的逻辑主语通常应是句子的主语。这一点要特别注意。

e.g. Seen form the hill, the city is beautiful.（过去分词短语作状语）

Seeing form the hill, you can see the whole city.（动词-ing 短语作状语）

Exercise 10: Select the best choice for each sentence.

1) The speaker raised his voice but still couldn't make himself _____.

    A. hear   B. to hear   C. hearing   D. heard

2) It was so cold that they kept the fire _____ all night.

    A. to burn   B. burn   C. burning   D. burned

3) We walked as fast as we could, _____ to get there on time.

    A. to hope   B. hoped   C. hoping   D. being hoped

4) The computer center, _____ last year, is very popular among the students in this school.

    A. open   B. opening

    C. having opened   D. opened

5) He didn't keep on asking me the time any longer as he had had his watch _____.

    A. to repair   B. repaired

    C. repairing   D. repair

6) As soon as she entered the room, the girl caught sight of the flowers _____ by her mother.

    A. buying   B. being bought

    C. were bought   D. bought

7) The missing boys were last seen _____ near the river.

    A. playing   B. be playing   C. play   D. played

8) The visiting Minister expressed his satisfaction with the talks, _____ that he had enjoyed his stay here.

    A. having added   B. to add   C. adding   D. added

9) The first textbooks _____ for teaching English as a foreign language came out in the 16ᵗʰ century.

    A.   having written   B. to be written

    C. being written   D. written

10) Seeing the sun _____ above the surface of the sea, we let out a shout of joy.

    A. to rise   B. rising   C. to raise   D. raising

11) When he came back again, the door remained _____.

    A. locked   B. closing   C. locking   D. to lock

12) My grandfather was taking a walk, _____ by me.

    A. being supported   B. supported

    C. supporting   D. to support

13) The _____ boy sat in the corner, _____.

    A. frightened, crying   B. frightening, crying

    C. frightening, cried   D. frightening, to cry

14) _____ a windy day, I decided to stay at home.

    A. Being   B. It being   C. It's   D. Been

15) They usually have their classes with the lights _____, even when it is quite bright in the room.

    A. burned   B. to brining   C. burning   D. burn

16) I got a letter from my sister, _____ me that she would visit us.

    A. tells   B. told   C. telling   D. to tell

17) _____ white, the kitchen looks much better than before.

    A. Paints   B. Painted   C. Painting   D. To paint

18) Nearly every great building in Beijing was built _____ south.

    A. facing   B. to face   C. to have faced   D. being facing

19) _____ what the situation would be like, they decided to keep silent.

    A. Having not known   B. Knowing not

    C. No know   D. Not knowing

20) _____ with the size of the whole earth, the highest mountain does not seem high at all.

    A. Comparing   B. To compare

    C. Compared   D. Having compared

Exercise 11: Fill in with best choice.

Dear Christine,

It was a pity that you __1)__ be here for the play last night. I think that it __2)__ very well, but I'm glad that it's over now because it was a lot of __3)__. Mrs. Johnson is the leader of the theatre group so she told everyone __4)__. My sister Penny had one of the big parts (she was the queen and she __5)__ but I only had __6)__ things to say. A lot of people came to see the play and we made over one hundred pounds. Mrs. Johnson asked everyone how ___7)___ spend it. We have agreed to organize a trip to one of the big theatres in London, but can't go now; It'll ___8)___ Christmas.

In your last letter you asked ___9)___ Jim's new address, but I'm afraid I don't know it. We must both wait until he ___10)___ to us.

I hope you are well. Write soon.

Love,

Brian

1) A. can't   B. couldn't   C. may not   D. mightn't

2) A. went   B. was going   C. was   D. has been

3) A. the work   B. work   C. job   D. the job

4) A. which to do   B. which they did   C. what to do   D. what they did

5) A. seemed very nicely   B. seemed very nice

   C. looked very nicely   D. looked very nice

6) A. few short   B. a few short   C. a short few   D. short few

7) A. we should   B. should we   C. shall we   D. we shall

8) A. must be at   B. must be in   C. have to be at   D. have to be in

9) A. from me   B. me for   C. to me   D. to me for

10) A. is going to   B. is writing   C. will write   D. writes

Unit 11　Energy Resources
Communicative Samples

Conversation 1

(Crystal and Jim are talking about the importance of water resources.)

Crystal: Hello, Jim. Do you know that water is one of the indispensable resources for the human beings to live on?

Jim: Of course. Water plays a very important role in our lives.

Crystal: But nowadays there are many cities that are short of water, especially in the northwest of China. The water shortage has greatly affected the life of the ordinary people there.

Jim: Yes. In some cities the supply of running water is limited to several hours a day. People there have no other choice but to get used to it.

Crystal: Does that mean every day people will set aside a specific period of time to do some washing, cleaning and store up some water for other purposes?

Jim: Yes, you're right. Their normal schedule is disturbed.

Crystal: What's the reason for the water shortage?

Jim: I think the underlying reason for the water shortage is that lots of water has been seriously polluted by human beings.

Crystal: How can we solve this problem?

Jim: We should value what nature has given us and learn to protect it.

Crystal: That's very true.

Conversation 2

(Two people are discussing some social problems.)

John: As we know, as rapid development takes place, we find ourselves encountering more and more problems.

Betty: Yes. Just think of the population explosion. If that continues at the present rate, we'll all be starving in future.

John: Oh, don't say that. Most countries are developing family planning programs now. At least there is a solution to the population explosion.

Betty: It's all very well to say that population growth will be controlled.

John: But I don't think the figures show any real improvement yet, and all the people alive now obviously want to have children.

Betty: You may be right. But there are other things that need controlling.

John: Give me some examples.

Betty: For example, as the population increases, more waste materials are produced; and industry puts out a lot of pollution too.

John: Yes. Industry is using up the world's natural resources faster and faster, especially fossil fuels for energy.

Betty: Did you know that millions of tons of oil are spilt into the sea every year? It's terrible!

John: Yes, I agree. Oil is a critical issue.

Betty: Let's hope the scientists can develop new sources of energy.

New Words and Expressions

energy	/ˈenədʒi/	n.	精力，精神
negative	/ˈnegətiv/	adj.	否定的，消极的
ordinary	/ˈɔːdinəri/	adj.	平常的，普通的
resource	/riˈsɔːs/	n.	资源，财力
shortage	/ˈʃɔːtidʒ/	n.	不足，缺乏
store	/stɔː/	vt.	贮藏，储备

Exercise 1: Complete the following sentences.

A: Alice, do you know that _____ (土地资源短缺很严重) today.

B: Yes. The time when people had more land to spare has gone.

A: I think the _____ (土地问题应尽快解决).

B: What shall we do to solve this problem?

A: The best way is to _____ (控制人口).

B: Absolutely right.

Exercise 2: Fill in the missing letters.

re_ource　　　nega_ive　　　un_erlying　　　st_re　　　_rdinary

_opulation　　　e_ergy　　　_pilt　　　shorta_e　　　exp_osion

Paragraph Reading A: Natual Resources

In a way, all of us are on a spaceship, the planet Earth. We move around the sun at 18 miles per second and never stop. On our spaceship we have five billion people and a limited supply of air, water, and land. These supplies have to be used carefully because we can't buy new air, water, or land from anywhere else.

The environment on our planet is a closed system; nothing new is ever added. Nature recycles our resources. Water, for example, evaporates and rises as visible drops to form clouds. This same water returns to the earth as rain or snow. The rain that falls today is actually the same water that fell on the land 70 million years ago.

Today, the Earth is in trouble. Factories pour dirty water into our rivers. Many fish die and the water becomes unhealthy for people to drink. Cars and factories put poisons into the air and cause plants, animals and people to get sick. People throw bottles and paper out of their car windows and the side of the road becomes covered with all sorts of waste. Over the years, people have changed the environment, and we have pollution.

To continue to survive, we must learn how to use the Earth's resources wisely. We have to change our habits and stop dumping such enormous amounts of industrial waste into the water and air. We must cooperate with nature and learn better ways to use, not abuse our environment.

New Words and Expressions

add	/æd/	vt.	增加，添加
amount	/ə'maunt/	n.	数量
billion	/'biljən/	n./adj.	十亿（的）
carefully	/'keəfuli/	adv.	小心地，谨慎地
cooperate	/kəu'ɔpəreit/	vi.	合作，协作
dump	/dʌmp/	vt.	倾倒（垃圾），倾卸
enormous	/i'nɔ:məs/	adj.	巨大的，庞大的
environment	/in'vaiərənmənt/	n.	环境，外界
evaporate	/i'væpəreit/	v.	（使）蒸发，消失
habit	/'hæbit/	n.	习惯，习性
industrial	/in'dʌstriəl/	adj.	工业的，产业的
poison	/'pɔizn/	n.	毒药
recycle	/ri:'saikl/	v.	使再循环，反复应用

spaceship	/ˈspeisʃip/	n.	太空船
supply	/səˈplai/	vt.	补给，供给
survive	/səˈvaiv/	v.	幸存，生还
unhealthy	/ʌnˈhelθi/	adj.	不健康的
visible	/ˈvizəbl/	adj.	看得见的，明显的
wisely	/ˈwaizli/	adv.	聪明地，精明地

Exercise 3: Select the answer that best expresses the main idea of the paragraph reading A.

1) On our spaceship we have five billion people and limited supply of _____.

    A. water and land   B. air and human being

    C. spaceship and land   D. land, water, and air

2) To the effective method to protect our environment, we can do these except _____.

    A. not pouring dirty water into our rivers

    B. not putting poisons into the air

    C. not letting plants, animals and people get sick

    D. not throwing bottles and paper out of their car windows and the roadside

3) In order to protect our planet earth, the author's attitude is _____.

    A. passive   B. indifferent   C. active   D. oppositive

4) As a student, what is the possible practical method to him?

    A. Not pouring dirty water into our rivers.

    B. Not putting poisons into the air.

    C. Not swimming in the rivers.

    D. Not throwing bottles and paper out of their car windows and the roadside.

5) What is the theme of the passage?

    A. We have to change our habits.

    B. We should stop dumping such enormous amounts of industrial waste into the water and air.

    C. We must cooperate with nature and learn better ways to use, not abuse our environment.

    D. Keeping the nature balance.

Exercise 4: Fill in the blanks with words and expressions given below. Change the form where necessary.

| in a way | visible | unhealthy | resource | abuse |
| survive | dump | habit | amount of | cooperate with |

1) He _____ her roundly for her neglect.

2) In developing countries, the exploration of natural _____ is often hampered by the lack of technicians.

3) _____ I can see what you mean, even though I don't share your point of view.

4) He can get any _____ help.

5) You can borrow some money this time but don't make a _____ of it.

6) With the help of the government, many people _____ after the flood in 1991.

7) We decided to _____ friends in starting a social club.

8) The town was so tall that it was _____ for several kilometers.

9) Some people just _____ their rubbish in the river.

10) Many fish die and the water becomes _____ for people to drink.

Exercise 5: Definitions of these words appear on the right. Put the letter of the appropriate definition next to each word.

1) _____ spaceship   a. of industry and the people who work in it

2) _____ add   b. to (cause to) change into steam and disappear

3) _____ supply   c. spacecraft

4) _____ recycle   d. to treat (a substance that has already been used) so that it is fit to use again

5) _____ resource   e. (a) substance that can cause illness or death if taken into the body

6) _____ evaporate   f. any of possessions or qualities of a person, an organization, or a country

7) _____ habit   g. join one thing to another

8) _____ poison   h. the action of polluting or the state of being polluted

9) _____ pollution   i. give sb.sth. that is needed or useful

10) _____ industrial   j. a tendency to behave in a particular way or do particular things

Exercise 6: Translate the following sentences.

1）我丢了钥匙，只得把门砸开。

2）我不记得参观过的那座大桥在哪儿。

3）你最好下午来，那时我有空。

4）你能找个人帮我一下吗？

5）事情越来越糟了。

Paragraph Reading B: Electricity

Electricity is very important in our life. Today many of our actions are connected with electricity. Without electricity, the recorder, the lamp, and even the electric stove could not be used in our school. Without it, we'd be in the dark all night. What's worse is that, wouldn't be able to watch TV or go to the movies in our spare time. And we would have to wash a lot of clothes by hand.

Without it, the factories would have to stop producing and therefore the workers wouldn't get enough wages.

But there is a shortage of electricity. We find two main reasons for this shortage. On the one hand, many factories are set up, which use a lot of electricity. And in our homes we have more and more electrical appliances such as air conditioners and refrigerators. On the other hand, the number of power of plants is not increasing fast enough, because they cost too much money. How can we solve this problem?

Scientists have proposed some good solutions. First, we should use as little electricity as possible in our homes. For example, we can try not to use air-conditioners or use them less. Second, in some factories coal and some other fuels may replace electricity. Finally, the government needs to build more big power plants as soon as possible. We believe this problem can be solved in near future.

New Words and Expressions

action	/ˈækʃən/	n.	动作，作用
air-conditioner		n.	空调
appliance	/əˈplaiəns/	n.	用具，器具
electricity	/ilekˈtrisiti/	n.	电流，电
fuel	/fjuəl/	n.	燃料
increase	/inˈkriːs/	vt.	增加，加大
lamp	/læmp/	n.	灯
produce	/prəˈdjuːs/	vt.	生产，制造
propose	/prəˈpəuz/	vt.	计划，建议
recorder	/riˈkɔːdə/	n.	记录员，录音
refrigerator	/riˈfridʒəreitə/	n.	电冰箱
solution	/səˈljuːʃən/	n.	解决办法
solve	/sɔlv/	vt.	解决，解答
spare	/spɛə/	adj.	多余的，剩下的
stove	/stəuv/	n.	炉子
wage	/weidʒ/	n.	工资
without	/wiðˈaut/	prep.	没有，不
worse	/wəːs/	adj.	更坏的，更恶劣的

Exercise 7: Select the answer that best expresses the main idea of the paragraph reading B.

1) Without electricity, we can play or use _____ in our school.

    A. the air-conditioner   B. the computer

    C. the elevator   D. the violin

2) To factories, what does the kind of direct result that no electricity can lead to?

    A. The factories would have to stop producing.

    B. Workers can have a good rest.

    C. The workers wouldn't get enough wages as a result.

    D. Workers will be glad to the situation of no electricity.

3) According to the scientists' proposal, which isn't the good solution to the shortage of electricity?

   A. Replacing electricity with other materials.

   B. Using less air-conditioner or other electrical appliances.

   C. The government needs to build more big power plants.

   D. Saving money to devote them for power of plants.

4) The following reason causes mainly the shortage of electricity except _____?

   A. many factories which use a lot of electricity are set up.

   B. we have more and more electrical appliances such as air conditioners and refrigerators in our homes.

   C. electricity is not fuel.

   D. the number of power of plants is not increasing fast enough.

5) From the passage, we can infer that _____.

   A. the shortage of electricity problem can't be solved in near future

   B. most persons hope not to use air-conditioners

   C. the number of power of plants will increase fast enough, because they cost too much money

   D. in some factories coal and some other fuels may replace electricity

Exercise 8: Fill in the blanks with words and expressions given below. Change the form where necessary.

connect with	shortage	set up	propose	replace
without	worse	on the one hand	such as	electricity

1) There's no _____ of skilled workers but there aren't enough jobs for them.

2) I know this job of mine isn't well paid, but _____ I don't have to work long hours.

3) I _____ the old adding machine with a computer.

4) He _____ a trust fund for his niece.

5) This flight _____ a flight for Paris.

6) We buy a lot of things, _____ pens, pencils, etc.

7) Last year's harvest was bad, but this year's may be even _____.

8) We wouldn't have done it _____ Jim.

9) We _____ an early holiday in the winter.

10) _____ is very important in our life.

Exercise 9: Translate the following sentences.

1）你愿意和我进城买东西吗？

2）我正巧在商店里碰到他，要不然我还得打电话告诉他会议的事情。

3）万一有什么事情，请及时通知我。

4）天天做操对你健康很有益处。

5）这件工作很艰苦，但他并不在乎。

Grammar Focus: Emphasis and Inversion 强调与倒装

一、强调

（1）强调句的基本句型。

It is/was+被强调的成分+that（who，whom）+其他成分

e.g. It is I who/that am right.

　　It is tomorrow that they will have a meeting.

（2）强调句型应注意事项。

1）强调句中通常强调主语、宾语（包括介词宾语）、状语，可以强调单个的词、短语和从句。It 本身没有词义。

2）强调句中的连接词一般只用 who，whom（代人），that（可代物，也可代人），即使在强调时间状语从句和地点状语从句时也如此。

3）that 或 who、whom 之后动词的人称和数要与它前面被强调的名词或代词一致（即人称和数要与原句中的一致）。

4）强调句中的时态只有两种，一般现在时和一般过去时。原句谓语动词是一般过去时，过去完成时和过去进行时，用 It was…，其余的时态用 It is…。

e.g. It was the way he asked that really upset me.

　　Was it during the Second World War that he died?

（3）强调词 it 和先行词 it 的判别。

可用恢复原句的方式来判别，即把 It is/was…that 取消后，如果剩下的字词仍能组成一个完整的句子，那么这就是强调句型，否则就不是。

e.g. It is there that accidents often happen.

分析：去掉 It is… that…后仍是完整的句子，由此可判断它是强调句，强调的是地点状语 there.

e.g. It is clear that not all boys like football.

分析：去掉 It is… that…后不是完整的句子，因此它不是强调句，而是由 it 作先行词引导的主语从句。

（4）not…until 句型的强调句。

1）基本用法。

句型：It is/was not until+被强调部分+that+其他成分

e.g. He didn't go to bed until/till ten o'clock.　　→It was not until ten o'clock that he went to bed.

I didn't realize she was a famous film star till/until she took off her dark glasses. →It was not until she took off her dark glasses that I realized she was a famous film star.

注意：此种强调句只能用 until，不能用 till，但如果这句不是强调句型，till 和 until 则可以通用。

2）与倒装句的转换。

原句：The bus will not go until all the people get on it.

强调句：Not until all the people get on it that the bus will go.

倒装句：Not until all the people get on it will the bus go.

（5）谓语动词的强调。

It is/was...that...结构不能强调谓语，如果需要强调谓语时，用助动词 do 或 did。

e.g. Do sit down.

He did write to you last week.

Do be careful when you cross the street.

I did go to see you when you were in Shanghai.

注意：此种强调只有 do 和 did，没有别的形式。过去时用 did，后面的谓语动词用原形。

二、倒装

句子的正常语序是主语在前，谓语在后。有时为了强调句子的某一部分或其他原因，谓语需要全部或部分移到主语之前。

（1）全部倒装，又称主谓倒装。

一般以地点状语（here，there 等）、时间副词（now，then 等）、拟声词或状语副词（away，down，in，out，up 等）放在句首，都能引起全部倒装。

e.g. There goes the bell.

Down jumped the man.

注意：当主语为人称代词时，不能将动词移前。

e.g. Away they go.

Here it is.

（2）部分倒装。

部分倒装又称主语与助动词或情态动词的倒装，即状语提前，后接一般疑问句。

e.g. Never have I heard such a story.

1）句首为否定词或遇到有否定意义的词语时，常用部分倒装。

e.g. Not a word would be say.

　　Not until yesterday did John change his mind.

常见的否定词或带有否定意义的词语有：at no time, by no means, few, hardly/scarcely… when…, in no way, little, never, no longer, no sooner…than…, nowhere, not a single word, not often, not until, rarely, seldom, only 等。

2）如把 so+形容词或副词+that 结构中的 so+形容词成副词置于句首时，需用部分倒装。

e.g. So happy did he look that he began to tell his story.

　　So quickly did the students finish their homework that they were praised.

3）neither，nor 表"也不"，so 表"也"，用于简短回答，置于句首，引起部分倒装。

e.g. I don't care much for sweets. Neither do I.

　　I enjoy the play. So did my parents.

注意：如果以 so 开头的简短回答是表示对对方所说的情况加以肯定时，不必倒装。

e.g. It is very cold today. So it is.

　　You are a student. So I am.

4）当虚拟语气条件句中有 should，had，were 等词时，如果省略 if，就要用倒装语序。

e.g. Had he answered the policeman honestly, he would not have been arrested.

5）用 as，though 引导让步状语从句时，可把表语提到主语之前，形成部分倒装（但连词后不跟一般疑问句）。

e.g. Small as the atom is, we can smash it.

　　Rich though he is, he is not happy.

Exercise 10: Select the best choice for each sentence.

1) —She is going swimming today.

　—So _____.

　A. I do　　　　　　B. I also　　　　　　C. am I　　　　　　D. do I

2) Never before _____ heard such an interesting story.

　A. am I　　　　　　B. was I　　　　　　C. have I　　　　　　D. shall I

3) Hardly _____ the house when he was caught.

　A. The thief had entered　　　　　　　B. had the thief entered

　C. the thief entered　　　　　　　　　D. had entered the thief

4) Seldom _____ stop to ask what a word means when they're listening to a story.

　A. do children　　　　　　　　　　　B. does children

　C. children do　　　　　　　　　　　D. children

5) _____ at the school than it began to snow.

    A. No sooner I arrived   B. No sooner had I arrived

    C. Hardly had I arrived   D. I no sooner arrived

6) Not only _____ this washing machine, but _____ it.

    A. can he run, can he repair   B. can he run, he can repair

    C. he can run, he can repair   D. he can run, can he repair

7) Only after I read the text over again _____ its main idea.

    A. I could understand   B. did I know

    C. I can catch   D. was I followed

8) Not far from the school _____.

    A. is the White Tower stands   B. stands the White Tower

    C. the White Tower stands   D. the White Tower is standing

9) —She didn't get up very early that morning.

    — _____.

    A. Neither did I   B. I didn't also   C. So did I   D. Nor I did

10) —John can hardly do it;

    — _____.

    A. So can Mary   B. Nor can't Mary   C. So can't Mary   D. Nor can Mary

11) — May I use your dictionary?

    — _____.

    A. Here is it   B. Here are you   C. Here you are   D. It is here

12) Under the tree _____.

    A. lay an old man   B. an old man lay

    C. laid an old man   D. an old man laid

13) _____ yesterday, he would get there by Friday.

    A. Would he leave   B. Was he leaving

    C. Had he left   D. If he leaves

14) Old _____ she was, she went on doing physical exercise.

    A. although   B. as   C. because   D. for

15) _____, she is brave.

    A. As she is a woman   B. A woman as she is

    C. Though is she a woman   D. Woman as she is

16) Not until began to work _____ how much time I had wasted.

    A. did I realize   B. didn't I realize

    C. I didn't realize   D. I realized

17) Little _____ who the woman was.

    A. he knew   B. did he know   C. he had known   D. is he know

18) There _____.

    A. comes she   B. she will come   C. does she come   D. she comes

19) Li Ping has been to Beijing, _____.

    A. so am I   B. so have I   C. so do I   D. so I have

20) So carelessly _____ that he almost killed himself.

    A. he drives   B. he drove

    C. does he drive   D. did he drive

Exercise 11: Fill in with best choice.

The price of hotels in Britain is going up __1)__ at any other time since the war. There are a number of reasons for this but the __2)__ all is the Government's economic policy. Managers in factories see __3)__, so they are attracted to the idea of owning __4)__ businesses. __5)__ Britain's weather is often disappointing, the tourist industry is growing. Many people __6)__ like to combine a __7)__ holiday with the opportunity of improving their English. It is therefore not surprising that businessmen are buying hotels. The only thing __8)__ worries me is the kind of treatment their guests are __9)__ to receive since __10)__ of them know anything about hotel management.

    1) A. more fast than   B. more fast that

       C. faster than   D. faster that

    2) A. most important of   B. more important of

       C. most important from   D. more important from

    3) A. to fall their standard of living   B. falling their standard of living

       C. their standard of living to fall   D. their standard of living falling

    4) A. his proper   B. his own   C. their proper   D. their own

    5) A. In spite of   B. Although   C. Even   D. However

    6) A. in the continent   B. in the overseas   C. abroad   D. foreign

    7) A. fortnight   B. fortnight's   C. two weeks   D. two weeks'

    8) A. that   B. what   C. as   D. who

    9) A. like   B. probable   C. probably   D. likely

    10) A. little   B. at little   C. few   D. a few

Unit 12　How to Learn
Communicative Samples

Conversation 1

(Mike and Lisa are talking about studying English.)

Mike: Hi, Lisa, what has kept you so busy lately?

Lisa:　Studying English.

Mike: Why do you study English so hard?

Lisa:　You know we're going to have PETS Level 3 next month. I'm afraid I won't pass it.

Mike: Your English is not so bad.

Lisa:　Thank you, but I'm afraid my writing is not good enough. I often make mistakes in sentence structures.

Mike: Sentence structures in English are quite different from those in Chinese. And there are so many idiomatic ways of speaking.

Lisa:　Our teacher said we should do drills as much as possible, and the more we use phrases, the more natural they will become.

Mike: Speaking, listening, reading and writing are all closely related to each other. We need to practice more. As you know, "Practice makes perfect."

Lisa:　That's a good suggestion. We should practice all the skills together. Only by doing so can we achieve great progress in the correct use of English.

Mike: Absolutely.

Conversation 2

(John and Peter are talking about using the library.)

John: Excuse me. Can you tell me how to find some books on African Education?

Peter: Sure. You see all these little drawers here and those that go all the way around the walls?

John: Yes.

Peter: These drawers contain cards describing every book in our library. Together they constitute

the library's "card catalog". You can see that these drawers run from one part of the alphabet to another.

John: So if I'm looking for a book called *African Education*, I'd just look under "A".

Peter: Yes, that's right.

John: What if I don't know the name of the book?

Peter: Then you can look under the author's name.

John: Can you give me some examples, please?

Peter: Ok. If you want to find a book by Theodore Dreiser, you'd look under "Dreiser" and then "Theodore"

John: I get it. Thank you very much.

Peter: Not at all.

New Words and Expressions

catalog	/ˈkætəlɔg/	n.	目录，目录册
drawer	/ˈdrɔːə/	n.	抽屉，画家
perfect	/ˈpəːfikt/	adj.	完美的，全然的
sentence	/ˈsentəns/	n.	句子
structure	/ˈstrʌktʃə/	n.	结构，构造

Exercise 1: Complete the following sentences.

A: Hi, Lisa. Why do you study English so hard?

B: You know we're going to have an English exam next month. _____ (我担心自己无法通过考试).

A: _____ (你英语不错啊).

B: Thank you, but I'm afraid my writing is not good enough.

A: You can write more at your spare time.

B: Yes. _____ (熟能生巧).

Exercise 2: Fill in the missing letters.

| str_cture | ⌐ ⌐fect | _chieve | cons_itut_ | c_talog |
| la_ely | wer | alpha_et | s_ntence | i_iomatic |

Paragraph Reading A: How to Read

One of the important problems in getting beginners to read is that of self-confidence. The key to really building learners' confidence in reading is to prepare them effectively to read. This means "warming them up", encouraging them to be interested in the subject of the reading text, and also pre-teaching the words they will need to really understand and enjoy the text. Similarly, learners can work together once they have read the text.

It is of course helpful to choose a text which is really interesting for the learners, because then they will be more willing to read. Find out what the students like, and then look for suitable reading material. Choosing really interesting material may mean that the text is a little above the level of the learners.

Developing reading abilities in the learners is not about testing them, but about helping them to become better readers. Another important point is in setting the task of reading in advance, so that learners know exactly what they are going to do. Thus, the chances are that the learners' confidence will be high and they will become better readers.

New Words and Expressions

above	/əˈbʌv/	adj.	上面的，上述的
advance	/ədˈvɑːns/	v.	前进，提前
beginner	/biˈginə/	n.	初学者
effectively	/iˈfektivli/	adv.	有效地，有力地
material	/məˈtiəriəl/	n.	材料，原料
prepare	/priˈpɛə/	v.	准备，预备
self-confidence	/selfˈkɔnfid(ə)ns/	n.	自信
similarly	/ˈsi",miləli/	adv.	同样地，类似于
subject	/ˈsʌbdʒikt/	n.	题目，主题
suitable	/ˈsjuːtəbl/	adj.	适当的，相配的
test	/test/	n.	测试，试验
text	/tekst/	n.	正文，原文
thus	/ðʌs/	adv.	因而，从而

Exercise 3: Select the answer that best expresses the main idea of the paragraph reading A.

1) One way to get beginners to read is that of _____.

　　A. pre-teaching the words

　　B. preparing books

　　C. self-confidence

　　D. warming up

2) The key to build learners' confidence in reading includes the followings, except _____.

　　A. encouraging them to be interested in the subject of the reading text

　　B. preparing them effectively to read

　　C. pre-looking the words in dictionary

　　D. warming them up

3) Why do we choose a text which is really interesting for the learners?

    A. Because the text is very interesting.

    B. Because they will be more willing to read.

    C. Because there are some good pictures in the text.

    D. Because students like reading it.

4) How to develop learners' reading abilities?

    A. Helping them to become better readers.

    B. Setting the task of writing.

    C. Asking learners to read.

    D. Testing them.

5) What is the main idea of the passage?

    A. How to choose a good text for readers.

    B. How to choose really interesting materials.

    C. How to find out what the students like to read.

    D. How to build learners' confidence in reading.

Exercise 4: Fill in the blanks with words and expressions given below. Change the form where necessary.

self-confidence	prepare	effectively	warm up	ability
be interested in	willing to	above	suitable	in advance

1) He is _____ us a meal.

2) She had lost all faith in her _____ to succeed.

3) He is really unselfish and _____ small jealousy and hatred.

4) Jim is _____ help his friends.

5) I am very _____ reading books.

6) _____, their response was a refusal.

7) We had to pay the rent three weeks _____.

8) Are you _____ for the job?

9) You can't help admiring the _____ way she stood up to speak to the big crowed.

10) The runners are _____ before the rice.

Exercise 5: Definitions of these words appear on the right. Put the letter of the appropriate definition next to each word.

1) _____ beginner   a. in an effective way

2) _____ text   b. something being considered, as in conversation

3) _____ encourage   c. the main body of writing in a book

4) _____ similarly   d. act of confiding in or to

5) _____ confidence   e. examine and measure the qualities

6) _____ subject   f. right or appropriate for a purpose or an occasion

7) _____ material   g. person learning sth. and without much knowledge of it yet

8) _____ test　　　　　h. give hope, courage or confidence to

9) _____ effectively　　i. facts, happenings, elements

10) _____ suitable　　　j. being similar

Exercise 6: Translate the following sentences.

1）中国首都北京是一座漂亮的城市。

2）我买到了教授推荐的字典。

3）你上班路上帮我把这封信丢在信筒里好吗？

4）你不该这么晚，讲座半小时前就开始了。

5）屋里这么吵，我几乎听不见你在说什么。

Paragraph Reading B: Learning a Foreign Language

A language is complicated and flexible. It is not easy to learn a foreign language, and it is this fact which causes some to frequently be asked how to successfully master a foreign language.

We should remember that a child can learn language very quickly. He listens to what people say and tries to imitate what he hears. When he wants something, he has to ask for it. He is speaking, thinking, and listening to the same language all the time. These are the reasons why he could master a language in a very short period of time. If we could learn a foreign language in the same way, it would not seem so difficult.

Language is social and flexible, so we should learn and use it in a flexible way and pay more attention to the particular situation. It's also important to remember that we learn our own language by listening at the beginning, not by reading. Through listening to other people speaking a certain language, especially those native speakers, we can feel and understand the social in-depth of this language. Based on this understanding we can later flexibly master this language through our own reading, writing, speaking and practicing.

So in order to learn a foreign language well, we should try to use and imitate the native speakers. At the same time, we should try to practice it whenever possible. Practice is a short-cut to master a new language, because practice makes perfect.

New Words and Expressions

certain	/ˈsəːtən/	adj.	确定的，某一个
complicated	/ˈkɔmplikeitid/	adj.	复杂的，难解的
flexible	/ˈfleksəbl/	adj.	柔韧性，易曲的

frequently	/ˈfriːkwəntli/	adv.	常常，频繁地
imitate	/ˈimiteit/	vt.	模仿，仿效
master	/ˈmɑːstə/	n.	主人，雇主
native	/ˈneitiv/	adj.	本国的，本地的
period	/ˈpiəriəd/	n.	时期，学时
remember	/riˈmembə/	vt.	回忆起，铭记
short-cut		n.	捷径
situation	/ˌsitjuˈeiʃən/	n.	情形，境遇
social	/ˈsəuʃəl/	adj.	社会的，爱交际的
through	/θruː/	prep.	穿过，通过
whenever	/(h)wenˈevə/	conj.	无论何时，随时

Exercise 7: Select the answer that best expresses the main idea of the paragraph reading B.

1) When we learn a language, we find its feature includes _____.

   A. complicated   B. flexible

   C. easy   D. both A and B

2) _____ make(s) a child grasp a language in a very short period of time.

   A. Listening to what others say and tries to imitate what he hears

   B. Asking for it when he wants something

   C. Speaking, thinking, and listening to the same language all the time

   D. All of above

3) In order to grasp a language, _____ is not mentioned in the passage.

   A. learning it in a flexible way

   B. remembering enough new words

   C. using it in a flexible way

   D. paying more attention to the particular situation

4) From _____, we can feel and understand the social in-depth of this language mainly.

   A. those native speakers   B. the local speakers

   C. new words and expressions   D. good friends

5) In the following statements, _____ is the most effective method to learn a language?

   A. more practice   B. more listening

   C. more speaking   D. more translating

Exercise 8: Fill in the blanks with words and expressions given below. Change the form where necessary.

| master | imitate | flexible | native | in order to |
| short cut | complicated | period | social | through |

1) His specialty is to _____ famous actors.

2) They had some opinions on various _____ questions.

3) We were late for school, so we took a _____ across the fields.

4) The government must be _____ in its handing of this dangerous state of affairs.

5) Agriculture was the only line where one could be _____ of all one did.

6) When will you be _____ with your work?

7) It's rather _____ to explain, but I will try.

8) The cost of living in the United States has risen at a rate of 6% per year during the last ten-year _____.

9) Are you a _____ here, or just a visitor?

10) _____ pass the exam, she works very hard.

Exercise 9: Translate the following sentences.

1）汤姆以优异的成绩从大学毕业。

2）外出吃饭有什么好处？

3）我给你打电话没有人接。

4）自打我买了这条狗，再没人到我们家里来玩了。

5）她手中的咖啡杯子掉在地上碎了。

Grammar Focus: Tag Question 反意疑问句

一、反意疑问句概述

反意疑问句，又称附加疑问句（tag question），是一种常用于口语的疑问句式，主要由"陈述句+附加疑问"构成，附加疑问部分的动词一般要与陈述部分的动词相对应，附加疑问部分的主语要与陈述部分的主语相对应。如果陈述部分的主语是名词词组，则附加疑问部分就应用相应的代词表示。反意疑问句主要有两种形式："肯定的陈述句+否定的附加疑问句"和"否定的陈述句+肯定的附加疑问句"。

二、反意疑问句有两种语调："降—升"和"升—降"

句中前面的陈述句部分总是用降调，其后的疑问句部分的语调有两种情况。

（1）当说话者对陈述部分表示怀疑、没有把握，或说话为了语气婉转，表示客气时，疑问尾句用升调。

e.g. You're coming, aren't you?

（说话者对所述事实没有把握。）

（2）当说话者坚信陈述部分是事实，只是用来强调或证实陈述句的事实，疑问尾句用降调。

e.g. Beijing is a beautiful city, isn't it?

（说话者只想强调或证实一下所述事实。）

三、反意疑问句的构成

（1）当陈述部分的主语是 everybody、everyone、someone、no one、nobody、somebody 等指人的不定代词，附加疑问部分的主语在正式文体中通常用 he，在非正式文体中可用 they；

如陈述部分的主语是 everything、something、anything、nothing 等指物的不定代词，附加疑问部分的主语一般为 it。

  e.g. Everybody knows the answer, doesn't he?(or don't they?)

    Nothing could prevent me going, could it?

  （2）若陈述部分是 there 存在句时，附加疑问句部分的主语用 there。

  e.g. There are some students playing table tennis, aren't there?

    There is no help for it, is there?

  （3）若陈述部分带有 seldom、hardly、never、rarely、few、little、no、nowhere、nothing 等否定词时，附加疑问部分的动词用肯定形式。

  e.g. Bob rarely goes to the library, does he?

    Few people know him, do they?

  （4）若陈述部分是 I'm...的结构，附加疑问部分一般用 aren't I。

  e.g. I'm late, aren't I?

  （5）若陈述部分是以不定代词 one 作主语，附加疑问部分的主语在正式文体中通常用 one，在非正式文体中可用 you。

  e.g. One can't be too careful, can one/ can you?

  （6）当陈述部分是一个带有 that 分句作宾语的主从结构时，附加疑问部分一般应与主句的主语和谓语动词保持对应关系。

  e.g. He thinks that he is going to be a teacher, doesn't he?

    She says that I did it, doesn't she?

  注意：当陈述部分的主句是 I suppose、I expect、I think、I believe、I imagine 等结构时，附加疑问部分往往与 that 分句的主语和谓语动词保持对应关系，但要注意否定转移。

  e.g. I suppose that he was ill, wasn't he?

    I don't think that she goes to bed very late, doesn't she?

  （7）当陈述部分带有 have 动词时，如 have 表示"拥有"，那么附加疑问部分即可用 have，也可用 do 构成问句；如 have 不表示"拥有"，那么只能用 do 构成问句。

  e.g. Your have a beautiful car, don't you/ haven't you?

    She had a good time yesterday, didn't she?

  （8）当陈述部分带有情态动词 ought to 时，附加疑问部分在英国英语中仍用 ought，但在美国英语中用 should。

  e.g. The child ought to read the text loud, oughtn't he?

    We ought to go there, shouldn't we?

（9）当陈述部分带有情态动词 used to 时，附加疑问部分既可用 used 的形式也可用 did 的形式。

     e.g. They used to live in the countryside, usedn't they?

        He used to smoke and drink a lot, didn't he?

（10）在由"祈使句+附加疑问"的句式中，附加疑问部分一般用 will you。

     e.g. Don't move the chair, will you?

        Let us have a seat, will you?

但在 Let's… 开首的祈使句中，附加疑问部分用 shall we。

     e.g. Let's go camping, shall we?

（11）当陈述句的主语是由 neither…nor 或 both… and 连接时，疑问尾句要用相应的复数形式。

     e.g. Neither you nor I am going on holiday, are we?

（12）each 作主语强调"单个"时，疑问尾句要用单数形式，强调"全体"时，疑问尾句要用复数形式。

     e.g. Each of the students has his own desk, hasn't (doesn't) he?

        Each of the students passed the exam, didn't they?

（13）当陈述句中的主语是不定式（短语）、动名词（短语）、词组或从句时，疑问尾句的主语要用 it。

     e.g. To drive cars is not easy, is it?

        Seeing is believing, isn't it?

        From Beijing to Shanghai is a long way, isn't it?

        That you are leaving soon is true, isn't it?

（14）如果陈述部分的主语是指示代词 this、that 或 these、those 时，疑问尾句的主语要用人称代词 it 或 they。

     e.g. This is very important, isn't it?

（15）当陈述部分的动词为 dare、need 或 have 时，若它们为实义动词，疑问尾句的动词用 do 的适当形式，若 dare、need 为情态动词，have 为助动词时，疑问尾句用 dare、need 或 have 构成。

     e.g. We need to do it, don't we?

        You daren't go there, dare you?

        Tom has just bought a new book, hasn't he?

（16）若陈述部分含有情态动词 must 的句子表示推测，作"想必"解时，疑问尾句要根据 must 所表示的时态来确定，不能用 mustn't。

e.g. You must be tired, aren't you?

（17）若 must 表示"有必要"时，疑问尾句要用 needn't。

e.g. You must go home right now, needn't you?

（18）若 must 表示禁止时，疑问尾句用 must。

e.g. You mustn't walk on grass, must you?

（19）若陈述句的谓语动词为"must have+过去分词"时，若尾句强调对过去事情的推测，疑问尾句的谓语动词用"didn't +主语"结构，若强调动作完成，疑问尾句部分的谓语动词用"haven't(hasn't)+主语"结构。

e.g. He must have met her yesterday, didn't he?

You must have seen the film, haven't you?

（20）反意疑问句中陈述部分谓语出现否定前（后）缀时，疑问尾句仍用否定结构。

e.g. He is unfit for his office, isn't he?

四、反意疑问句中，疑问尾句的其他表示方式

疑问尾句有时可用 right?、am I right?、don't you think?、isn't that so? 等表示。

e.g. They forget to attend the lecture, am I right?

Exercise 10: Select the best choice for each sentence.

1) —Close the door, _____?

—Of course.

A. would you   B. will you   C. wouldn't you   D. might you

2) You'd rather watch TV this evening, _____?

A. isn't it   B. hadn't you   C. wouldn't you   D. won't you

3) Let's have a rest, _____?

A. are we   B. do we   C. shall we   D. will we

4) It seldom rains there, _____?

A. is it   B. isn't it   C. does it   D. doesn't

5) There used to be many trees in the garden, _____?

A. usedn't there   B. wasn't there   C. were there   D. did there

6) I think he hardly makes spelling mistakes, _____?

A. does he   B. doesn't he   C. do I   D. don't I

7) There is little tea in the cup, _____?

A. isn't it   B. is there   C. hasn't it   D. isn't there

8) What a lovely day, _____?

A. doesn't it   B. isn't it   C. is it   D. hasn't it

9) I don't believe she knows it, _____?

    A. do I   B. does she   C. doesn't she   D. don't I

10) Miss Li seldom goes shopping on weekdays, _____ he?

    A. does   B. doesn't   C. is   D. isn't

11) I don't think the little boy can finish it, _____?

    A. do I   B. can't he   C. can he   D. does he

12) He had to accept the present, _____?

    A. hadn't he   B. wouldn't he   C. didn't he   D. shouldn't he

13) Let me think it over, _____?

    A. don't you   B. will   C. do I   D. shall we

14) Mary had a meeting at school yesterday, _____?

    A. had she   B. hadn't she   C. did she   D. didn't she

15) Bill has bought a new computer, _____?

    A. has he   B. hasn't he   C. does he   D. doesn't Bill

16) Your cousin doesn't like singing, _____?

    A. doesn't he   B. does he   C. do you   D. don't you

17) I'm late, _____?

    A. am not I   B. am I   C. don't I   D. aren't I

18) Don't tell her about it, _____?

    A. will you   B. did you   C. don't you   D. do you

19) Your father seldom goes to the bar, _____?

    A. do you   B. seldom he   C. doesn't he   D. does he

20) Nobody came here yesterday, _____?

    A. did he   B. didn't he   C. didn't they   D. did they

Exercise 11: Fill in with best choice.

A: —Hello, daring. What ___1)___ for dinner tonight?

B: —I don't mind.

A: —We could have steak but we ___2)___ had that this week. I thought you ___3)___ like a change.

B: —Ask me later, ___4)___ you? I'm very busy at the moment.

A: —But ___5)___ to the shops. It will be too late to talk about it when I ___6)___ back.

B: —How about some fish? It's a long time since we ___7)___ fish.

A: —All right, then. Why ___8)___ some fish.

B: —But if you'd rather ___9)___ steak, say so. Don't say you'll have fish just ___10)___ me.

A: —No, fish will be fine.

  1) A. would you want B. would you like   C. would you   D. are you wanting

  2) A. already   B. yet   C. have yet   D. have already

  3) A. could   B. can   C. must   D. might

 4) A. do   B. are   C. shall   D. will

 5) A. I've gone out   B. I've gone away   C. I'm going out   D. I'm going away

 6) A. get   B. shall get   C. will get   D. am getting

 7) A. had   B. have had   C. were having   D. are having

 8) A. aren't you getting B. don't you get   C. not to get   D. not be getting

 9) A. to have   B. have   C. having   D. that we have

10) A. so you' re pleasing   B. for pleasing

    C. please   D. to please

Glossary

A

ability	/ə'biliti/	*n.*	能力，才干	1A
above	/ə'bʌv/	*adj.*	上面的，上述的	12A
absurd	/əb'sə:d/	*adj.*	荒谬的，可笑的	6B
abuse	/ə'bju:z/	*v.*	滥用，虐待	4B
academic	/ˌækə'demik/	*adj.*	学院的，理论的	3A
accept	/ək'sept/	*vt.*	接受，认可	1A
accomplishment	/ə'kɔmpliʃmənt/	*n.*	成就，完成	7A
account	/ə'kaunt/	*n.*	计算，账目	8B
achieve	/ə'tʃi:v/	*vt.*	完成，达到	7A
acknowledge	/ək'nɔlidʒ/	*vt.*	承认，答谢	10B
action	/'ækʃən/	*n.*	动作，作用	11B
adapt	/ə'dæpt/	*vt.*	使适应	1A
add	/æd/	*vt.*	增加，添加	11A
addition	/ə'diʃən/	*n.*	增加，加法	8A
additionally	/ə'diʃənlli/	*adv.*	加之，又	4B
advance	/əd'va:ns/	*v.*	前进，提前	12A
advanced	/əd'va:nst/	*adj.*	先进的，事先的	1A
advantage	/əd'va:ntidʒ/	*n.*	优势，有利条件	1B
advertisement	/əd'və:tismənt/	*n.*	广告，做广告	8B
aggressive	/ə'gresiv/	*adj.*	好斗的，侵略性的	4B
ahead	/ə'hed/	*adj.*	在前，向前	8
air-conditioner	/ɛə-kən'diʃənə/	*n.*	空调	11B
alert	/ə'lə:t/	*adj.*	提防的，警惕的	9A
alive	/ə'laiv/	*adj.*	活着的，活泼的	7
alongside	/ə'ɔŋ'said/	*adv.*	在旁边	2A
amaze	/ə'meiz/	*vt.*	使吃惊	6B
amount	/ə'maunt/	*n.*	数量	11A
annual	/'ænjuəl/	*adj.*	一年一次的	4B
anxiety	/æŋg'zaiəti/	*n.*	忧虑，焦急	4B
appear	/ə'piə/	*vi.*	出现，看来	8B
appliance	/ə'plaiəns/	*n.*	用具，器具	11B
application	/ˌæpli'keiʃən/	*n.*	请求，申请	1A
apply	/ə'plai/	*vt.*	申请，应用	2
appreciate	/ə'pri:ʃieit/	*vt.*	鉴赏，感激	5A

approach	/əˈprəutʃ/	n.	逼近，走进	9
approaching	/əˈprəutʃiŋ/	n.	接近，逼近	4A
arise	/əˈraiz/	vi.	出现，发生	6B
article	/ˈɑːtikl/	n.	文章，物品	8
asleep	/əˈsliːp/	adj.	睡着的，睡熟的	1
associate	/əˈsəuʃieit/	vi.	交往，结交	4B
attempt	/əˈtempt/	vt.	尝试，企图	8B
attend	/əˈtend/	vt.	出席，参加	1A
attention	/əˈtenʃən/	n.	注意，关心	4B
attitude	/ˈætitjuːd/	n.	态度，看法	1A
authority	/ɔːˈθɔriti/	n.	权威，威信	3A
automatically	/ɔːtəˈmætikli/	adv.	自动地，机械地	9
autumn	/ˈɔːtəm/	n.	秋天	4
average	/ˈævəridʒ/	adj.	一般的，通常的	2B
avert	/əˈvəːt/	v.	转移	10B
aware	/əˈwɛə/	adj.	意识到的	2A

B

backward	/ˈbækwəd/	adv.	向后地，退步	9A
banner	/ˈbænə/	n.	旗帜，横幅	8B
basic	/ˈbeisik/	n.	基本，基础	1
battlefield	/ˈbæt(ə)lfiːld/	n.	战场，沙场	6B
beginner	/biˈginə/	n.	初学者	12A
behave	/biˈheiv/	vi.	举动，举止	5B
behavior	/biˈheivjə/	n.	举止，行为	4B
benefit	/ˈbenifit/	vt.	有益于，有助于	8B
billion	/ˈbiljən/	n./adj.	十亿（的）	11A
bold	/bəuld/	adj.	大胆的	7A
boring	/ˈbɔːriŋ/	adj.	令人厌烦的，枯燥的	1
bounce	/bauns/	v.	（使）反跳，弹起	4A
branch	/brɑːntʃ/	n.	分支，分部	7B
brief	/briːf/	adj.	简短的，短暂的	10B

C

carefully	/ˈkeəfuli/	adv.	小心地，谨慎地	11A
catalog	/ˈkætəlɔg/	n.	目录，目录册	12
certain	/ˈsəːtən/	adj.	确定的，某一个	12B
change	/tʃeindʒ/	vt.	改变，变革	2A
changeable	/ˈtʃeindʒəbl/	adj.	可改变的	4

channel	/'tʃænl/	n.	路线	7A
character	/'kæriktə/	n.	特性，性质	6A
characteristic	/ˌkæriktə'ristik/	adj.	特有的，典型的	3A
chat	/tʃæt/	v.	聊天	3B
chief	/tʃi:f/	n.	首领，领袖	2B
childhood	/'tʃaildhud/	n.	孩童时期	2
civilization	/ˌsivilaî'zeiʃən/	n.	文明，文化	9A
climate	/'klaimit/	n.	气候，风土	2B
coach	/kəutʃ/	n.	四轮大马车，教练	9B
collect	/kə'lekt/	v.	收集，聚集	8B
comfort	/'kʌmfət/	n.	安慰，舒适	5B
common	/'kɔmən/	adj.	共同的，公共的	1B
communicate	/kə'mju:nikeit/	v.	沟通，通信	3A
compared	/kəm'pɛə/	v.	比较，相比	4B
compete	/kəm'pi:t/	vi.	比赛，竞争	1B
competition	/kɔmpi'tiʃən/	n.	竞争，竞赛	1B
complicated	/'kɔmplikeitid/	adj.	复杂的，难解的	12B
conceited	/kən'si:tid/	adj.	自以为是的	5B
concept	/'kɔnsept/	n.	观念，概念	8A
concern	/kən'sə:n/	vt.	涉及，关系到	1B
concrete	/'kɔnkri:t/	n.	混凝土	6B
conductor	/kən'dʌktə/	n.	领导者，售票员	9B
confuse	/kən'fju:z/	vt.	困惑，使糊涂	1A
conservative	/kən'sə:vətiv/	adj.	保守的，守旧的	2B
consideration	/kənsidə'reiʃən/	n.	体谅，考虑	5B
consist	/kən'sist/	vi.	由…组成	9B
consume	/kən'sju:m/	vt.	消耗，消费	2A
contest	/'kɔntest/	n.	论争，竞赛	6B
convenience	/kən'vi:njəns/	n.	便利，方便	9B
cooperate	/kəu'ɔpəreit/	vi.	合作，协作	11A
cooperation	/kəuˌɔpə'reiʃən/	n.	合作，协作	9A
correct	/kə'rekt/	adj.	正确的，恰当的	10A
correspondence	/ˌkɔris'pɔndəns/	n.	函授，信件	8A
couple	/'kʌpl/	n.	（一）双，夫妇	7
courage	/'kʌridʒ/	n.	勇气，精神	6A
craze	/kreiz/	n.	狂热	3
create	/kri'eit/	vt.	创造，创作	6B
cricket	/'krikit/	n.	板球	6B
critical	/'kritikəl/	adj.	评论的，批评的	3A

crowded	/ˈkraudid/	adj.	拥挤的，塞满的	9B
culture	/ˈkʌltʃə/	n.	文化，文明	5A
current	/ˈkʌrənt/	adj.	当前的，通用的	2A
customize	/ˈkʌstəmaiz/	v.	[计] 定制，用户化	8A

D

daily	/ˈdeili/	adj.	每日的，日常的	7A
dangerous	/ˈdeindʒrəs/	adj.	危险的	2A
deal	/diːl/	vi.	处理，应付	3
decade	/ˈdekeid/	n.	十年，十	8A
declare	/diˈklɛə/	vt.	断言，宣称	10B
deduce	/diˈdjuːs/	vt.	推论，演绎出	6B
deed	/diːd/	n.	行为，事实	9A
degree	/diˈgriː/	n.	程度，学位	1
demand	/diˈmɑːnd/	n.	要求，需求	6A
depend	/diˈpend/	vi.	依靠，依赖	7A
describe	/disˈkraib/	vt.	描写，记述	4A
despite	/disˈpait/	prep.	不管，尽管	3A
destination	/ˌdestiˈneiʃən/	n.	目的地	9B
detect	/diˈtekt/	vt.	察觉，侦查	4A
determine	/diˈtəːmin/	v.	决定，确定	1A
detest	/diˈtest/	vt.	厌恶，憎恨	1B
develop	/diˈveləp/	vt.	发展，进步	2A
diploma	/diˈpləumə/	n.	文凭，毕业证书	1B
dirt	/dəːt/	n.	污垢，泥土	4
disappear	/ˌdisəˈpiə/	vi.	消失，不见	2
disappoint	/ˌdisəˈpoint/	vt.	使失望	10B
discipline	/ˈdisiplin/	n.	纪律，学科	6A
disgrace	/disˈgreis/	n.	耻辱，丢脸的人（或事）	6B
dislike	/disˈlaik/	vt.	讨厌，不喜欢	5B
disposal	/disˈpəuzəl/	n.	处理，布置	7A
distance	/ˈdistəns/	n.	距离，远离	8A
dominate	/ˈdomineit/	v.	支配，占优势	1B
dozen	/ˈdʌzn/	n.	一打，十二个	8A
dramatically	/drəˈmætikəli/	adv.	戏剧地，引人注目地	2B
drawer	/ˈdrɔːə/	n.	抽屉，画家	12
dream	/driːm/	v.	梦见，梦想，	2
drop	/drɔp/	v.	滴下，落下	4A
due to		adv.	由于，应归于	9A

| dump | /dʌmp/ | vt. | 倾倒（垃圾），倾卸 | 11A |

E

effect	/iˈfekt/	n.	作用，影响	6A
effectively	/iˈfektivli/	adv.	有效地，有力地	12A
efficient	/iˈfiʃ ənt/	adj.	生效的，有效率的	1B
electricity	/ilekˈtrisiti/	n.	电流，电	11B
electronic	/ilekˈtrɔnik/	adj.	电子的	3B
embarrass	/imˈbærəs/	vt.	使困窘，使局促不安	6
emerge	/iˈməːdʒ/	vi.	显现，浮现	1B
emotion	/iˈməuʃən/	n.	情绪，情感	4B
emperor	/ˈempərə/	n.	皇帝，君主	7A
employer	/imˈplɔiə/	n.	雇主，老板	10B
enable	/iˈneibl/	vt.	使能够	9A
enclose	/inˈkləuz/	vt.	放入封套，装入	10B
encourage	/inˈkʌridʒ/	vt.	鼓励	2A
endurance	/inˈdjurəns/	n.	忍耐（力），持久（力）	6A
energy	/ˈenədʒi/	n.	精力，精神	11
engage	/inˈgeidʒ/	vi.	答应，从事	4B
engine	/ˈendʒin/	n.	发动机，机车	2A
enormous	/iˈnɔːməs/	adj.	巨大的，庞大的	11A
enroll	/inˈrəul/	vt.	登记，入学	1A
entirely	/inˈtaiəli/	adv.	完全地，全然地	9A
envelope	/ˈenviləup/	n.	信封，封套	10B
environment	/inˈvaiərənmənt/	n.	环境，外界	11A
equipment	/iˈkwipmənt/	n.	装置，设备	6
especially	/isˈpeʃəli/	adv.	特别，尤其	6A
evaporate	/iˈvæpəreit/	v.	（使）蒸发，消失	11A
eventually	/iˈventjuəli/	adv.	最后，终于	2B
evidence	/ˈevidəns/	n.	明显，显著	2B
exaggerate	/igˈzædʒəreit/	v.	夸大，夸张	8
exhibit	/igˈzibit/	vt.	展出，陈列	3A
exhilarating	/igˈziləreitiŋ/	adj.	令人喜欢的	9B
exist	/igˈzist/	vi.	存在，生存	5B
expand	/iksˈpænd/	vt.	使膨胀，扩张	8A
experience	/iksˈpiəriəns/	vt.	经验，体验	5A
expert	/ˈekspəːt/	n.	专家，行家	4A
explanation	/ˌekspləˈneiʃən/	n.	解释，解说	10B
express	/iksˈpres/	vt.	表达，表示	9B

| extra | /ˈekstrə/ | adj. | 额外的 | 7 |
| extremely | /iksˈtriːmli/ | adv. | 极端地，非常地 | 9B |

F

famous	/ˈfeiməs/	adj.	著名的，出名的	7A
favorite	/ˈfeivərit/	adj.	喜爱的，宠爱的	7
field	/fiːld/	n.	旷野，领域	1
figure	/ˈfigə/	n.	数字，形状	2B
fireplace	/ˈfaiəpleis/	n.	壁炉	5
fit	/fit/	adj.	合适的，恰当的	6A
flexible	/ˈfleksəbl/	adj.	柔韧性，易曲的	12B
forecast	/ˈfɔːkɑːst/	n.	预测，预报	2B
foreigner	/ˈfɔrinə/	n.	外国人，外地人	5A
forest	/ˈfɔrist/	n.	森林，林木	7B
formally	/ˈfɔːməli/	adv.	正式地，形式上	5A
frankly	/ˈfræŋkli/	adv.	坦白地，真诚地	6B
freely	/ˈfriːli/	adv.	自由地，直率地	5A
frequent	/ˈfriːkwənt/	adj.	频繁的	9B
frequently	/ˈfriːkwəntli/	adv.	常常，频繁地	12B
frightened	/ˈfrait(ə)nd/	adj.	受惊的，受恐吓的	1A
fuel	/fjuəl/	n.	燃料	11B
further	/ˈfəːðə/	adj.	更远的，更多的	2A
future	/ˈfjuːtʃə/	n.	将来，前途	1

G

gain	/gein/	vt.	得到，增进	8B
gasoline	/ˈgæsəliːn/	n.	汽油	2A
generally	/ˈdʒenərəli/	adv.	一般，通常	4A
get rid of		v.	摆脱，除去	2A
global	/ˈgləubəl/	adj.	球形的，全球的	2B
goodwill	/gudˈwil/	n.	善意，亲切	6B
govern	/ˈgʌvən/	v.	统治，支配	1B
graduate	/ˈgrædjueit/	n.	毕业生，研究生	1A
graphical	/ˈgræfikəl/	adj.	绘画的	8B
guest	/gest/	n.	客人，来宾	5A

H

| habit | /ˈhæbit/ | n. | 习惯，习性 | 11A |
| hang | /hæŋ/ | vt. | 悬挂，附着 | 5 |

harm	/hɑ:m/	vt.	伤害，损害	1B
hatred	/ˈheitrid/	n.	憎恨，乱意	6B
health	/helθ/	n.	健康，健康状态	6A
hiking	/haikiŋ/	n.	徒步旅行	5
hit	/hit/	vt.	打击，碰撞	3
hole	/həul/	n.	洞，孔	6
honesty	/ˈɔnisti/	n.	诚实，正直	5A
host	/həust/	n.	主人	5A
humid	/ˈhju:mid/	adj.	充满潮湿的，湿润的	4
humidity	/hju:ˈmiditi/	n.	湿气，潮湿	4A
hungry	/ˈhʌŋgri/	adj.	饥饿的，渴望的	7B

I

illness	/ˈilnis/	n.	疾病，生病	2
imitate	/ˈimiteit/	vt.	模仿，仿效	12B
immediately	/iˈmi:djətli/	adv.	立即，马上	3B
impact	/ˈimpækt/	n.	冲击，影响	2B
impersonal	/imˈpə:sənl/	adj.	非个人的	10B
impolite	/impəˈlait/	adj.	无礼的，粗鲁的	10B
inclination	/ˌinkliˈneiʃən/	n.	倾向，爱好	6B
include	/inˈklu:d/	vt.	包括，包含	9
increase	/inˈkri:s/	vt.	增加，加大	11B
indirectly	/ˌindiˈrektli/	adv.	间接地，拐弯抹角地	8B
indulge	/inˈdʌldʒ/	v.	纵情于，放任，迁就	1B
industrial	/inˈdʌstriəl/	adj.	工业的，产业的	11A
inferior	/inˈfiəriə/	adj.	差的，次的	1B
influence	/ˈinfluəns/	vt.	影响，改变	3
informally	/inˈfɔ:məli/	adv.	非正式地	5A
innovative	/ˈinəuveitiv/	adj.	创新的	8A
insect	/ˈinsekt/	n.	昆虫	7
instance	/ˈinstəns/	n.	实例，建议	8B
instant	/ˈinstənt/	adj.	立即的，直接的	3B
instead	/inˈsted/	adv.	代替，改为	6A
institution	/ˌinstiˈtju:ʃən/	n.	协会，制度	8A
instructor	/inˈstrʌktə/	n.	教师，讲师	8A
insured	/inˈʃuəd/	n.	被保险者，保户	10
integrated	/ˈintigreitid/	adj.	综合的，完整的	8A
interact	/ˌintərˈækt/	vi.	互相作用，互相影响	8A
interactive	/ˌintərˈæktiv/	adj.	交互式的	8A

interview	/'intəvju:/	vt.	接见，面试	1A
introduce	/,intrə'dju:s/	vt.	介绍，传入	5A
invention	/in'venʃən/	n.	发明，创造	9A
inventor	/in'ventə/	n.	发明家	2A
invite	/in'vait/	vt.	邀请，引起	5A
involve	/in'vɔlv/	vt.	包括，笼罩	6B
irritable	/'iritəbl/	adj.	易怒的，急躁的	4B
issue	/'isju:/	n.	问题，结果	9A

<h1 style="text-align:center">J</h1>

job-hunter	/dʒɔb-'hʌntə/	n.	求职的人，找工作的人	10B
journey	/'dʒə:ni/	n.	旅行，旅程	9B

<h1 style="text-align:center">K</h1>

kilometer	/'kiləmi:tə/	n.	千米，公里	3B

<h1 style="text-align:center">L</h1>

lamp	/læmp/	n.	灯	11B
latitude	/'lætitju:d/	n.	纬度，范围	4
leaf	/li:f/	n.	叶，树叶	7B
limit	/'limit/	vt.	限制，限定	7A
link	/liŋk/	vt.	连接，联合	3B
literature	/'litəritʃə/	n.	文学（作品），文献	1
loose	/lu:s/	adj.	宽松的，自由的	3A

<h1 style="text-align:center">M</h1>

magnitude	/'mægnitju:d/	n.	数量，巨大	7A
maintain	/men'tein/	vt.	维持，维修	9A
major	/'meidʒə/	vi.	主修	1A
manager	/'mænidʒə/	n.	经理，管理人员	10B
manner	/'mænə/	n.	礼貌，风格	5B
mark	/mɑ:k/	vi.	作记号	5B
mass	/mæs/	adj.	大规模的，集中的	3A
master	/'mɑ:stə/	n.	主人，雇主	12B
match	/mætʃ/	n.	相配，比赛	9B
material	/mə'tɪəriəl/	n.	材料，原料	12A
maximum	/'mæksiməm/	adj.	最高的，最多的	2B
melt	/melt/	v.	（使）融化，（使）熔化	2B
memorize	/'meməraiz/	v.	记住，记忆	9

message	/ˈmesidʒ/	n.	消息，通信	10
methods	/ˈmeθəd/	n.	方法	3B
misty	/ˈmisti/	adj.	有薄雾的	4A
modern	/ˈmɔdən/	adj.	近代的，现代的	9A
motorcycle	/ˈməutəsaikl/	n.	摩托车，机车	6
multimedia	/ˌmʌltiˈmiːdjə/	n.	多媒体的采用	8A

N

native	/ˈneitiv/	adj.	本国的，本地的	12B
naturally	/ˈnætʃərəli/	adv.	自然地	5B
negative	/ˈnegətiv/	adj.	否定的，消极的	11
nervous	/ˈnəːvəs/	adj.	神经紧张的，不安的	1B
network	/ˈnetwəːk/	n.	网络	3A
noise	/nɔiz/	n.	喧闹声，噪声	7B

O

object	/ˈɔbdʒikt/	n.	物体，目标	4A
observe	/əbˈzəːv/	vt.	观察，遵守	4B
obtain	/əbˈtein/	vt.	获得，得到	1B
occasional	/əˈkeiʒnəl/	adj.	偶然的，非经常的	4B
occupy	/ˈɔkjupai/	vt.	占用，占领	7A
occurrence	/əˈkʌrəns/	n.	发生，出现	9A
odor	/ˈəudə/	n.	气味，名声	4A
offend	/əˈfend/	v.	犯罪，冒犯	5B
offer	/ˈɔfə/	vt.	提供	1A
official	/əˈfiʃəl/	n.	官员，公务员	10A
online	/ˈɔnlain/	n.	联机，在线式	3B
opportunity	/ˌɔpəˈtjuːniti/	n.	机会，时机	8A
ordinary	/ˈɔːdinəri/	adj.	平常的，普通的	11
organization	/ˌɔːgənaiˈzeiʃən/	n.	组织，机构	3A
own	/əun/	adj.	自己的，特有的	10A

P

package	/ˈpækidʒ/	n.	包裹，包	10
pale	/peil/	adj.	苍白的，暗淡的	1B
participant	/pɑːˈtisipənt/	n.	参与者，共享者	8A
particular	/pəˈtikjulə/	adj.	特殊的，特别的	4B
pavement	/ˈpeivmənt/	n.	人行道，公路	9A
pedestrian	/peˈdestriən/	n.	步行者	9A

perfect	/ˈpəːfikt/	adj.	完美的，全然的	12
perhaps	/pəˈhæps/	adv.	或许，多半	5A
period	/ˈpiəriəd/	n.	时期，学时	12B
permit	/pə(ː)ˈmit/	v.	许可，允许	3B
personal	/ˈpəːsənl/	adj.	私人的，个人的	8B
phenomenon	/fiˈnɔminən/	n.	现象	4B
physical	/ˈfizikəl/	adj.	身体的，物质的	3A
planet	/ˈplænit/	n.	行星	2B
poison	/ˈpɔizn/	n.	毒药	11A
poisonous	/ˈpɔiznəs/	adj.	有毒的	2A
policy	/ˈpɔlisi/	n.	政策，方针	10B
politely	/pəˈlaitli/	adv.	客气地，斯文地	5B
pollution	/pəˈluːʃən/	n.	污染，玷污	2A
pour	/pɔː/	v.	灌注，倾泻	9
practice	/ˈpræktis/	n.	实践，惯例	2A
predict	/priˈdikt/	v.	预知，预言	2B
prepare	/priˈpɛə/	v.	准备，预备	12A
president	/ˈprezidənt/	n.	总统，会长	10A
pressure	/ˈpreʃə(r)/	n.	强制，紧迫	4A
prevent	/priˈvent/	v.	防止，预防	6A
previously	/ˈpriːvjuːsli/	adv.	先前，以前	2B
principle	/ˈprinsəpl/	n.	法则，原则	5B
probably	/ˈprɔbəb(ə)li/	adv.	大概，或许	5A
procedure	/prəˈsiːdʒə/	n.	程序，手续	1A
produce	/prəˈdjuːs/	vt.	生产，制造	11B
product	/ˈprɔdəkt/	n.	产品，产物	3B
professional	/prəˈfeʃənl/	adj.	专业的，职业的	8A
professor	/prəˈfesə/	n.	教授	1
profile	/ˈprəufail/	n.	侧面，外形	8B
progress	/ˈprəugres/	vi.	前进，进步	2A
promise	/ˈprɔmis/	vt.	允诺，答应	6
propose	/prəˈpəuz/	vt.	计划，建议	11B
protect	/prəˈtekt/	vt.	保护	3
protocol	/ˈprəutəkɔl/	n.	草案，协议	3A
provide	/prəˈvaid/	v.	供应，供给	3B
provider	/prəˈvaidə/	n.	供给者，供应者	8B
public	/ˈpʌblik/	n.	公众，公共场所	9B

Q

quench	/kwentʃ/	vt.	结束，熄灭	7A

R

rage	/reidʒ/	n.	愤怒，情绪激动	4B
rapidly	/'ræpɪdli/	adv.	迅速地	8A
rate	/reit/	n.	速度，价格	10
reality	/ri(:)'æliti/	n.	真实，事实	3A
realize	/'riəlaiz/	vt.	了解，实现	5A
reasonably	/'ri:zənəbli/	adv.	适度地，相当地	10B
recorder	/ri'kɔ:də/	n.	记录员，录音	11B
recycle	/ri:'saikl/	v.	使再循环，反复应用	11A
refrigerator	/ri'fridʒəreitə/	n.	电冰箱	11B
register	/'redʒistə/	vt.	记录，登记，注册	1A
regulation	/regju'leiʃən/	n.	规则，规章	10
relative	/'relətiv/	adj.	有关系的，相对的	5
relax	/ri'læks/	vi.	放松，休息	5A
release	/ri'li:s/	vt.	释放，解放	4A
reluctant	/ri'lʌktənt/	adj.	不顾的，勉强的	10B
remember	/ri'membə/	vt.	回忆起，铭记	12B
remove	/ri'mu:v/	vt.	移动，开除	10B
rent	/rent/	v.	租，租借	5
replace	/ri(:)'pleis/	vt.	取代，替换	2A
reply	/ri'plai/	n.	答复，报复	10A
representative	/ˌrepri'zentətiv/	n.	代表	1A
require	/ri'kwaiə/	vt.	需要，要求	1A
research	/ri'sə:tʃ/	n./vi.	研究，调查	3B
researcher	/ri'sɜ:tʃə(r)/	n.	研究员	2B
resource	/ri'sɔ:s/	n.	资源，财力	11
respective	/ris'pektiv/	adj.	分别的，各自的	7A
respond	/ris'pɔnd/	v.	回答，响应	10B
responsible	/ris'pɔnsəbl/	adj.	有责任的，可靠的	9A
retire	/ri'taiə/	vi.	退休，引退	7
rough	/rʌf/	adj.	粗糙的，粗略的	5B
route	/ru:t/	n.	路线，路程	5
rude	/ru:d/	adj.	粗鲁的，无礼的	5B
rush	/rʌʃ/	vi.	冲，奔	9B

S

sailor	/ˈseilə/	n.	海员，水手	4A
sandal	/ˈsændl/	n.	凉鞋	6
savage	/ˈsævidʒ/	adj.	野蛮的，未开化的	5B
scare	/skɛə/	v.	惊吓，受惊	6
schedule	/ˈʃedjuːl/	n.	时间表，进度表	9B
scholar	/ˈskɔlə/	n.	学者	7A
secretary	/ˈsekrətri/	n.	秘书，书记	10A
security	/siˈkjuəriti/	n.	安全	3
seek	/siːk/	v.	寻找，探索	5B
self-assured	/selfəˈʃuəd/	adj.	有自信的	1B
self-confidence	/selfˈkɔnfid(ə)ns/	n.	自信	12A
selfish	/ˈselfiʃ/	adj.	自私的	5B
senses	/sens/	n.	感觉，判断力	4A
sentence	/ˈsentəns/	n.	句子	12
serious	/ˈsiəriəs/	adj.	严肃的，认真的	2A
service	/ˈsəːvis/	n.	服务	3B
shortage	/ˈʃɔːtidʒ/	n.	不足，缺乏	11
short-cut		n.	捷径	12B
shout	/ʃaut/	v.	呼喊，呼叫	7B
sidewalk	/ˈsaidwɔːk/	n.	人行道	9A
sign	/sain/	n.	标记，符号	4A
signal	/ˈsignl/	n.	信号	7B
significant	/sigˈnifikənt/	adj.	有意义的，重大的	6B
similarly	/ˈsiriləli/	adv.	同样地，类似于	12A
simulation	/ˌsimjuˈleiʃən/	n.	仿真，假装	2B
site	/sait/	n.	地点，场所	8B
situation	/ˌsitjuˈeiʃən/	n.	情形，境遇	12B
skating	/ˈskeitiŋ/	n.	溜冰	6A
skyscraper	/ˈskaiskreipə(r)/	n.	摩天楼	2
snowball	/ˈsnəubɔːl/	n.	雪球	4
social	/ˈsəuʃəl/	adj.	社会的，爱交际的	12B
soft	/sɔft/	adj.	柔软的，温和的	7B
solution	/səˈluːʃən/	n.	解决办法	11B
solve	/sɔlv/	vt.	解决，解答	11B
spaceship	/ˈspeisʃip/	n.	太空船	11A
spare	/spɛə/	adj.	多余的，剩下的	11B
special	/ˈspeʃəl/	adj.	特别的，特殊的	10A

spectator	/spek'teitə/	n.	观众	6B
speed	/spi:d/	n.	迅速，速度	9B
spell	/spel/	vt.	拼写，拼成	10
spill	/spil/	n.	溢出，溅出	2
spirit	/'spirit/	n.	精神，勇气	5B
standard	/'stændəd/	n.	标准，规格	3A
status	/'steitəs/	n.	身份，地位	3A
sticky	/'stiki/	adj.	黏的，黏性的	9B
stocking	/'stɔkiŋ/	n.	长袜	5
store	/stɔ:/	vt.	贮藏，储备	11
stove	/stəuv/	n.	炉子	11B
straight	/streit/	adj.	直的，诚实的	4A
strength	/streŋθ/	n.	力量，力气	6A
structure	/'strʌktʃə/	n.	结构，构造	12
subject	/'sʌbdʒikt/	n.	题目，主题	12A
submerge	/səb'mə:dʒ/	v.	浸没，淹没	2B
subtitle	/'sʌbtaitl/	n.	副题（书本中的）	8
success	/sək'ses/	n.	成功，成就	7A
suitable	/'sju:təbl/	adj.	适当的，相配的	12A
sunny	/'sʌni/	adj.	阳光充足的	4B
superficially	/sju:pə'fiʃəli/	adv.	浅薄地	5A
supply	/sə'plai/	vt.	补给，供给	11A
support	/sə'pɔ:t/	vt.	支持，支援	8A
suppressed	/sə'pres/	vt.	镇压，抑制	4A
surf	/sə:f/	vi.	冲浪	3A
survey	/sə:'vei/	n.	测量，调查	8
survive	/sə'vaiv/	v.	幸存，生还	11A
suspicion	/səs'piʃən/	n.	猜疑，怀疑	10B
symbol	/'simbəl/	n.	符号，记号	3A
sympathize	/'simpəθaiz/	vi.	同情，共鸣	9A
symptom	/'simptəm/	n.	症状，征兆	4B
system	/'sistəm/	n.	系统，体系	9B

T

tangible	/'tændʒəbl/	adj.	切实的	8B
task	/tɑ:sk/	n.	任务，作业	1A
taste	/teist/	v.	品尝，体验	7
teamwork	/'ti:mwɜ:k/	n.	联合作业，协力	6A
technique	/tek'ni:k/	n.	技术，技巧	9

technology	/tek'nɔlədʒi/	*n.*	科技，技术	2
teenager	/'tiːnˌeidʒə/	*n.*	十几岁的青少年	6
telecommunication	/'telikəmjuːni'keiʃən/	*n.*	电信，无线电通信	3A
temperature	/'tempritʃə(r)/	*n.*	温度	2B
test	/test/	*n.*	测试，试验	12A
text	/tekst/	*n.*	正文，原文	12A
thirst	/θəːst/	*n.*	口渴，渴望	7A
through	/θruː/	*prep.*	穿过，通过	12B
throughout	/θruː(ː)'aut/	*prep.*	遍及，贯穿	4
thus	/ðʌs/	*adv.*	因而，从而	12A
tool	/tuːl/	*n.*	工具，用具	3B
tour	/tuə/	*v.*	旅行，游历	9
track	/træk/	*n.*	跟踪，足迹	6A
transportation	/ˌtrænspɔː'teiʃən/	*n.*	运输，运送	9B
type	/taip/	*n.*	类型，典型	10A

U

uncomfortable	/ʌn'kʌmfətəbl/	*adj.*	不舒服的，不安的	5A
underground	/'ʌndəgraund/	*n.*	地铁	9B
unhealthy	/ʌn'helθi/	*adj.*	不健康的	11A
unique	/juː'niːk/	*adj.*	唯一的，独特的	8A
urban	/'əːbən/	*adj.*	城市的，市内的	4B

V

vacancy	/'veikənsi/	*n.*	空白，空缺	10B
vain	/vein/	*adj.*	徒然的，无益的	5B
valuable	/'væljuəbl/	*adj.*	贵重的，有价值的	6A
value	/'væljuː/	*n.*	价值，估价	6A
various	/'vɛəriəs/	*adj.*	不同的，各种各样的	6A
vast	/vɑːst/	*adj.*	巨大的，辽阔的	9B
vehicle	/'viːikl/	*n.*	交通工具，车辆	9A
victim	/'viktim/	*n.*	受害人，牺牲者	9A
view	/vjuː/	*n.*	景色，观点	3B
virtual	/'vəːtjuəl/	*adj.*	虚的，实质的	8A
virtue	/'vəːtjuː/	*n.*	德行，美德	6B
virus	/'vaiərəs/	*n.*	[微]病毒	3
visible	/'vizəbl/	*adj.*	看得见的，明显的	11A
volleyball	/'vɔlibɔːl/	*n.*	排球	6A

W

wage	/weidʒ/	n.	工资	11B
warfare	/ˈwɔːfɛə/	n.	战争，竞争	6B
waste	/weist/	vt.	浪费，消耗	7A
website	/ˈweb ˌsait/	n.	网站	8
whatsoever	/wɔtsəuˈevə/	pron.	无论什么	8B
whenever	/(h)wenˈevə/	conj.	无论何时，随时	12B
whistle	/(h)wisl/	n.	口哨，汽笛	7B
wisely	/ˈwaizli/	adv.	聪明地，精明地	11A
without	/wiðˈaut/	prep.	没有，不	11B
wonder	/ˈwʌndə/	vt.	对…感到惊讶，惊奇	10B
worse	/wəːs/	adj.	更坏的，更恶劣的	11B
worth	/wəːθ/	adj.	值钱的	10A
worthwhile	/ˈwəːðˈ(h)wail/	adj.	值得做的	3A

Model Test 1

Part I Reading Comprehension (40%)

Directions: There are three passages in this part. Each passage is followed by some questions or unfinished statements. For each of them there are four choices marked A, B, C and D. you should decided on the best choice and mark the corresponding letter on the Answer Sheet with a single line through the center.

Passage 1

Questions 1 to 5 are based on the following passage:

Movies are the most popular form of entertainment for millions of Americans. They go to see the movies to escape their normal every day existence and to experience a life more exciting than their own. They may choose to see a particular film because they like the actors or because they have heard the film has a good story. But the main reason why people go to see the movies is to escape. Sitting in a dark theater, watching the images on the screen, they enter another world that is real to them. They become involved in the lives of the characters in the movie, and for two hours, they forget all about their own problems. They are in a dream world where things often appear to be more romantic and beautiful than in real life.

The biggest "dream factories" are in Hollywood, the capital of the film industry. Each year, Hollywood studios make hundreds of movies that are shown all over the world. American movies are popular because they tell stories and they are well-made. They provide the public with heroes who do things the average person would like to do but often can't. people have to cope with many problems and much trouble in real life, so they feel encouraged when they see the "good guys" win in the movies.

1) The Americans go to see the movies mainly because they want _____.

    A. to enjoy a good story   B. to experience an exciting life

    C. to see the actors and actresses   D. to escape their daily life

2) Which of the following is people's normal response to the movies they watch?

    A. They feel that everything on the screen is familiar to them.

    B. They try to turn their dreams into reality.

    C. They become so involved that they forget their own problems.

    D. They are touched by the life stories of the stories of the actors and actresses.

3) It is obvious that real life is _____.

    A. less romantic than that in the movies   B. more romantic than that in the movies

    C. as romantic as that in the movies   D. filled with romantic stories

4) The American movies are popular because _____.

   A. they are well-made and the stories are interesting

   B. the characters in the movies are free to do whatever they like

   C. the heroes have to cope with many problems and frustrations

   D. good guys in the movies always win in the end

5) People enjoy seeing the movies because they _____.

   A. are tired of their everyday lives

   B. feel inspired by the heroic deeds of the good guys

   C. want to see who win in the end

   D. have to cope with many problems in their lives

Passage 2

Questions 6 *to* 10 *are based on the following passage*:

After a busy day of work and play, the body needs to rest. Sleep is necessary for good health. During this time, the body recovers from the activities of the previous day. The rest that you get while sleeping enables your body to prepare itself for the next day.

There are four levels of sleep, each being a little deeper than the one before. As you sleep, your muscles relax little by little. Your heart beats more slowly, and your brain slows down. After you reach the fourth level, your body shifts back and forth from one level of sleep to the other.

Although your mind slows down, from time to time you will dream. Scientists who study sleep state that when dreaming occurs, your eyeballs begin to move more quickly (although your eyelids are closed). This stage of sleep is called REM, which stands for rapid eye movement. If you have trouble falling asleep, some people recommend breathing very slowly and very deeply. Other people believe that drinking warm milk will help make you drowsy. There is also an old suggestion that counting sheep will put you to sleep.

6) A good title for this passage is _____.

   A. Sleep   B. Good Health

   C. Dreams   D. Work and Rest

7) The word "drowsy" in the last paragraph means _____.

   A. sick   B. stand up   C. asleep   D. a little sleepy

8) This passage suggests that not getting enough sleep might make you _____.

   A. dream more often   B. have poor health

   C. nervous   D. breathe quickly

9) During REM, _____.

   A. your eyes move quickly   B. you dream

   C. you are restless   D. both A and B

10) The average number of hours of sleep that an adult needs is _____.

   A. approximately six hours   B. around ten hours

   C. about eight hours   D. not stated here

Passage 3

Questions 11 *to* 15 *are based on the following passage*:

The agriculture revolution in the nineteenth century involved two things: the invention of labor-saving machinery and the development of scientific agriculture. Labor-saving machinery naturally appeared first where labor was scarce. "In Europe", said Thomas Jefferson, "the object is to make the most of their land, labor being sufficient; here it is to make the most of our labor, land being abundant". It was in America, therefore, that the great advances in nineteenth-century agricultural machinery first came. At the opening of the century, with the exception of a crude plow, farmers could have carried practically all of the existing agricultural tools on their backs. By 1860, most of the machinery in use today had been designed in an early form. The most important of the early inventions was the iron plow. As early as 1890 Charles Newbolt of New Jersey had been working on the idea of a cast-iron plow and spent his entire fortune in introducing his invention. The farmers, however, would home none of it, claiming that the iron poisoned the soil and made the weeds grow. Nevertheless, many people devoted their attention to the plow, until in 1869, James Oliver of South Bend, Indiana, turned out the first chilled-steel plow.

11) The word "here"(Para. 1, Line 4) refers to _____.

    A. Europe   B. America

    C. New Jersey   D. Indiana

12) Which of the following statements is NOT true?

    A. The need for labor helped the invention of machinery in America.

    B. The farmer rejected Charles Newbolt's plow for fear of ruin of their fields.

    C. Both Europe and America had great need for farmer machinery.

    D. It was in Indiana that the first chilled-steel plow was produced.

13) The passage is mainly about _____.

    A. the agriculture revolution

    B. the invention of labor-saving machinery

    C. the development of scientific agriculture

    D.the farming machinery in America

14) At the opening of the nineteenth-century, farmers in America _____.

    A. preferred light tools

    B. were extremely self-reliant

    C. had many tools

    D. had very few fools

15) It is implied but not stated in the passage that _____.

    A. there was a shortage of workers on America farms

    B. the most important of the early invention was the iron plow

    C. after 1869, many people devoted their attention to the plow

    D. Charles Newbolt had made a fortune by his cast—iron plow

Part II　Vocabulary and Structure (30%)

Directions: In this part there are 30 incomplete sentences. For each sentence there are four choices marked A, B, C and D. Choose the ONE answer that best completes the sentence. Then mark the corresponding letter on the Answer Sheet with a single line through the center.

16) "What date will tomorrow be?" "It will be _____."

  A. a fine day   B. April the sixth   C. Saturday   D. April six

17) There are six engineers in our team. _____ are from Japan.

  A. The six of them B. Six of them   C. Six they   D. All six

18) He was so poor that he had _____ than one hundred dollars.

  A. no less   B. not less   C. no more   D. not more

19) There was a knock at the door. It was the second time someone _____ me this evening.

  A. interrupted   B. had interrupted   C. would interrupt   D. interrupt

20) Don't leave the room until the television _____.

  A. will be turned off   B. is being turned off

  C. has turned off   D. is turned off

21) This out-of-date teaching method _____.

  A. must do away with   B. must have done away with

  C. must being done away with   D. must be done away with

22) Hardly _____ for his destination.

  A. I had reached the airport when he started

  B. had I reached the airport when did he start

  C. I had reached the airport when did he start

  D. had I reached the airport when he started

23) Jane said that yesterday she had a good time, _____?

  A. didn't she   B. did she   C. hadn't she   D. was she

24) To do morning exercises has helped improve our health, _____?

  A. hasn't it   B. has it   C. doesn't it   D. does it

25) _____ had Bob reached school than the bell rang.

  A. No sooner   B. Only when   C. Rarely   D. Hardly

26) Only recently _____ to deal with the problem.

  A. something has done   B. has something done

  C. has something been done   D. something has been done

27) In my opinion, he's _____ imaginative of all the modern poets.

  A. quite the most   B. by far the most

  C. very the most   D. rather the most

28) When I saw him yesterday, he was reading _____.

    A. an exciting, detective, old story   B. an old, exciting, detective story

    C. an exciting, old, detective story   D. a detective, old, exciting story

29) There are forty students in their class. Ten of them are girls and _____ are boys.

    A. third forth   B. third fourths

    C. three fourth   D. three fourths

30) Will you buy me _____ stamps when you go out?

    A. some   B. any   C. a little   D. a few of

31) The factory will be _____ Dr. Johnson next week when the director's away.

    A. in the charge of   B. in chare of   C. in charge   D. free of charge

32) Barbara tried _____ in the door but _____ worked.

    A. every of her keys, none   B. all of her keys, not everyone

    C. all of her keys, none   D. her all keys, not all

33) _____ the scholarship really surprised me.

    A. Mike got   B. Mike getting

    C. Mike's getting   D. Mike gets

34) It's _____ I expected.

    A. a lot more big than   B. much bigger that

    C. a lot more big that   D. much bigger than

35) We _____ any physical training classes this week.

    A. haven't had   B. hadn't had   C. had not   D. did not have

36) What _____ on Saturdays?

    A. Susan usually does   B. does Susan usually do

    C. does Susan usually   D. usually does Susan do

37) Rapid progress _____ in physical education in recent years.

    A. has been made   B. have been made

    C. has made   D. will be made

38) I promise you that I _____ you a present next week.

    A. will to give   B. will have given

    C. shall give   D. shall have given

39) The students are told _____ machines.

    A. not stop   B. don't stop   C. to stop not   D. not to stop

40) Today there _____ a number of telephone calls from the applicants for the position.

    A. have been   B. is having   C. has been   D. are to have

41) "What is he?" "He is _____."

    A. a singer and a composer   B. singer and composer

    C. the singer and composer   D. a singer and composer

42) A new doctor was sent to the village in place of _____ one who had retired.

    A. a   B. the   C. an   D. its

43) Can you tell me _____ a new passport?

    A. to obtain   B. how to obtain   C. obtaining   D. to be obtained

44) _____ by the police, the robbers had no choice but to surrender.

    A. To be surrounded   B. Surrounded

    C. Having surrounded   D. Surrounding

45) Let's go to see the film, _____?

    A. will you   B. won't you   C. shall we   D. shan't we

Part III Identification (10%)

Directions: *Each of the following sentences has four underlined parts marked A, B, C and D. identify the one that is not correct. Then mark tile corresponding letter on the Answer Sheet with a single line through the center.*

46) In Hawaii, people are friendly and always warmly welcomed visitors.

        A   B   C   D

47) It was in this school where he had studied for four years.

      A   B   C   D

48) Being felt that she had done something wonderful, she sat down to rest.

     A   B   C   D

49) She was angry, went out, and slamming the door behind her.

         A   B   C   D

50) He jumped over the fence, ran across the field, and disappearing into the woods.

       A   B   C   D

51) The meeting was interesting to some people, and to me it was boring.

               A B   C   D

52) Find answers to these questions is something like a detective story.

       A   B   C   D

53) This morning I got up late, so I came to school ten minutes later.

          A B C   D

54) I'm old enough not to let my trouble to interfere with my work.
         A   B   C   D

55) Where did the accident in which your friend was hurt took place?
    A   B   C   D

Part IV Cloze (10%)

Directions: *there are* 20 *blanks in the following passage, and for each blank there are* 4 *choices marked* A, B, C *and* D *at the end of the passage. You should choose ONE answer that best fits into the passage. Then mark the corresponding letter on the Answer Sheet with a single line through the center.*

The measure of a man's real character is what he would do if he knew he would never be found out. Thomas Macaulay. Some thirty years ago, I was studying in a public school in New York. One day, Mrs. O'Neil gave a math __56)__ to our class. When the papers were __57)__ she discovered that twelve boys had make exactly the __58)__ mistakes throughout the test.

This is nothing really new about __59)__ in exams. Perhaps that was why Mrs. O'Neil __60)__ even say a word about it. She only asked the twelve boys to __61)__ after class. I was one of the twelve.

Mrs. O'Neil asked __62)__ questions, and she didn't __63)__ us either. Instead, she wrote on the blackboard the __64)__ words by Thomas Macaulay. She often ordered us to __65)__ these words into our exercise books one hundred times.

I don't know about other eleven boys. Speaking for myself I can say: it was the most important single __66)__ of my life. Thirty years after being introduced to Macaulay's words, they __67)__ seem to me the best yardstick, because they give us a __68)__ to measure ourselves rather than others. __69)__ of us are asked to make great decisions about nations going to war or armies going to battle. But all of us are called __70)__ daily to make a great many personal decisions should the wallet, found in the street, be put into a pocket __71)__ turned over to the policeman? Should the __72)__ change received at the store be forgotten or __73)__? Nobody will know except __74)__. But you have to live with yourself, and it is always __75)__ to live with some you respect.

    56) A. test   B. problem   C. paper   D. lesson
    57) A. examined   B. completed   C. marked   D. answered
    58) A. easy   B. funny   C. same   D. serious
    59) A. lying   B. cheating   C. guessing   D. discussing
    60) A. didn't   B. did   C. would   D. wouldn't
    61) A. come   B. leave   C. remain   D. apologize

62) A. no	B. certain	C. many	D. more
63) A. excuse	B. reject	C. help	D. scold
64) A. above	B. common	C. following	D. unusual
65) A. repeat	B. get	C. put	D. copy
66) A. chance	B. incident	C. lesson	D. memory
67) A. even	B. still	C. always	D. almost
68) A. way	B. sentence	C. choice	D. reason
69) A. All	B. Few	C. Some	D. None
70) A. out	B. for	C. up	D. upon
71) A. and	B. or	C. then	D. but
72) A. extra	B. small	C. some	D. necessary
73) A. paid	B. remembered	C. shared	D. returned
74) A. me	B. you	C. us	D. them
75) A. easier	B. more natural	C. better	D. more peaceful

Part V Translation (20%)

Section A

Directions: *in this part there are five sentences which you should translate into Chinese. These sentences are all taken from the 3 passage you have just read in the part of Reading Comprehension. You can refer back to the passages so as to identify their meanings in the context.*

76) American movies are popular because they tell stories and they are well-made. (passage 1)

77) The rest that you get while sleeping enables your body to prepare itself for the next day. (passage 2)

78) If you have trouble falling asleep, some people recommend breathing very slowly and very deeply. (passage 2)

79) The agriculture revolution in the nineteenth century involved two things: the invention of labor-saving machinery and the development of scientific agriculture. (passage 3)

80) By 1860, most of the machinery in use today had been designed in an early form. (passage 3)

Section B
Directions: *In this part there are five sentences Chinese. You should translate them into English. Be sure to write clearly.*

81）他们试图想出一个解决这个问题的办法。

82）今年他们建造的房子跟去年一样多。

83）我们的新产品非常受欢迎，对此我们感到十分自豪。

84）使我感到惊奇的是，他的英语说得如此的好。

85）无论多么困难，我也不会失去信心。

Model Test 2

Part I   Reading Comprehension (40%)

Directions: There are three passages in this part. Each passage is followed by some questions or unfinished statements. For each of them there are four choices marked A, B, C and D. you should decided on the best choice and mark the corresponding letter on the Answer Sheet with a single line through the center.

Passage 1

Questions 1 to 5 are based on the following passage:

In the United States, 30 percent of the adult population has a "weight problem". To many people, the cause is obvious: they eat too much. But scientific evidence does little to support this idea. Going back to the America of the 1910s, we find that people were thinner than today, yet they ate more food. In those days people worded harder physically, walked more, used machines much less and didn't watch television.

Several modern studies, moreover, have shown that fatter people do not eat more on the average than thinner people. In fact, some investigations, such as the 1979 study of 3,545 London office workers, report that, on balance, fat people eat less than slimmer people.

Studies show that slim people are more active than fat people, a study by a research group at Stanford University School of Medicine found the following interesting facts:

The more the men ran, the more body fat they lost.

The more they ran, the greater amount of food they ate.

Thus, those who ran the most ate the most, yet lost the greatest amount of body fat.

1) The physical problem that many adult Americans have is that _____.

    A. they are too slim   B. they work too hard

    C. they are too fat   D. they lose too much body fat

2) According to the article, given 500 adult Americans, _____ people will have a "weight problem".

    A. 30   B. 50   C. 100   D. 150

3) Is there any scientific evidence to support that eating too much is the cause of a "weight problem"?

    A. Yes, there is plenty of evidence.

    B. Of course, there is some evidence to show this is true.

    C. There is hardly any scientific evidence to support this.

    D. We don't know because the information is not given.

4) In comparison with the adult American population today, the Americans of the 1919s _____.

    A. ate more food and had more physical activities

    B. ate less food but had more activities

    C. ate less food and had less physical exercise

    D. had more weight problems

5) Modern scientific researches have reported to us that _____.

    A. fat people eat less food and are less active

    B. fat people eat more food than slim people and are more active

    C. fat people eat more food than slim people but are less active

    D. thin people run less, but have greater increase in food intake

Passage 2

Questions 6 to 10 are based on the following passage:

We use both words and gestures to express our feelings, but the problem is that these words and gestures can be understood in different ways.

It is true that a smile means the same thing in any language. So does laughter or crying. There are also a number of striking similarities in the way different animals show the same feelings. Dogs, tigers and humans, for example, often show their teeth when they are angry. This is probably because they are born with those behavior patterns.

Fear is another emotion that is shown in much the same way all over the world. In Chinese and in English literature, a phrase like "he went pale and begin to tremble" suggests that the man is either very afraid or he has just got a very big shock. However, "he opened his eyes wide" is used to suggest anger in Chinese whereas in English it means surprise. In Chinese "surprise" can be described in a phrase like "they stretched out their tongues!" sticking out your tongue in English is an insulting gesture or expresses strong dislike.

Even in the same culture, people differ in ability to understand and express feelings. Experiments in America have shown that women are usually better than men at recognizing fear, anger, love and happiness on people's faces. Other studies show that older people usually find it easier to recognize or understand body language than younger people do.

6) According to the passage, _____.

    A. we can hardly understand what people's gestures mean

    B. we can not often be sure what people mean when they describe their feelings in words or gestures

    C. words can be better understood by older people

    D. gestures can be understood by most of the people while words can not

7) People's facial expressions may be misunderstood because _____.

    A. people of different ages may have different understanding

    B. people have different cultures

    C. people of different sex may understand a gesture in a different way

    D. people of different countries speak different languages

8) In the same culture, _____.

    A. people have different ability to understand and express feelings

    B. people have the same understanding of something

    C. people never fail to understand each other

    D. people are equally intelligent

9) From this passage, we can conclude _____.

    A. words are used as frequently as gestures

    B. words are often found difficult to understand

    C. words and gestures are both used in expressing feelings

    D. gestures are more efficiently used than words

10) The best title for this passage may be _____.

    A. Words and Feelings   B. Words, Gestures and Feelings

    C. Gestures and Feelings   D. Culture and Understanding

Passage 3

Questions 11 to 15 are based on the following passage:

Thousands of years ago, in the middle of an ocean, miles from the nearest island, an undersea volcano broke out. The hot liquid piled higher and higher and spread wider and wider. In this way, an island rose up in the sea.

As time went on, hot sun and cool rains made the rock split and break to pieces. Sea waves dashed against the rock. In this way, soil and sand came into being.

Nothing lived on the naked soil. And then the wind and birds brought plant seeds, spiders and other little creatures there. Only plants could grow fast. Only they, in sunlight, could produce food from minerals of the soil, water and air. While many animals landed on the island, they could find no food. A spider spun its web in vain, because there were no insects for its web to catch. Insects couldn't stay until there were plants for them to eat. So plants had to be the pioneer life on this island.

11) The passage centers on _____.

    A. how an undersea volcano broke out

    B. how an island rose up in the sea

    C. how soil was formed on a new island

    D. how life began on a volcano-produced island

12) According to the passage, the island got its first soil from _____.

    A. sea waves   B. its own rock

    C. the sand brought by the wind   D. cool rains

13) The word "naked" (in paragraph 3) could be replaced by _____.

    A. hidden   B. new   C. mysterious   D. bare

14) The order of coming into being on the island is _____.

    A. soil, plants and animals   B. soil, little creatures and plants

    C. soil, birds and plants   D. soil, human beings and animals

15) According to the passage, which of the following is **TRUE**?

    A. Spiders were the first life that could live on the island.

    B. The island is far away from any piece of land.

    C. Insects could not live on the island without plants.

    D. Plants were brought to the island by human beings.

Part II   Vocabulary and Structure (30%)

Directions: *In this part there are* 30 *incomplete sentences. For each sentence there are four choices marked* A, B, C *and* D. *Choose the ONE answer that best completes the sentence. Then mark the corresponding letter on the Answer Sheet with a single line through the center.*

16) She never told us why she would come, _____ ?

    A. didn't she   B. wouldn't she   C. would she   D. did she

17) Not until Columbus discovered America _____ to Europe.

    A. bananas were brought   B. bananas brought

    C. bananas had been brought   D. were bananas brought

18) The man in the corner admitted to _____ a lie to the manager of the company.

    A. have told   B. be told   C. being told   D. having told

19) When he _____ all the letters, he took them to the post office.

    A. had been writing   B. had written

    C. was wrote   D. has written

20) _____ is a good meal and a good rest.

    A. That you really need   B. What you really need

    C. How you are really needing   D. What you are really needed

21) _____ do you meet each other?

    A. How many days   B. How often

    C. How long   D. How much time

22) About _____ of the students in our school are League members.

    A. five ninths   B. fifths nine

    C. fifths ninth   D. five ninths

23) What _____ would happen if the director knew you felt that way?

    A. will you suppose   B. you suppose

    C. do you suppose   D. you would suppose

24) "So far _____ ."

    "That is too bad."

    A. we receive nothing from him   B. there is nothing from him

    C. nothing from him has been received   D. he sent no message to us

25) He had an accident while he _____.
    A. was driving   B. drove
    C. drive   D. driving

26) This book is so long that I _____.
    A. haven't finished it yet   B. haven't finished it already
    C. still have finished it   D. still haven't finished it already

27) The more we looked at the picture, _____.
    A. the less we liked it   B. better we liked it
    C. we liked it less   D. it looked better

28) It seems to me that the cold weather came _____ this year than last year.
    A. more earlier   B. most earliest
    C. much earlier   D. much more earlier

29) Then percent of the workers in this city _____ now on a strike.
    A. is   B. are   C. is to be   D. are to be

30) There is very _____ hope that he will survive the car accident.
    A. few   B. a few   C. many   D. little

31) Something is difficult in your life, _____?
    A. is it   B. isn't it   C. are they   D. aren't they

32) It wasn't until Smith criticized him _____.
    A. when he became aware of his mistake
    B. when his mistake became obvious
    C. that did he realize his mistake
    D. that he became aware of his mistake

33) The children were _____ by the story since the story was _____.
    A. amused, amusing   B. amusing, amused
    C. amused, amused   D. amusing, amusing

34) A new car _____ her by her father as a birthday present.
    A. will be buying   B. is going to buy
    C. will buy   D. will be bought for

35) If you smoke in a non-smoking section, people _____.
    A. have objected   B. will object
    C. objected   D. must object

36) I went to _____ bed to pick up some books that I had left on it.
    A. the   B. a   C. an   D. /

37) _____ have gone into the building of the hall.
    A. Millions of dollars   B. Millions of dollar
    C. Million dollars   D. Millions dollars

38) The photographs of Mars taken by satellite are _____ than those taken from the earth.
    A. clearest   B. the clearest   C. much clearer   D. more clearer

39) After searching for half an hour, she realized that her glasses _____ on the table all the time.

    A. were lain   B. had been lain

    C. have been lied   D. had been lying

40) "I can't see the blackboard very well."

    "Perhaps you ought _____."

    A. to examine your eyes   B. to have examined your eyes

    C. having your eyes examined   D. to have your eyes examined

41) It is only when you nearly lose someone _____ fully conscious of how much you value him.

    A. do you become   B. then you become

    C. that you become   D. have you become

42) Let me help you with your English study, _____?

    A. could I   B. shall I

    C. will you   D. would you

43) Why is there _____ traffic on the streets in winter than in summer?

    A. less   B. fewer   C. few   D. little

44) Mrs. Smith spent all evening talking about her latest book, _____ none of us had ever read.

    A. which   B. that   C. of what   D. of that

45) After the battle they buried _____ and brought with them _____.

    A. the death, the wounded   B. the deadly, the wounded

    C. the died, the wounding   D. the dead, the wounded

Part III   Identification (10%)

Directions: Each of the following sentences has four underlined parts marked A, B, C and D. identify the one that is not correct. Then mark tile corresponding letter on the Answer Sheet with a single line through the center.

46) <u>Red and green</u> light, <u>if mixing</u>, <u>in</u> the right proportion, <u>will give</u> us yellow.

        A   B   C   D

47) <u>Arriving</u> for the lecture early <u>is better than</u> <u>to take</u> the chance of <u>being late</u>.

      A   B   C   D

48) <u>If you</u> <u>try to learn</u> too many things <u>at a time</u> you may get <u>confusing</u>.

    A   B   C   D

49) You <u>have</u> <u>heard from</u> him <u>since</u> last month, <u>have</u> you?
　　　　A　　B　　　　　　C　　　　　　　D

50) I was just <u>falling</u> <u>sleep</u> last night <u>when</u> I heard a knock <u>at</u> the door.
　　　　　　　　A　　　B　　　　　　C　　　　　　　　　　D

51) <u>Despite</u> they are <u>small,</u> the horses are <u>strong</u> and <u>have</u> great energy.
　　A　　　　　　　B　　　　　　　　　C　　　　D

52) <u>Having returned</u> from <u>Berlin</u>, he received no <u>telephone call</u>, <u>neither</u>.
　　　　A　　　　　　　B　　　　　　　　　　　　　　C　　　　　　D

53) <u>It is</u> <u>in</u> his spare time <u>when</u> Robert teaches <u>himself</u> English and Japanese.
　　A　B　　　　　　　C　　　　　　　　　D

54) It is <u>driving</u> <u>on the left</u> <u>what</u> causes visitors to Britain the <u>most</u> trouble.
　　　　　A　　　　B　　　　C　　　　　　　　　　　　　　　　D

55) Some people find swimming <u>more enjoyable</u> than <u>to sit</u> <u>at</u> home <u>reading</u>.
　　　　　　　　　　　　　　　　　A　　　　　　　　B　　C　　D

Part IV　Cloze (10%)

Directions: there are 20 blanks in the following passage, and for each blank there are 4 choices marked A, B, C *and* D *at the end of the passage. You should choose ONE answer that best fits into the passage. Then mark the corresponding letter on the Answer Sheet with a single line through the center.*

"I was going to be late ___56)___ the manager wasn't going to be ___57)___. Thank God!" The bus ___58)___ round the corner and I got on. At 9:25 I was walking into the ___59)___ where I work. "I ___60)___ the manager doesn't notice. But no ___61)___ luck!"

"Smith!" shouted the manager. "Late again! What's your ___62)___ this time?" "I'm afraid the bus was late, Mr. Brown." "___63)___ up earlier tomorrow! Anyway, get to ___64)___ at the counter. We'll be opening in a few minutes."

My first customer was a pretty girl ___65)___ a red dress. Behind her was a young man carrying something ___66)___ with brown paper. ___67)___ few seconds he looked towards the main entrance. The girl asked about opening a bank account. I gave her the necessary information and she walked out. Turning to my next customer, I was terrifies to see a gun sticking out of his coat.

Then a loud noise __68)__ my ears … __69)__ seemed a very long time, I opened my eyes and found myself in bed! __70)__ shaking from the memory of this terrible dream, I got dressed and ran out of the house. As __71)__, the bus wasn't on time, and I arrived at 9:25.

"Smith!" the manager cried out in a voice like __72)__. "Late again! Go and start your work at once!" To my __73)__, the first customer was a girl __74)__ a red dress and behind her stood a man carrying something wrapped in brown paper. The dream! __75)__ that the surprise of my life!

56) A. as	B. but	C. and	D. or
57) A. pleased	B. worried	C. sorry	D. patient
58) A. ran	B. came	C. rode	D. drove
59) A. hotel	B. shop	C. bank	D. restaurant
60) A. believe	B. expect	C. guess	D. hope
61) A. much	B. such	C. more	D. this
62) A. excuse	B. idea	C. reply	D. answer
63) A. Hurry	B. Come	C. Catch	D. Get
64) A. business	B. job	C. place	D. spot
65) A. having on	B. wearing	C. putting on	D. dressing
66) A. hidden	B. rolled	C. filled	D. covered
67) A. A	B. Some	C. Every	D. Each
68) A. took	B. shook	C. filled	D. tore
69) A. It	B. When	C. What	D. Which
70) A. Even	B. Still	C. Just	D. Ever
71) A. usual	B. past	C. such	D. yet
72) A. noise	B. thunder	C. shot	D. shout
73) A. belief	B. surprise	C. dream	D. regret
74) A. of	B. with	C. on	D. in
75) A. Was	B. Is	C. Wasn't	D. Isn't

Part V Translation (20%)

Section A

Directions: in this part there are five sentences which you should translate into Chinese. These sentences are all taken from the 3 passage you have just read in the part of Reading Comprehension. You can refer back to the passages so as to identify their meanings in the context.

76) Thus, those who ran the most ate the most, yet lost the greatest amount of body fat. (passage 1)

77) Fear is another emotion that is shown in much the same way all over the world. (passage 2)

78) Other studies show that older people usually find it easier to recognize or understand body language than younger people do. (passage 2)

79) Thousands of years ago, in the middle of an ocean, miles from the nearest island, an undersea volcano broke out. (passage 3)

80) A spider spun its web in vain, because there were no insects for its web to catch. (passage 3)

Section B

Directions: In this part there are five sentences Chinese. You should translate them into English. Be sure to write clearly.

81）我已了解清楚，他的结论是以事实为依据的。

82）物体离我们越远，看起来就越小。

83）每个人都知道，学习对一个人的成长是至关重要的。

84）尽管有许多困难，我们仍然决心执行我们的计划。

85）你能说话大声点好让每个人都听得见吗？

Answer Keys

Unit 1

Exercise 1:

B: I'm trying to <u>take an English literature course</u> for this term.

A: Take Professor Holt's class. <u>I had hers last year.</u>

A: <u>Fantastic!</u> I think she's really a good teacher.

Exercise 2:

literature	professor	future	degree	asleep
fantastic	boring	basics	attention	field

Exercise 3: 1)~5) B A D B D

Exercise 4: 1) applications 2) attitude 3) attend 4) determined 5) enroll 6) interview

7) procedure 8) register 9) representative 10) requires

Exercise 5: 1)~5) b e h g a 6)~10) j c i d f

Exercise 6:

1) Hardly had they arrived at the airport when their teacher told them the good news.

2) It took the students two hours and a half to work out the math problem.

3) I think it no use crying for his death now.

4) Being /As a Chinese, we should devote ourselves to our motherland.

5) Last week we visited the house where the scientist used to live.

Exercise 7: 1)~5) C C D C C

Exercise 8: 1) advantage 2) competing for 3) concerns 4) diploma 5) dominated

6) emerged 7) indulge in 8) inferior 9) obtained 10) detests

Exercise 9:

1) The man whom she met is a doctor.

2) He used to have a walk along the river after supper.

3) Compared with cars, bicycles have many advantages.

4) She not only sings well but also dances beautifully.

5) My parents kept encouraging me to study hard.

Exercise 10: 1)~ 5) C C A B D 6)~10) A D A C C

11)~15) D C B A C 16)~20) C C D A C

Exercise 11: 1)~ 5) C C A D C 6)~10) C D B D D

Unit 2

Exercise 1:

A: <u>Everyone is aware of</u> the dangers of air pollution.

A: Governments <u>are taking some measures</u> to solve it.

B: <u>Good idea.</u>

Exercise 2:

childhood   dreamed   skyscraper   bacteria   disappear   flyover

apply   illness   spill   technology

Exercise 3: 1)～5) C   B   D   D   B

Exercise 4: 1) consumed   2) current   3) encourage   4) aware of   5) practice

6) progress   7) replaced   8) get rid of   9) serious   10) further

Exercise 5: 1)～5) c   f   d   b   i   6)～10) h   a   j   e   g

Exercise 6:

1) Yesterday it took us about two hours to finish that job. (or) Yesterday we spent about two hours finishing that job.

2) It's important for children to learn English and computer well.

3) He didn't work hard last term, as a result, he failed in his math exam.

4) The students were very interested in what the reporter said.

5) When they got to the cinema, the film had already begun.

Exercise 7: 1)～5) B   ·C   C   A   D

Exercise 8: 1) evidence   2) melted   3) conservative   4) previously   5) Eventually

6) Global   7) more than   8) maximum   9) submerge   10) average

Exercise 9:

1) Beijing is one of the most beautiful cities she has visited.

2) Having lived in Beijing for many years, they are used to the weather here.

3) We are sure that our wish will come true if we work hard.

4) The teacher told us that this novel was worth reading.

5) My friend asked me whether I had any difficulty in my work.

Exercise 10:   1)～ 5) D   A   A   D   D   6)～10) B   C   B   C   D

11)～15) B   C   A   A   C   16)～20) D   A   B   B   C

Exercise 11:   1)～ 5) A   D   A   B   C   6)～10) C   C   C   A   B

Unit 3

Exercise 1:

B: <u>There is something wrong with my computer.</u>

A: Don't worry. <u>Let me have a check.</u>

A: Yes, <u>there are viruses in your computer.</u> But I have removed them.

Exercise 2:

craze   hit   influence   deal   protect

security   absence   beloved   virus   addict

Exercise 3: 1)～5) C   D   D   A   B

Exercise 4: 1) communicate   2) symbol, symbol   3) physical   4) internal   5) worthwhile

6) surfing   7) loose   8) exhibited   9) despite   10) critical

Exercise 5: 1)～5) c　i　b　g　e　　　　6)～10) a　f　h　d　j

Exercise 6:

1) She told me that she had been to Shanghai three times.

2) The problem is how we can get there on time.

3) I don't know whether she is fit for the job.

4) My bike is broken. May I use yours?

5) On my way home yesterday I met an old friend of my father's.

Exercise 7: 1)～5) B　C　D　C　A

Exercise 8: 1) view　2) chatted　3) kilometers　4) Online　5) research
　　　　　6) links　7) permit　8) service　9) provides　10) instant

Exercise 9:

1) If I were you, I would not change my idea/mind.

2) This is the tape that they are looking for.

3) When I entered into the room, she was writing to her friend.

4) She didn't go to work because of her illness the day before yesterday.

5) She prefers to stay at home rather than go to see the meaningless film.

Exercise 10:　1)～5) A　B　D　B　A　　　　6)～10) B　B　D　A　A
　　　　　　11)～15) D　A　D　B　A　　　　16)～20) C　D　D　B　B

Exercise 11:　1)～5) A　B　A　B　B　　　　6)～10) B　C　D　D　A

Unit 4

Exercise 1:

A: Hi, Alice. <u>It's a sunny day today,</u> isn't it?

A: <u>You really know how to enjoy yourself.</u>

A: Maybe you're right. <u>Can I join you?</u>

Exercise 2:

latitude　　　autumn　　　temperature　　　snowball　　　changeable

predict　　　throughout　　　dirt　　　agreeable　　　humid

Exercise 3: 1)～5) B　C　D　D　A

Exercise 4: 1) released　2) bounced　3) comes up　4) pressure　5) describe　6) detected
　　　　　7) generally　8) sign　9) senses of　10) suppressed

Exercise 5: 1)～5) f　d　g　a　c　　　　6)～10) j　b　e　i　h

Exercise 6:

1) They have already decided to put off the meeting to next Wednesday.

2) In fact, most traffic accidents can be avoided.

3) By the end of last term, they had learned twenty units.

4) The students always keep the classroom clean.

5) Today it is quite necessary for people to master one or two foreign languages.

Exercise 7: 1)～5) C　C　D　D　D

Exercise 8: 1) play a very important role   2) sunny   3) compared with   4) occasional

5) emotions   6) attention   7) annual   8) aggressive   9) additionally   10) irritable

Exercise 9:

1) She spoke English so fast that many students could not understand.

2) Remember to turn off the lights when you leave the classroom.

3) Today computer has been widely used in people's daily life.

4) I think it very important for university students to spend one or two hours doing physical exercises every day.

5) Please speak slowly so that everyone can understand you.

Exercise 10:   1)～ 5) C   D   B   D   C   6)～10) A   D   D   B   A

11)～15) B   A   D   C   A   16)～20) B   B   D   D   D

Exercise 11:   1)～ 5) B   D   D   A   B   6)～10) B   D   A   C   A

Unit 5

Exercise 1:

A: Lisa, Easter is coming. May I ask you some questions?

B: Of course, go ahead.

B: Sorry, I don't know. Can you tell me about that?

Exercise 2:

hiking	rougher	stocking	relative	wrapping
route	rent	hang	fireplace	daybreak

Exercise 3: 1)～5) C   C   A   B   D

Exercise 4: 1) introduced   2) invited   3) uncomfortable   4) relax   5) experienced   6) cultures

7) realized   8) honesty   9) formally   10) appreciated

Exercise 5: 1)～5) e   c   h   g   d   6)～10) b   i   a   f   j

Exercise 6:

1) We hope you will be a teacher in the future.

2) She is three years older than her sister.

3) I can't afford any time to see films.

4) When I went to see her yesterday, she was busy with her homework.

5) Do you believe what he said is true?

Exercise 7: 1)～5) B   B   D   C   A

Exercise 8: 1) offended   2) exists   3) dislike   4) conceited   5) manner   6) behaving

7) comfort   8) selfish   9) grow up   10) principle

Exercise 9:

1) You must be careful, or you will hurt yourself.

2) Don't take it for granted to be late for class.

3) Comrade Zhang was always ready to help others; he never thought of himself first.

4) This is the boy of whom we were talking yesterday.

5) I don't know the true reason why he didn't come to attend the meeting.

Exercise 10: 1)~ 5) D   D   B   A   C   6)~10) C   C   C   A   A

           11)~15) B   C   C   D   C   16)~20) B   C   C   B   A

Exercise 11: 1)~ 5) C   B   B   C   B   6)~10) B   D   A   C   B

Unit 6

Exercise 1:

B: <u>Physical exercise can make you body strong.</u>

B: Yes, of course. <u>I like playing golf.</u>

B: <u>Let's go.</u>

Exercise 2:

equipment   promise   sandal   scare   hole

parachute   motorcycle   teenager   embarrassed   bungee

Exercise 3: 1)~5) D   B   A   D   D

Exercise 4: 1) valuables   2) not only…but also   3) endurance   4) what's more   5) take part in

         6) courage   7) prevent …from   8) Instead of   9) various   10) demand

Exercise 5: 1)~5) i   c   d   j   f   6)~10) a   h   b   e   g

Exercise 6:

1) It is no use asking him to come now, because he is very busy.

2) Don't forget to lock the door before you go to bed.

3) We consider it useless only to study theories, they must always be combined with practice.

4) Scientists are trying their best to prevent the atmosphere from being polluted.

5) She would rather stay at home than go swimming.

Exercise 7: 1)~5) A   A   C   B   D

Exercise 8: 1) at any rate   2) inclination to   3) spectators   4) lead to   5) goodwill   6) disgraced

         7) contesting   8) absurd   9) mimic   10) amazed

Exercise 9:

1) They kept on working in spite of heavy rain.

2) The doctor suggested the patient give up smoking as soon as possible.

3) Looking at the sleeping child, Mary could not help thinking of her own childhood.

4) Coming into the classroom, the teacher found the students reading English.

5) They were determined to finish this work by the end of the month.

Exercise 10: 1)~ 5) D   A   C   B   A   6)~10) B   D   D   C   A

           11)~15) B   A   C   D   A   16)~20) B   C   D   D   A

Exercise 11: 1)~ 5) C   A   B   A   C   6)~10) D   A   D   A   D

Unit 7

Exercise 1:

A: Hi, Maria, <u>would you like to see a picture?</u>

B: Yes, I'd love to. Oh, how nice! Now, <u>who's this?</u>

B: <u>She is a lovely girl.</u> Who is this?

Exercise 2:

| couple | repellent | extra | favorite | warmer |
| retired | taste | insect | alive | tent |

Exercise 3: 1)～5) A C A D D

Exercise 4: 1) occupies 2) made use of 3) thirst 4) particular 5) accomplishments 6) success 7) as a whole 8) at best 9) respective 10) depending…on

Exercise 5: 1)～5) e h c i a   6)～10) b j f d g

Exercise 6:

1) The doctor said drinking too much would do harm to health.

2) At last he came to know why he had been criticized.

3) She got up very late this morning, and she had to go to work without breakfast.

4) My friend doesn't like football, but he's fond of swimming.

5) My father will go to the station to see his friends off tomorrow evening.

Exercise 7: 1)～5) A C B D B

Exercise 8: 1) cover up 2) noises 3) get into 4) shout 5) signal 6) forests 7) leaves 8) whistled 9) branches 10) kept on

Exercise 9:

1) Could you go over my composition and see if I need to make any changes?

2) My brother will graduate from his university next year.

3) This little girl is smarter than the boy.

4) It is said the bridge will be completed next month.

5) She didn't finish her homework until 10:00 last night.

Exercise 10: 1)～ 5) D B A C A   6)～10) D A B B D
11)～15) B C A B C   16)～20) C B A C D

Exercise 11: 1)～ 5) C C B A C   6)～10) A B A A A

Unit 8

Exercise 1:

A: Hi, Jim. <u>What does CAI mean?</u>

A: <u>Do you know the advantage of Computer Assisted Instruction?</u>

B: Ok. It can give a student <u>immediate feedback.</u>

Exercise 2:

| ahead | website | article | survey | online |
| technique | engine | exaggerate | subtitle | happenings |

Exercise 3: 1)～5) C D C D B

Exercise 4: 1) professional 2) concepts of 3) interact 4) In general 5) dozen of 6) expanded 7) In addition to 8) allows… to 9) unique 10) so on

Exercise 5: 1)～5) d c i j b   6)～10) h e f a g

Exercise 6:

1) The teacher asked the students whether they had any problems in their studies.

2) Besides these, you should write down your telephone number and address.

3) She will have to work for 8 hours a day if she gets this job.

4) Please tell her not to be late again.

5) Today is the first day of the new term, the teacher and the students are introducing themselves to each other.

Exercise 7: 1)～5) B   B   D   C   A

Exercise 8: 1) banners   2) at the end of   3) profile   4) personal   5) attempt   6) for instance   7) in return   8) advertisement   9) site   10) providers

Exercise 9:

1) As soon as she had trouble in her work, she went to ask her friend for help.

2) My friend plans to apply for a job in a foreign company in Beijing.

3) She doesn't like dancing, nor do I .

4) Because of their hard work they completed the plan in 8 days instead of 10 days.

5) She has worked for many years in this factory, and she has a lot of practical experience.

Exercise 10: 1)～ 5) A   B   A   A   C   6)～10) D   B   B   C   D

   11)～15) A   D   A   B   B   16)～20) A   B   D   C   A

Exercise 11: 1)～ 5) D   B   A   A   A   6)～10) D   B   D   D   C

Unit 9

Exercise 1:

   B: Yes? Is there anything I can help you, Ma'am?

   B: You can take the subway 9.

   B: You're welcome.

Exercise 2:

approaches	dollar	tour	automatically	plastic
timetable	subway	include	guide	pour

Exercise 3: 1)～5) A   D   B   A   C

Exercise 4: 1) issue   2) did away with   3) lessening   4) due to   5) achieved   6) maintain   7) cannot help   8) pavement   9) Deeds   10) On behalf of

Exercise 5: 1)～5) c   h   g   j   b   6)～10) e   i   f   d   a

Exercise 6:

1) It is important for us to first know the difference between the two languages.

2) I want to know why we must do this job.

3) We are looking forward to seeing our new teacher as soon as possible.

4) I'm sorry to have kept you waiting for such a long time.

5) She looks ill. Please send for a doctor.

Exercise 7: 1)～5) B   A   C   C   D

Exercise 8: 1) match   2) rush   3) journey   4) sticky   5) express   6) crowded   7) ended up   8) convenience   9) extremely   10) consists of

Exercise 9:

  1) The teacher asked who was in charge of the cleaning work of the class.

  2) I suggest he do the work in different ways.

  3) It is said there will be more students in our school next year.

  4) What the teacher said at the beginning of the meeting was very important.

  5) Please tell us in advance if you can't come to attend the meeting.

Exercise 10: 1)～ 5) D C B C A   6)～10) D D D C B

               11)～15) C A B B B   16)～20) C C D A B

Exercise 11: 1)～ 5) D B B A A   6)～10) A A A C B

Unit 10

Exercise 1:

  B: Yes. Could you tell me <u>how much it is to send a telegram?</u>

  A: <u>Where do you send it to?</u>

  A: It's three dollars for <u>the first twenty words</u> and seventeen cents for each additional word.

Exercise 2:

  parcel   insured   regulation   message   expense

  additional   telegram   rate   spell   package

Exercise 3: 1)～5) C B A D D

Exercise 4: 1) special   2) own   3) reply   4) received   5) favorite   6) According to

         7) electronic   8) correspondence   9) official   10) less than

Exercise 5: 1)～5) c f h e b   6)～10) i j g a d

Exercise 6:

  1) We should avoid making the same mistakes again.

  2) This is a very happy family, and they have been to many countries.

  3) If they had left school earlier, they would not have missed the bus.

  4) Tom apologized to his classmates and teacher for being late.

  5) The teacher said the homework must be handed in in the next morning.

Exercise 7: 1)～5) A C B A A

Exercise 8: 1) suspicion   2) sent off   3) acknowledge   4) respond   5) If only   6) removed

         7) impersonal   8) reluctant to   9) applications   10) wonder

Exercise 9:

  1) Without your help, we could not have made so great progress.

  2) The school provides the students with the classrooms and reading-rooms.

  3) Neither she nor her friend can typewrite in English.

  4) We had hardly got to school when it began to rain.

  5) He regrets not having gone to the evening party yesterday.

Exercise 10: 1)～ 5) D C C D B   6)～10) D A C D B

               11)～15) A B A B C   16)～20) C B A D C

Exercise 11: 1)～5) B A B C D   6)～10) B A C B D

Unit 11

Exercise 1:

A: Alice, do you know that <u>land shortage is serious</u> today.

A: I think the <u>land problem should be solved as quickly as possible.</u>

A: The best way is to <u>control the population.</u>

Exercise 2:

resource	negative	underlying	store	ordinary
population	energy	spilt	shortage	explosion

Exercise 3: 1)～5) D C C D C

Exercise 4: 1) abused   2) resources   3) In a way   4) amount of   5) habit   6) survived

        7) cooperate with   8) visible   9) dump   10) unhealthy

Exercise 5: 1)～5) c g i d f   6)～10) b j e h a

Exercise 6:

1) I lost my key and had to force the door open.

2) I forget where the bridge that we visited is.

3) You'd better come in the afternoon when I'll be free.

4) Could you get someone to help me?

5) Things are getting worse and worse.

Exercise 7: 1)～5) D A D C D

Exercise 8: 1) shortage   2) on the one hand   3) replaced   4) set up   5) connects with

        6) such as   7) worse   8) without   9) propose   10) Electricity

Exercise 9:

1) Would you like to go shopping in town with me?

2) I happened to meet him in the shop. Otherwise I would have to phone to tell him about the meeting.

3) Please let me know in case anything happens.

4) It would do you a lot of good to do some exercise every day.

5) It was a hard job, but he did not mind.

Exercise 10: 1)～ 5) C C B A B   6)～10) B B B A D

        11)～15) C A C B D   16)～20) A B D B D

Exercise 11: 1)～ 5) C A D D B   6)～10) A B A D C

Unit 12

Exercise 1:

B: You know we're going to have an English exam next month. <u>I'm afraid I won't pass it.</u>

A: <u>Your English is not so bad.</u>

B: Yes. <u>Practice makes perfect.</u>

Exercise 2:

structure	perfect	achieve	constitute	catalog
lately	drawer	alphabet	sentence	idiomatic

Exercise 3: 1)～5) C C B A D

Exercise 4: 1) preparing   2) ability   3) above   4) willing to   5) be interested in
       6) Effectively   7) in advance   8) suitable   9) self-confident   10) warming up

Exercise 5: 1)～5) g c h j d   6)～10) b i e a f

Exercise 6:

1) Beijing, the capital of the China, is a beautiful city.

2) I have bought the dictionary our professor recommended.

3) Would you mind dropping this letter into the mail-box for me on your way to work?

4) You shouldn't have come so late. The lecture started half an hour ago.

5) It's so noisy in the room that I can hardly hear what you are saying.

Exercise 7: 1)～5) D D B A A

Exercise 8: 1) imitate   2) social   3) short-cut   4) flexible   5) master   6) through
       7) complicated   8) period   9) native   10) In order to

Exercise 9:

1) Tom left college, having won great honours.

2) What's the advantage of dining out?

3) I phoned you but nobody answered it.

4) Nobody has come to see us since we bought this dog.

5) The coffee cup dropped out of her hand and broke on the floor.

Exercise 10:   1)～ 5) C C B A B   6)～10) B B B A D
         11)～15) C A C B D   16)～20) A B D B D

Exercise 11:   1)～ 5) C A D D B   6)～10) A B A D C

Model Test 1

Part Ⅰ Reading Comprehension

   1)～ 5) D C A A B   6)～10) A D B D D
   11)～15) B C B C A

Part Ⅱ Vocabulary and Structure

   16)～20) B B C B D   21)～25) D D A A A
   26)～30) C B C D A   31)～35) A C C D A
   36)～40) B A C D A   41)～45) D B B B C

Part Ⅲ Identification

   46)～50) D C A C D   51)～55) C A D C D

Part Ⅳ Cloze

   56)～60) A C C B A   61)～65) C A D A A
   66)～70) C B A B D   71)～75) B A D B C

Part Ⅴ Translation

76）美国电影因为情节和制作精良而受到欢迎。

77）睡眠时获得的能量使你的身体为第二天做准备。

78）如果你入睡困难，有些人建议慢慢进行深呼吸。

79）19 世纪的农业革命包括两个方面：省力农业机械的发明和科学农业的发展。

80）到 1980 年人们就已经设计出许多今天仍在使用的机器的雏形。

81) They are trying to find a solution to this problem.

82) They have built as many houses this year as they did last year.

83) We are proud that our new products are popular among consumers.

84) To my great surprise, his English is so good.

85) No matter how difficult it is, I will never lose my confidence.

Model Test 2

Part Ⅰ Reading Comprehension

  1)～ 5) C D C A A   6)～10) B B A C B

11)～15) D B D A C

Part Ⅱ Vocabulary and Structure

16)～20) D D D B B   21)～25) B D C C A

26)～30) A A C C D   31)～35) B D A D B

36)～40) A A C D D   41)～45) C C A A D

Part Ⅲ Identification

46)～50) B C D D B   51)～55) A D C C B

Part Ⅳ Cloze

56)～60) C A B C D   61)～65) B A D A B

66)～70) D C C A B   71)～75) A B B D C

Part Ⅴ Translation

76）因此，运动量最大的人吃得也最多，但同时消耗的体内脂肪也最多。

77）恐惧、害怕是另一种世界各国的人们表达方式非常相似的情感。

78）还有其他研究显示老人比年轻人更容易识别或理解肢体语言。

79）数千年之前，在海洋的中央，离海岛只有数米远的地方一个海底火山爆发了。

80）蜘蛛网也没有任何意义，因为根本就没有昆虫可捕捉。

81) I know for sure that his conclusion is based on truth.

82) The farther an object is away from us, the smaller it looks.

83) It is known to all that studying is of vital importance to a person's growing-up.

84) Even though there are a lot of difficulties, we still insist on carrying out our plan.

85) Could you speak louder to make yourself heard?